ALP

"This is a pho
to say that it is black where the actual scene is white and vice versa. Those objects are astronomical. The picture was taken from our Briareus Twelve satellite near the orbit of Jupiter, on its way out to Neptune four months ago. The central object is the star Alpha Centauri. It was photographed with a special instrument which filters out most of the light from the star; the instrument is electronic in nature and performs somewhat like the well-known coronascope which is used for photographing prominences on our own Sun. We hoped that by this means we might be able actually to photograph the planet Alpha-Aleph. We were successful, as you can see."

The flash pointer laid its little arrow next to the nearest small dot to the star.

"That, gentlemen and ladies, is Alpha-Aleph. It is precisely where we predicted it to be from radio-telescope data."

"This is rollicking hard-core Pohl, offering us lots of fun to distract us from brooding too much on our doom."

—Washington Post Book World

THE CRITICS LOVED

STARBURST

"Here's a new science-fiction novel in the old, traditional mold: a story about science and scientists—a story about motivation; about ways of thinking and learning and living, and about what is good for us . . . a well-crafted, well-paced yarn by one of the old masters."

—*St. Louis Post-Dispatch*

"Like Pohl's *Man Plus*, *Starburst* comments upon the natures of man and superman. Highly recommended."

—*Library Journal*

"Another example of Pohl at his finest . . . *Starburst* may well give the most effective expression to themes which have been troubling/delighting Pohl for a long time."

—*Extrapolation*

"Pohl at his best, blending science, speculation and satire to fascinate us from first page to last."

—*Publishers Weekly*

Starburst

Frederik Pohl

A Del Rey Book

BALLANTINE BOOKS • NEW YORK

A Del Rey Book
Published by Ballantine Books

Library of Congress Catalog Card Number: 81-17624

ISBN 0-345-27537-3

Manufactured in the United States of America

First Hardcover Edition: June 1982

First Paperback Edition: December 1983

Cover art by David B. Mattingly

1

EVEN THE STURDY OLD WALLS OF THE WHITE HOUSE DID NOT keep out all the winter drafts. The great gold drapes of the Grand Ballroom rippled slightly, though the windows were closed, and some of the arriving guests had cherry cheeks and frosty noses. They did not relish standing in the blowing snow on the White House lawn for the obligatory identity check and weapons search. But, like everyone else in America, they had got used to the Troubles and to the lower-case troubles the Troubles made for everybody. Besides, this was a jolly occasion. Dr. Dieter von Knefhausen rubbed his hands and beamed as he greeted each new dignitary. "A great day for your country, Dieter." "Jawohl, Herr Doktor Präsident! For all our countries!" "My deepest congratulations, Dr. von Knefhausen, from myself personally and from all France." "Merci, M. l'Ambassadeur!" Oh, they were all there to see his triumph, and he almost hopped with excitement.

Technically, to be sure, the guests of honor were many and von Knefhausen was only ninth in precedence among them—well, tenth, if you gave the President of the United States a place. He was not jealous. There was glory enough for all. Because the eight principal guests had a hard several weeks ahead of them, not to mention the rather unprecedented several years which would follow, the receiving line was kept mercifully short. Even so, it was more than two hours from the time the first of the guests shook the hand of the smiling, mellow President of the United States, at the head of the line, until the last of them paid his respects to Science Advisor Dieter von Knefhausen, at the end. It was a long line. In between President and Science Advisor were the First Lady, sleek in gold lamé, the Vice President and his eldest daughter—he had no wife at the moment—and, of course, the four bright young couples who were about to devote their lives to making a trip to another star. They were the real celebrities. Unfortunately, they had had less practice at it than the politicians, and as the short winter day waned they waned too.

They were a handsome and impressive lot. Two of the men and one of the women had distinguished military careers. Seven of the eight held pilot's ratings, ranging from Eve Barstow's Saturday afternoon sports flying to Colonel Jackman's eight thousand command hours, including chief piloting in five deep-space missions. Among the eight of them they held nineteen earned and seven honorary degrees; and every one of them was very good to look at. "May I suggest," boomed the Soviet Ambassador affably as he pumped Dr. von Knefhausen's hand, "that one of your criteria for selecting these wonderful young people must have been the way they photographed?"

"Your Excellency may certainly suggest it," beamed the Science Advisor, as dapper and delighted clasping the hand of his enemy as with any friend. "But I fear you are mistaken. Nevertheless! Since they are to be the parents, perhaps, of a whole new human race on Alpha-Aleph, why not be sure that these new human generations will be quite handsome?"

A cloud passed over the Ambassador's face. "As to that," he said slowly, "let us speak instead of the weather."

Since the day was, more than anything else, Knefhausen's personal triumph, he could afford to be generous to a foe. In any case, there was a delay in the receiving line, as the daughter of the Canadian ambassador was presenting wreaths of roses and maple leaves to each of the four astronaut wives. Knefhausen allowed the Russian to chatter of the snow in Washington as contrasted with the snow in Moscow. "Ah," said Knefhausen genially, "but one knows nothing of snow unless one has experienced the winters of Kiel! When I was a boy—" And he told the patient Ambassador of the winds that came down the Kattegat, and the bitter Januarys of his childhood. At the time of which he spoke his nation and the Ambassador's had been grinding each other to powder all across the Ukraine, and both of them knew it. Generously Knefhausen forebore to mention the thousand Russian POWs his unit of the Hitler Youth drove across the frozen fields to scour out each last overlooked turnip and wizened potato. There were things about that time that were best not mentioned anymore. Though there was nothing to be ashamed of! Not in the least! Young Dietz von Knefhausen was a member of the Youth, certainly, but he had never believed in the *Führerprinzip,* or even in the war. One joined such organizations because one wished to survive, even to thrive; but even in early adolescence he had understood that such things were to be used by him, not he by them, no matter what blood-chilling oaths one spoke. His unit leader had been no harder to manipulate than any other nominal superior in von Knefhausen's long life. Including the one who now stood at the head of this line. "I beg your pardon?" he said, recalled from the reverie of the sound of his own voice as he saw that the Russian was peering past him.

"Only a small accident, I think," the Ambassador smiled. The young Canadian girl was picking herself off the floor, very near to tears. "Ah, the poor little thing! While she was handing the flowers to Mrs. Barstow she perhaps tripped on her mother's train. Well. I have enjoyed our chat, Dr. von Knefhausen, but now you have other guests. We will continue it, I think, at another time."

The astronauts got one big break. They were excused early. That was not charity on the part of the protocol experts of the White House, it was only bowing to necessary reality. At a quarter to five the whir of a helicopter came from the landing pad. The eight starfarers exited to a round of applause and well-wishing, bundled up against the winter, and dashed through the blowing snow. The chopper lifted rapidly. No pilot wanted to stay on the White House grounds any longer than he had to. The four young couples were jounced against their seat belts so violently that Ann Becklund gasped and clutched at her husband's arm, and Will Becklund hastily found her an airsick bag. But she didn't need it, quite. At Dulles they transferred to Air Force One without incident. The feared demonstrations had not materialized, and the identity checks were almost perfunctory. In less than ten minutes they were cleared for Patrick Air Force Base in Florida, and airborne.

As the big jet leveled off, Jim Barstow left the third pilot's seat to come back to where his wife was sitting, in the private Presidential lounge. He bounced cheerfully on the leather couch. "Hey, this is luxury, hon!" He stretched, and yawned, and finally noticed his wife's damp cheek. "Aw, Eve. What's the matter?" She smiled and shook her head. "No, come on. Scared? I can't blame you for that!"

"No—anyway," she added honestly, "no more than I've been all along. I guess it was that little Canadian girl. She was so sweet."

He squeezed her shoulders sympathetically. They had talked all that out, of course. They had agreed that giving up any real chance of raising a family was certainly painful. Still, when you measured it objectively against the chance to be the first human beings to visit a planet of another star, it just was not really important. A steward came by to save him the necessity of talking about it. "Anything for you folks, sir?"

"No, thanks. Yes." It wasn't every day you flew in Air Force One. "I changed my mind. I'll have a very dry Martini, Beefeater's, with a key-lime twist, and for the lady a banana Daiquiri." Watching the steward's white-jacketed back go away, he said, "Might as well enjoy it while we can, hon."

"That's affirmative," Eve Barstow said, sitting up and looking more lively. "What does Will want?" The Becklunds were turning over a stubby chrome object; from the weeks of drill in nomenclature and repair, Eve recognized it as a spare part of the refrigerant circuits for the plasma jet. Will was looking toward them.

"Wants a real expert, I guess," her husband called, and swayed over to join them around a teak veneer coffee table. Eve was glad enough to let him go. He was a fine person, her husband; they were all fine persons, and had proved it over and over again in the long months of training for the mission. But Eve liked to be by herself sometimes. What terrified her about the next ten years most of all was that there would be no good place in their little spacecraft to do that.

Shef Jackman came back from where he had replaced Barstow in the third pilot's seat. "All squared away. We're climbing through twenty-five thousand, and it's going to be clear skies once we get past Hatteras. We'll ETA Patrick by seven o'clock, get to the Cape at eight, in bed by ten."

"I can stand some clearing up," his wife said. "I've been freezing for the last ten days."

Jackman sat down beside her, grinning. "Cheer up, Flo. We'll be warm enough in another couple of weeks."

The Space Shuttle launch was no longer newsworthy in itself, there had been so many of them, but this one was special. The VIP galleries were full, and out across the Banana River the shore was lined with ordinary citizens, watching eight human beings start the longest trip ever made by man. A million and a half people, at least. There was a difference between the audiences on the two sides of the river. The VIPs were festive and congratulatory. The citizens along the river were a mixed bag. Among them there were hundreds of placards, hard to read from the launch pad. But no one had to read them. They would all say the same thing, even though the words were different in a hundred ways: Unemployed Need Help! Cut Back Welfare Cutbacks! Stop the Andaman Islands War! Pass ERA! Do! Don't! Stop! Ban! They were all peremptory orders to a government that most of the watchers on the riverbank perceived as an enemy, and each one carried the unspoken alternative: Or Else! The nation had never been more divided. Everyone had had plenty of time to get used to division, but nothing had healed. The last time the condition of the country could have been called joyful was—when? The end of World War II? The President could not remember exactly, but he was sure that it had certainly not been within his own administration.

The President could see the riverside crowds out of the corner of his eye if he let himself. He did not. He had trained his eyes not to look at what it was best not to notice, just as he had trained his smile muscles never to ache no matter how long they had to maintain the look of joy. Well, damn it, this was a day for joy! He was entitled! Some individual occasions could be pleasing even now—as long as no crank with paranoia in his mind and a grudge in his heart appeared—as long as you did not look too far into the worrisome future—

The smile on his face flickered for a second, but he brought it back. Nothing was going to spoil this day! His chief aide, Murray Amos, helped all he could by bringing a constant stream of encouraging statistics. There were more than 4,000 accredited press people present, passing the early

Apollo record of 3,497. They had run out of the 500-page press kits, and copies were selling as high as $300 each on the black market. It was taking more than 200 chartered buses to bring the dignitaries in. Eighty ambassadors. Fifteen heads of state. Two hundred and fifty television stars. More than 3,000 "legislative guests"—it worked out to better than five apiece for every Representative and Senator. The official count was 22,000 spectators authorized, not counting the million-plus who were rumbling and chanting and sometimes firing off what looked like firecrackers—the President hoped they were firecrackers—across the Banana River. "Good, good," said the President. "Go tell Knefhausen, Murray."

"Yes, Mr. President," Amos said obediently. Not enthusiastically. He located Knefhausen, wheeling and dealing among the celebrities, accepting a ritual kiss from the head of the French space program, another one from a blonde singing star in see-through hiphuggers, clapping the back of the representative of the British Royal Society, exchanging bows and handshakes with the Japanese group.

Knefhausen glanced at Amos, gave him half a quick nod, and accepted the slip of paper from the Public Information Office. "Ah, yes, good," he said, dismissing the aide. A sullen little piece of goods, that one, von Knefhausen told himself. But not important. Murray Amos was not one of the people who knew anything. He was close enough to the President to know, however, that there was something he didn't know, and that was no doubt what made him sullen. It did not matter. In a very short time now, the voyage would be launched, the program would be begun, success was then in the hands of the gods. The wife of the President of Argentina was clamoring for his attention, in any case.

"Ah, yes, my dear lady," Knefhausen said when he had understood her question, "you wish to know why it is that when this ship is to go so far away from the Sun it begins by going so quite close? Yes. A paradox, it seems. But by circling quickly around the Sun, you see, we steal some of its very great force; the ship goes faster as a result and, in the long run, reaches the star Alpha Centauri much sooner. You see? Now you understand as much as the greatest astronomer!"

The Argentinian President's lady dimpled prettily, and put a hand on his arm to detain him. "It will be such a great adventure," she said wistfully.

"Indeed! To be sure! And they will see such sings—things! Can you imagine, dear lady, all of the stars in the sky sweeping together in a glorious rainbow of color? Yes. That is one thing. A starbow! Can you imagine, also, that for each one of them time itself will slow down? Yes. It is so! Not a great deal, but they will come back only about twenty-two years older than they leave, while all of us will age by twenty-four—excepting, of course, your charming self, dear lady!" A lie, of course—or if you wanted the truth of it, two lies. But she would not know that.

Yet she was looking at him curiously. "You do not mention that they will see this marvelous new planet, Alpha-Aleph, as you call it."

"But to be sure!" he said quickly, and caught sight of the CBS news team coming purposefully in his direction, not a moment too soon. "Ah, I fear duty calls me now. Adieu, my dear lady." And to the newscaster: "How good to see you, Alfred! Are you getting all the cooperation you need?"

"Oh, yes, just fine, Dr. Knefhausen." The cameras were panning the crowd, and the newsman's microphone was lowered. "I just wondered. Can you tell me who it is the Russian Ambassador is talking to?"

Knefhausen peered over the newsman's shoulder and scowled. "Yes, of course, Alfred. It is Dr. Hauptmann, the astronomer from our Farside Base on the Moon, who has been personally responsible for the discovery of the planet of Alpha Centauri."

"It looks as though the Ambassador's giving him a hard time. Do you know why?"

What pests these media persons were! But useful when properly managed, so Knefhausen said cheerfully, "Because he is a Russian, to be sure! It is a great occasion for us in America but, you understand, not as great for our competitors. Do you wish a statement?"

It was the easiest way to get rid of anyone from the media. "Another time, Doctor," the CBS man said; and as soon as he had turned away Knefhausen walked briskly past the astronomer and the Ambassador. He only glanced at them once, and then sat down in one of the VIP armchairs. He fixed his gaze on the President and his perpetual farmhand's grin. One could see the utility of this as a means of concealing the man's appalling overbite, but how like an American President to grin like a golliwog all the time! A true leader could be more serious. He looked up courteously as the man from the Moon joined him, but did not rise or offer his hand. "A splendid day, eh, Hauptmann? Although I perceive our Russian friends are seeking to dampen it for you?"

The astronomer shrugged morosely. "Same as always, Knefhausen."

Now here was a man who would be improved by a smile! What a weakling this creature was. But Knefhausen said kindly, "It does not matter. In a moment they will launch. Look, the outer hatches are secured and the gantry is pulling away. In six hours they will be in orbit; in another twenty they will be transshipped and on their way. And then all the world will see what a great, I could even say what a perfect, achievement this will be. And then, for all of us, you will see! Fame, lecture contracts, no doubt an honorary degree or two!"

The man refused to be cheered up. "I certainly hope so," he said, and turned, gaze lackluster, to confront the explosion of light and the great wash of sound as the old shuttle began its rise into the sky.

2

Message received from Lt Col Sheffield N Jackman, USAF, commanding U.S. Starship Constitution. *Day 40.*

ALL'S WELL, FRIENDS. THANKS TO ALL THE GOOD BUDDIES AT Mission Control for the batch of personal messages. We enjoyed the concert you beamed us, in fact we recorded most of it so we can play it over again a little farther along, in case communication gets hairy.

We are now approaching the six-week point in our expedition to Alpha Centauri, and have opened up the drive to

.75 G acceleration—close enough to our Earthside weight that we move about quite easily and comfortably. As nearly as Letski could figure, we exceeded the distance from Earth of any other manned vehicle eight days ago. We were all excited about that. But now we're really beginning to feel we're on our way! Our latest navigation check confirms Mission Control's plot, and we estimate we should be crossing the orbit of Pluto, or where the orbit of Pluto would be if it were as tipped to the ecliptic as we are, at approximately 1631 hours, ship time, of Day 40. Which is today! Letski has been keeping track of the time dilation effect, which is beginning to be significant now that we are traveling about some 6 percent of the speed of light. He says this would make it approximately a quarter of two in the morning, your time, Mission Control.

Now, that's a significant thing, and we have voted to consider it the "coastal waters" mark. From then on we will have left the solar system behind, and thus we will be the first human beings to enter upon the deeps of interstellar space.

So we plan to have a ceremony. Letski and Ann Becklund have made up an American flag and we will jettison it at that point through the Number Three survey port, along with the prepared stainless-steel plaque containing the President's commissioning speech. We are also each throwing in some private articles. I am contributing my Air Academy class ring.

There is little change since previous reports. We are settling down nicely to our routine. The *Constitution*'s outer skin temperature is now in close radiation equilibrium with the inputs from starlight and what's left of the heat from the Sun. It's certainly a lot better than when we were rounding the Sun for gravitational acceleration, and all getting pretty nervous as the heat began to seep through! I don't know if you could tell from our reports, but it was scary. Still, it was all within operational tolerances. We picked up the predicted delta-Vs, and the fusion drive never faltered.

Since then it's been pretty slow. We finished up all our postlaunch checks weeks ago, and as Dr. Knefhausen predicted, we began to find time hanging heavy on our hands. I remember him coming down to Huntsville and saying, "Between Sol and Alpha there is nothing to do, nothing!

So time will hang heavily!" Well, in between the centrifuge and the do-it-yourself medical courses we just couldn't imagine that at the time, but he was right. The spaceship really runs itself.

So we tried going along with Kneffie's proposed recreational schedule, using the worksheets prepared by the NASA Division of Flight Training and Personnel Management. At first—I think the boys back in Houston are big enough to know this!—it met with what you might call a cool reception. The first syllabus section called for studying things like number theory and the calculus of statement. Well, imagine that for openers! I'm afraid we just couldn't hack it, and we weren't desperate enough to give it the real effort it needed. So I have to say we just fooled around. Ann and Will Becklund played a lot of chess, sometimes with one of the rest of us but mostly together. Dot Letski began—wait for it!—writing a verse adaptation of *War and Peace*. The rest of us hacked around with equipment checks, and making astronomical observations, and just gabbing, and, you know, Kneffie was right. It began to get tiresome, just as he had briefed us.

So we got together one night over dinner, and we talked it over. Jim Barstow practically repeated Kneffie's speech word for word. He said mathematical questions had occupied some of the finest minds of the human race for thousands of years, and they could occupy ours fully and satisfyingly if we gave them a chance—besides which, considered purely as recreation, that had the advantage of no mass to transport, no competitive elements to get tempers disturbed, and so on. It all began to make sense. Plus we were frankly getting a little bit bored.

So we gave it a try. Now Letski is in his tenth day of trying to find a formula for primes, and my own dear Flo is trying to prove Goldbach's Conjecture by means of the theory of congruences. This is the girl who two months ago couldn't add up a laundry list! I have to admit that it certainly passes the time.

Also things are looking up in other respects. The first crop of new carrots and spring peas is coming in from the hydroponics system, so we're eating a little better. You can get pretty tired of dehydrated rations! We take turns cooking, and Flo is teaching me how to make everything come out at the same time—first time I cooked we ate in installments. Medically we are all fit. Psychologically, within predicted limits. But you know all that from the cardiovascular-respiratory monitors and so on; there was a little tension for a while, I admit, as the Sun got smaller and smaller and the time ahead began looking longer. But I think we're over the worst of it.

And we're grateful for the chance you've given us! Particularly to our godfather, the good Doctor von Knefhausen.

That's about all for now; I'll append the detailed data on our blood pressures, pulses, and so on, as well as the tape from the power plant and navigation systems readouts. I'll report again as scheduled. Take care of the Earth for us—we're looking forward to seeing it again, in twenty years or so!

3

THERE WAS A LULL IN THE URBAN GUERRILLA WAR IN Washington that week. Dr. von Knefhausen's chopper was able to float right in to the South Lawn of the White House—no sniper fire, no heat-seeking missiles. No one was even throwing rocks from the fence. Of course there was a demonstration going on. When was there not? But only a small demonstration, only a tiny newborn puppy of a demonstration: a knot of tired pickets trudging in the rain under the eye of twice as many police. They did not look militant. Probably Gay Lib or, who knew what, maybe nature food or single tax, there was no limit to the concerns with which these foolish people obsessed themselves. At any rate there were no rocks, as there would be from the peace people or the race people. All that came from them was a little disorganized booing as the helicopter landed.

Knefhausen hopped nimbly out of the chopper, bowed sardonically to *Herr Omnes*, and got out of the way as the aircraft took off again. Which it did at once. You did not risk a valuable machine for long on the South Lawn.

There was here a question of pride, so Knefhausen did not trouble to run to the White House. He strolled. He did not fear these simple people, even if the helicopter pilot did. Also he was not really eager to keep his appointment with the President.

The aide de camp who frisked him did not smile. The orderly who conducted him to the West Terrace did not salute. No one relieved him of the dispatch case with his slides and papers, although it was heavy. You could tell right away when you were in the doghouse, he thought, ducking his head from the rotor blast as the pilot circled the White House to gain altitude before venturing back across the untrustworthy city streets.

It had been a lot different just a few months ago! How soon they forgot! But Knefhausen did not forget. It was right here, this portico, where he had stood beside the President before all the world's press and photographers to tell them about the Alpha-Aleph Project. He had seen his picture on all the front pages, watched himself on the TV newscasts, as he filled their eyes with stars and shared his own glorious vision. Or part of it. A New Earth! An entire planet to be colonized by Americans, four light-years away! He remembered the launch into low orbit, foreign statesmen and scientists eating their hearts out with envy, American leaders jovial with pride. The orderlies saluted then, all right. His lecture fees had gone clear out of sight. There was even talk of making him the Vice Presidential candidate in the next election—and it could have been serious, too, if the election had been right then, and if there hadn't been this question of his having been born in another country. Then, six weeks ago, the actual launch of the interstellar spacecraft itself, from its parking orbit, spiraling down toward the Sun; yes, even then there had been many expressions of congratulation and joy, even though it was not quite the same as the Cape, and now—

Now it was all different. They took him up to the meeting in the service elevator! Astonishing. It was not so much that Knefhausen minded all of this for his own sake, he told himself, but by what means did the word get out so quickly that there was trouble? Was it only the newspaper stories? Was there a leak?

They showed him to a washroom—a public washroom!—

and he ran a comb through his thinning hair, tightened his plump cheeks, nodded once, and was ready. "Come, let us go in," he said sternly to the Marine orderly. The private knocked once on the big door of the Cabinet room, and it was opened from inside. Knefhausen entered, stern and self-assured.

There was no "Come in, Dieter, boy, pull up a pew," from the President. No Vice President jumping up to grab his arm and slap his back. His greeting was thirty silent faces turned toward him. Some were frankly hostile. Some were only reserved. The full Cabinet was there, along with half a dozen department heads and the President's personal action staff, and the most hostile face around the big oval table was the President's own.

Knefhausen bowed. No, he thought justly, I was wrong; it is better when he smiles. Such teeth! An atavistic longing for lyceum-cadet jokes made him think of clicking his heels and adjusting a monocle, but he didn't have a monocle and, in any case, did not yield to such impulses. He merely moved toward the foot of the table. There was an empty chair but he chose to stand. When the President nodded, Knefhausen said, "Yes, good morning, gentlemen. And ladies. I assume you want me to clarify the record as to the stupid lies the Russians are spreading about the Alpha-Aleph program."

Roobarooba, they muttered to each other. The President said in his sharp tenor, "So you are certain they are lies."

"Lies or mistakes, Mr. President, what's the difference? We are right and they are wrong, that's all."

Roobaroobarooba. The Secretary of State looked inquiringly at the President, got a nod, and said, "Dr. Knefhausen, you know I been on your team a long time. I don't want to disagree with any statement you care to make, but are you so sure about that? They's some mighty persuasive figures comin' out of the Russians."

"They are false, Mr. Secretary."

"Ah, well, Dr. Knefhausen, I might be inclined to take your word for it, but they's others might not. Not cranks or Commies, Dr. Knefhausen, but good, decent people. Do you have any evidence for such as them?"

"To be sure. With your permission, Mr. President?"

The President nodded again. Knefhausen unlocked his dispatch case and drew out a slim sheaf of slides. He handed them to a major of Marines, who looked to the President for approval and then did what Knefhausen told him. The room lights went down, a screen slid out of the ceiling at the back of the room, and, after some fiddling with the focus, the first slide was projected over Knefhausen's head. It showed a huge array of Y-shaped metal posts, stretching away into the distance of a bleak, powdery-looking landscape.

"This picture is our radio telescope on Farside, on the Moon," he said. "It is never visible from the Earth, because that portion of the Moon's surface is permanently turned away from us. For this reason it was selected for the site of the radio telescope. There is no electrical interference of any kind. The instrument is made up of 33 million separate dipole elements, aligned with an accuracy of one part in some millions. Its actual size is an approximate circle eighteen miles across, but by virtue of the careful positioning its performance is effectively equal to a telescope with a diameter of some twenty-six miles. Next slide, please."

Click. The picture of the huge radio-telescope array swept away and was replaced by another similar—but visibly smaller and shabbier—construction.

"This is the Russian instrument, gentlemen. And ladies. It is approximately one quarter the size of ours in diameter. It has less than one-tenth as many elements, and our reports—these are classified, but I am informed this gathering is cleared to receive this information, yes?—our reports indicate the alignment is very crude. Even terrible, you could say.

"The difference between the two instruments in information-gathering capacity is roughly a hundred to one, in our favor. Lights, please.

"What this means," he went on smoothly, smiling at each of the thirty persons around the table in turn as he spoke, "is that if the Russians say no and we say yes, bet on yes. Our radio telescope can be trusted. Theirs cannot."

The meeting shifted uneasily in its leather armchairs. They were as anxious to believe Knefhausen as he was to convince them, but they were not sure.

Representative Belden, the Chairman of the House Ways and Means Committee, was near Knefhausen at the foot of the table. He spoke up for all of them. "Nobody doubts the quality of your equipment. Especially since we've still got the bruises from paying for it all. But the Russians made a flat statement. They said that Alpha Centauri can't have a planet larger than three hundred miles in diameter, or nearer than eight hundred million miles to the star. I have a copy of the Tass release here. It admits that their equipment is inferior to our own, but they have a statement signed by twenty-two academicians that says their equipment could not miss on any object larger or nearer than what I have said, or on any body of any kind which would be a suitable landing place for our astronauts. Are you familiar with this statement?"

"Yes, of course, I have read it."

"Then you know that they state positively that the planet you call Alpha-Aleph does not exist."

"Yes, that is what they state."

"Moreover, statements from authorities at the Paris Observatory and the UNESCO Astrophysical Center at Trieste and from England's Astronomer Royal at Herstmonceux all say that they have checked and confirmed their figures."

Knefhausen nodded cheerfully. "That is correct, Representative Belden. They confirm that if the observations are as stated, then the conclusions drawn by the Soviet installation on Farside at Novy Brezhnevgrad naturally follow. I don't question the arithmetic. I only say that the observations are made with inadequate equipment, and thus the Soviet astronomers have come to a false conclusion. But I do not want to burden your patience with an unsupported statement," he added hastily as there were stirrings all around the table and the Congressman opened his mouth to speak again, "so I will tell you all there is to tell. What the Russians say is theory. What I have to counter this is not merely better theory, but also objective fact. I know that Alpha-Aleph is there because I have seen it! Lights again, Major, and the next slide, if you please!"

The screen lit up and showed glaring bare white with a sprinkling of black dots, like ink spatters on a blotter. A large one appeared in the exact center of the screen, with a few lesser ones sprinkled around it. Knefhausen picked up a flash pointer and aimed its little red arrowhead of light at the central dot.

"This is a photographic negative," he said, "which is to say that it is black where the actual scene is white and vice versa. Those objects are astronomical. The picture was taken from our Briareus Twelve satellite near the orbit of Jupiter, on its way out to Neptune four months ago. The central object is the star Alpha Centauri. It was photographed with a special instrument which filters out most of the light from the star; the instrument is electronic in nature and performs somewhat like the well-known coronascope which is used for photographing prominences on our own Sun. We hoped that by this means we might be able actually to photograph the planet Alpha-Aleph. We were successful, as you can see." The flash pointer laid its little arrow next to the nearest small dot to the star. "That, gentlemen and ladies, is Alpha-Aleph. It is precisely where we predicted it to be from radio-telescope data."

There was another buzz from the table. In the dark it was louder than before. The Secretary of State cried sharply, "Mr. President! Can't we release this photograph?"

"We will release it immediately after this meeting," said the President.

Roobarooba. Knefhausen pressed his advantage. "If I may just add," he said, "there arises the question the President has touched on, lies or mistakes? One hesitates to say 'lies,' but we are realists here, is that not true? And one can see a motivation. The Russians read our newspapers. They know what the polls say. They are aware that this project of ours, this Alpha-Aleph—this New Earth that we have and they do not—it is the single most significant source of pride for all we Americans. If they can tarnish it, how excellent for them! We live in gravely troubled times—"

"We are all aware of the Sacramento riots and the Toledo bombing, Dr. Knefhausen—and of the public-opinion polls, too," the President interrupted. "Perhaps we should stick to this one simple subject. Are there any further questions?"

Pause. These politicians were sensitive to unspoken strains and they could perceive that there was one here, even if they did not understand it. Then the committee chairman again, looking back and forth from Knefhausen to the President, but addressing his question to the head of the table: "Mr. President, I'm sure if you say that's the planet we want, then it's the planet. But others outside this room may wonder, for indeed all those dots look about alike to me. I wonder if Knefhausen could satisfy a layman's curiosity. *How* do we know that that thing is Alpha-Aleph?"

Knefhausen kept his face impassive, although his heart was filled with glee. "Slide number four, please—and keep number three in the carriage." The same scene, subtly different. "Note that in this picture, gentlemen, that one object, there, is in a different position. It has moved. You know that the stars show no discernible motion, of course. The object has moved because this picture was taken several months later —just a few days ago, in fact—also from our Briareus Twelve spacecraft; the computer-processing has just been completed, and we see that the planet Alpha-Aleph has revolved in its orbit. This is not theory, this is evidence, and I add that the original tapes from which the photoprint was made are stored in Goldstone, so there is no question that arises of foolishness." *Roobarooba*, but in a higher and excited key. Gratified, Knefhausen nailed down his point. "So, Major, if you will now return to slide three, yes— And if you will flip back and forth, between three and four, as fast as you can— Thank you." The little black dot called Alpha-Aleph bounced back and forth like a tennis ball, while all the other star points remained motionless. "This is what is called the blink comparator process, you see. I point out that if what you are looking at is not a planet, it is, excuse me, Mr. President, the damnedest funniest star you ever saw. Also it is exactly at the distance and with exactly the orbit velocity we specified based on the RT data. Now, are there any more questions?"

"No, sir!" "That's great, Kneffie!" "Clear as a cow's ass to the stud bull!" "I think that wraps it up." "That'll show the Commies where to get off!"

The President's voice overrode them all.

"I think we can have the lights on now, Major Merton," he said. "Dr. Knefhausen, thank you. I'd appreciate it if you would remain nearby for a few minutes, so you can join me in the study to check over the text of our announcement before we release these pictures." He nodded sober dismissal to his Chief Science Advisor and then, confronted by the happy faces of his cabinet, remembered to bare his overbite in a smile of pleasure.

4

Message received from Sheffield Jackman, Starship Constitution, *Day 95.*

According to Letski we are now traveling at just about 15 percent of the speed of light, almost 30,000 miles per second. Of course, we don't feel that, and there aren't any telephone poles going by outside the window; as far as we can tell, we're pretty much standing still. The fusion thrust is operating smoothly and well. We've got ourselves a new operating engineer, because Will Becklund has taken quite an interest in plasma physics and gets Letski to teach him the drill. So the two of them spend a lot of time back at the shield. Fuel, power, and life-support indices are right on the curve. There's no sweat of any kind with the ship, or, actually, with anything else.

Dot Letski calculated the other day that we've accumulated more than 35,000 mph in delta-Vs now (of course, it doesn't all show up in relative speed), so that we've passed escape velocity from the Sun. Up until then if we'd just cut the motors we'd have fallen back—sooner or later. Now we'd just go on forever. Interesting thought. What we do see out the ports is interesting, too. Relativistic effects have begun to show up as predicted. Jim Barstow's spectral studies show the stars in front of us are showing a shift to the blue end, and the Sun and the other stars behind us are shifting to the red. Without the spectroscope you can't see much, though. Beta Circini looks a little funny, maybe. As for the Sun, it's still very bright—Jim logged it as minus-six magnitude the other day—and as I've never seen it quite that way before, I can't tell whether the color looks right or not. It certainly isn't the golden yellow I associate with type G0, but neither is Alpha Centauri ahead of us, and I don't really see a difference between them. I think the reason is simply that they are so bright that the color impressions are secondary to the brightness impressions, although the spectroscope, as I say, does show the differences. It doesn't look a whole lot like the "starbow" Dr. Knefhausen promised us, but maybe it's early yet. We've all taken turns at looking back. Naturally enough, I guess. We can still make out the Earth and even the Moon in the telescope, but it's chancy. Ski almost got an eyeful of the Sun at full light-gathering aperture yesterday because the visual separation is only about twelve seconds of arc now. In a few more days they'll be too close to separate.

Let's see, what else?

We've been having a fine time with the recreational math program. Ann has taken to binary arithmetic like a duck to water. She's been involved in what I take to be some sort of statistical experimentation (we don't pry too much into what the others are doing until they're ready to talk about it—since we don't really have privacy, we have to make some), and, of all things, she demanded that we produce coins for her to flip. Well, naturally none of us had taken any money with us! Except that it turns out two of us did. Ski had a Russian silver ruble that his mother's uncle had given him for luck, and I found an old Philadelphia transit token in my pocket. Ann rejected my token as too light to be reliable, but she now spends happy hours flipping the ruble, heads or tails, and writing down the results as a series of six-place binary numbers, heads for 1 and tails for 0. After about a week my curiosity got too much for me so I began hinting to find out what she was doing. When I ask she says things like, "By means of the easy and the simple we grasp the laws of the whole world." When I say that's nice but what laws does she hope to grasp by flipping the coin? she says, "When the laws of the whole world are grasped, therein lies perfection." So, as I say, we don't press each other, and anyway it keeps her off the streets. I leave it there. It probably has something to do with her books. We all brought some, of course, in our personal allowances, and mostly we made them common property right away, but Ann kept a couple out. That's all right, though. The common ones have got pretty familiar to all of us already. When she's ready to share the others they'll be like Christmas presents, and we can all use a little surprise now and then.

Kneffie would be proud of himself if he could see how our recreation keeps us busy. None of us has managed to prove Fermat's Last Theorem yet or anything like that. But of course that's the whole point. If we could solve the problems, we'd have used them up. And then what would we do for recreation? The stuff does exactly what it was intended to. It keeps us mentally alert on this long and intrinsically rather dull boat ride.

Now we come to the parts that never get dull! I refer, of course, to what you call "personal relationships." They are really jes' fine, fellows, jes' fine. A lot better than any of us actually hoped, back there at the personal-hygiene briefings at the Houston Space Center. We follow the book. The girls take the stripy pills every day until just before their periods, then they take the green pills for four days, then they lay off pills for four days (what we call the "Weekend in Vegas"). Then back to the stripes. There was a little embarrassed joking about it at first, but we got over that. Now it's strictly routine, like brushing the teeth. We men take our red pills every day (Ski calls them "stoplights") until our wives tell us they're about to lay off. Then we take the Blue Devil (that's what we call the antidote) and have a hell of a time until the girls are on the stripes again. None of us thought any of this would work, you know. But it works fine. I don't even think sex until Flo kisses my ear and tells me she's ready to, excuse the expression, come in heat. And then like wow! Same with everybody. The aft chamber with the nice wide bunks we call "Honeymoon Hotel." It belongs to whoever needs it, and never once have both bunks been used. The rest of the time we just sleep wherever is convenient, and nobody gets uptight about it.

Excuse my getting personal, but you told me you wanted to know everything, and there's not much else to tell. We eat and sleep and look out the ports and the plasma jet thrums right along at our point-seven-five Gee, and nothing has given any trouble, or even looked as though it might be thinking about giving trouble later on. So we get quite into personal things.

But they're all right, really. We've even got used to the recycling system. None of us thought we'd get with the suction toilet, not to mention what happens to the contents, but we did. It was a little, well, annoying, at first—no, "annoying" isn't the word. Say "sordid." But now it's fine. The treated product goes into the sludge tanks, feces and urine together. The sludge from the algae goes into the hydroponic tanks, but of course by that time it's nothing but greeny-brown sort of decaying-looking vegetable matter. My father used to get worse than that out of his mulch beds every fall. That's all handled pretty much automatically anyway, so our first real physical contact with the system comes in the kitchen. By that time it's all cosmetically clean. The food we eat comes in the form of nice red tomatoes and crispy little carrots and stuff like that. (We do miss animal protein a little. The frozen stores have to last a long time, so each hamburger is a ceremonial feast. We only have them once a week or so.) The water we drink comes actually out of the air, condensed by the dehumidifiers into the reserve tanks, where we pipe it out to drink. It's all chilled and aerated, and it tastes fine. Of course, the way it gets into the air in the first place is by being sweated out of our pores or transpired from the plants (which are irrigated direct from the treated product of the reclamation tanks after the solids have settled out). We all know perfectly well, when we stop to think of it, that every drop we drink has passed through all our kidneys, and will go on doing so for ten years. But not without stops along the way. That's the point. What we drink is clear, sweet dew. And if it was once something else, well, can't you say the same of Lake Erie?

There's probably a million other things I ought to tell you about, but—

Shef Jackman clicked off the dictating switch and looked around at Ann Becklund, grinning. "But you'd bust his chops," she said dreamily, without looking up from her ruble. She was spinning it on her library shelf, and when it slowed and toppled its ringing was softer and mellower than on Earth.

Jackman shrugged, meaning that he took her point, and agreed with it, but nevertheless wanted to think it out for himself; they had all come to know each other well enough to dispense with a lot of talking. Jackman leaned back, taking his time to think the matter through. The privilege of doing that, of being able at any time to do that, was something new to him. Since the only thing they really had to do for the next several years was to stay alive there was no fidgety timetabling, no deadlines, no pressures; long elliptical thoughts could round themselves out at their own pace.

"Could tell old Dieter about everybody getting bombed," he offered slyly. For answer to that Ann needed no words at all, only a glance out of the corner of her eye. She closed her eyes for a moment, bored with her ruble, and Jackman allowed himself to close his. It was very peaceful where they were, in the communications corner of the plotting/control/instrument room. Although *Constitution* was smaller than a two-bedroom bungalow, it had crannies where eight people could almost lose themselves. Letski and Ann's husband, Will Becklund, were back as close to the plasma chamber as the shielding would let them get. The Barstows were off to Vegas, the others who knew where; Jackman and Ann Becklund were alone.

When Jackman opened his eyes he reflected that it was not entirely true, what he had told Dieter von Knefhausen about not thinking of sex at *all* when you were taking your pills. Ann had roused and uncurled herself and she was doing some sort of languid, slow-motion stretching exercises. They had all got quite informal about what they wore. Even Shef had come down to a pair of suntan uniform shorts and, sometimes, socks. So had all four of the women. All four of them had been foxy to begin with and bustwise, Shef decided appreciatively, the three-quarters gravity had made them even foxier. The only thing the pills did was that although you didn't stop thinking about making love, you didn't have the need to do anything about it.

Or had not so far, at least.

Ann lurched, and scowled at Jackman. Jackman had felt the same hiccough in the acceleration that held them down; he scowled back in agreement and reached for the intercom. "Will, Ski," he called, "what the hell?"

There was a sort of giggle from the other end, and a brief whispering. Then Will's voice said, "Maintenance check." He was giggling again when he switched off.

"Don't blow the old Kraut's mind," said Ann softly, and

Jackman nodded agreement. He picked up the dictation microphone again and finished his transmission:

"—but you've probably got the idea by now. We're happy in the service, and we all thank you for this pleasure cruise, every one!"

5

THERE WAS NO HELICOPTER FOR DR. DIETER VON KNEFhausen this time, no, not even a car! He had to take, can one believe such things?, the subway! And then to scuttle like some hunted rodent from the station to the White House perimeter; and then to mingle with those rabble along the fence, actually pretending to be one of them, until the captain of the mortar squad at the gate recognized him and tipped him a wink. And then he had to run, actually *run* like a fugitive criminal, all the way up the driveway, with the catcalls and the imprecations and even the thrown rocks and bits of offal following him all the way! Disgraceful! To be more exact, he corrected himself, disgracing; it was no accident that he was treated so shabbily, he was meant to feel humiliation.

Well . . . Inside the White House he settled himself and asked politely for the use of a washroom. What could one do? For every rise there was always some fall; he had known this, he had merely not expected it would be so quick. It made nothing! There could yet be still another rise, a rise that would astonish them all!

He combed his pale hair meticulously before the mirror. Knefhausen was a realist. He knew that for someone to be taken seriously it was valuable to have the appearance of someone who deserved to be taken seriously. The broad forehead and wide-set eyes, the strong bones of his face were of great value. Mature Polish men sometimes looked like this, and once the First Lady had asked if some drop of Polish blood explained that look of serene authority. "My family, it is true, came originally from Stettin," he acknowledged, "and that is now the Polish city of Sczeczin. But from what I know of my grandfather, if there was any flow of genes, Madam, it was quite in the opposite direction!"

He was breathing normally and in full possession of himself when he emerged from the washroom, and reconciled in advance to the fact that he would be told to cool his heels for a time before the President was ready. So he was. He sat, alert and upright but quite relaxed under the eyes of the guards with the Uzis, and opened his briefcase with the air of a man who is grateful for this unexpected chance to perform certain very necessary duties. And by and by, rereading the communique from the spaceship, he no longer had to pretend to be cheerful, he was so in fact. He even chuckled to himself a time or two at certain passages. "Happy in the service." "Like wow." "Kneffie would be proud of himself" —indeed Kneffie was! And proud of them as well, those little wonders out there! So brave, so strong!

He put down the crisp blue typescript from the NASA Mission Control and gazed unseeingly past the Marine guard, his expression pleased and proud. Knefhausen took as much pride in his eight little goslings as though they had been his own flesh and blood—no, more, even! Everybody knew that the Alpha-Aleph project was Knefhausen's baby. Not everyone knew, because he did not advertise it, that in his own mind they were his children. They were the pick of the western world, without question! And he had picked them, he had put them where they were.

His eyes focused as something fluttered past the window—good heavens, a kite, with something quite disgusting painted on it! What a difference between those clean, true spacefarers and *Herr Omnes*! He could hear the distant chanting; such people, they had nothing better to do than to harass the people who were making the world go, such great lumps! Dirty hair, dirtier morals. But the heavens belonged only to angels, and it was Dieter von Knefhausen who had chosen who the angels should be!

He snorted loudly, startling the Marine lieutenant, whose attention had been drifting. The chopper in his hand swerved toward Knefhausen, but he did not notice. Yes, he had done it! He had established the selection procedures. (And if he had done some things that could perhaps be criticized to make sure the procedures worked, then what of it?) It was he who had conceived and adapted the very recreation schedule, and above all he who had persuaded the President to make the entire project come true! That was what really counted. The hardware? It was nothing, only money. The basic scientific concepts were known. Most of the components were even on the shelves already, it took only will to put them together. That will would not have existed if it had not been for Knefhausen's own will. It was Knefhausen who created the program; Knefhausen who announced Hauptmann's discovery of the planet Alpha-Aleph from his radio-observatory on Farside—Knefhausen even who named the observatory that, although as everyone realized he could have called it by any name he chose, even his own. It was Knefhausen who carried on the fight for the project by every means available until the President bought it.

It had been a hard, bitter struggle. He reminded himself with courage that the worst was still ahead. No matter! Whatever it cost, it was now begun. And it was worthwhile. These reports from the *Constitution* already proved it. Everything was going as planned—

He paused and corrected himself justly. Not everything. No. It was yet possible for all to go awry. But he would not let it, be sure of that!

"Excuse me, Dr. Knefhausen."

He looked up, snatched back from almost half a light-year away.

"I said the President will see you now, Dr. Knefhausen," the usher repeated.

"Ah," said Knefhausen. "Oh, yes, to be sure. I was deep in thought."

"Yes, sir. This way, sir."

She led the way, and as Knefhausen rose to follow the lieutenant and two Marine privates fell in behind. This was new! To be marched along with guards fore and aft, like a condemned felon on his way to the headsman! And they did not take him at once to the President. The usher conducted him to a small, bare room and remained outside while the Marines crowded in behind. They ordered him to strip. Down to bare skin, while the privates handed each garment to the lieutenant and the lieutenant turned out every pocket and investigated every seam, and then they searched the bare skin! Yes, like a mother checking a child's armpits, or a doctor looking for hemorrhoids!

This, now. Yes, this was really new.

And when they were through he was allowed to dress and invited to sit in a straight-backed wooden chair, in that same room, while the Marines waited for some signal from outside, and the weapons were openly in their hands.

In spite of that silly young woman's use of the word "now," the signal did not come at once. Through a little window Knefhausen had time to observe what there was to see in the White House grounds. This was not much. The action was beyond the fence, where the demonstrators seemed to be increasing in numbers and in vigor.

Perhaps, Knefhausen thought wryly, he had chosen a poor time to join the councils of the mighty. Power was seeping away from the organs of government, and erupting in places which were worrisome and distasteful. Such goings-on! A black riot in Atlanta, Georgia, with twenty-two dead and some of the handsomest new buildings torched to the ground. A power failure in Chicago, and the whole Loop in the hands of looters and muggers for six long, frightful nights.

The police were barely in control. Perhaps they were not in control at all, except where there survived still some consensus of obedience to law, and those places were more rare each day. If one took the Washington subway, as Knefhausen had just done, one could see the spectrum of police authority. In downtown, governmental Washington there was no smoking on the subway, no spitting, no loud playing of radios, and the transit cops wrote out summonses for offenders. Between D Street and Georgetown police eyes were closed against minor violations, but still the person and property of the riders was safe. From Georgetown on the smoking was widespread. And not only of tobacco. And not only smoking. The works came out at Georgetown, and the eager addicts sought their needles, and the cops rode two in a car, and only in one car of a train. In the rest of the train King Mob made his own rules, and what any transit cop sought in that section was not glory. It was only survival.

It was quite a shame. Even one's well-earned perquisites

were devalued. Sometimes abolished entirely. His lecture tour had been interrupted, and finally terminated, by ridiculous demonstrators. In Pittsburgh it was illegal aliens demanding an end to deportation to Mexico. In Cleveland, Detroit, and two universities in Ohio, it was protest against the President's decision to assist friendly African governments against their Moslem revolutionaries. In every city, everywhere, there was a constant outcry from the unemployed and the welfare clients. And such terrible injustice! For none of these things, not one of them, was in any sense the proper responsibility of Dieter von Knefhausen! In the fabric of society the seams were pulling loose!

But, of course, Knefhausen had not chosen this time. It was simply the time he had been born in. The prudent man wasted no tears in bemoaning the absence of what simply no longer existed. The prudent man used his strength on achieving what was possible, and Dieter von Knefhausen had achieved very, very much!

The door opened, and the usher looked in. Knefhausen shook himself and focused on what had been before his unseeing eyes all along: new turmoil at the outside gates, a thin blue cloud of tear gas, distant, furious shouting. "Ah, King Mob is busy," he observed.

The woman glanced at him incuriously. "There's no danger, sir. Through here, please."

The President was in his private study, but to Knefhausen's surprise he was not alone. There was yet another Marine corporal with a weapon, which one could understand. But there were four other men in the room. Knefhausen recognized them as Murray Amos, the President's personal secretary; the Secretary of State; the Speaker of the House; and, of all people, the Vice President. How extraordinary, Knefhausen thought, for what was described as a confidential briefing for the President alone! But he rallied quickly.

"Excuse me, Mr. President," he said cheerfully. "I thought you were ready for our little talk, but perhaps that silly girl has brought me in too soon."

"No, I'm ready, Knefhausen," said the President. The cares of his years in the White House rested heavily on him today. He looked very old and tired, and the famous overbite was very clear. "You will tell these gentlemen what you would have told me."

"Ah, yes, I see," said Knefhausen, to conceal the fact that he did not see at all. Surely the President did not mean what his words said; therefore it was necessary to try to understand what was in his thoughts. "Yes, to be sure. Here is something, Mr. President. A new report from the *Constitution*! Very gratifying! It was received by burst transmission from the Lunar Orbiter via Goldstone just an hour ago, and has just come from the decoding room. Let me read it to you. Our brave astronauts are proceeding splendidly, just as we planned. They say—"

"Don't read it to us just now," said the President harshly. "We'll no doubt want to hear it, but first there's something else. I want you to tell this group the full story of the Alpha-Aleph project."

"Ah, yes, Mr. President, the full story." Knefhausen hung on gamely. "Of course. You wish me to begin with the very beginning, when first we realized at the lunar observatory that we had located a planet—"

"No, Knefhausen. Not the cover story. The truth."

"Mr. President!" cried Knefhausen in sudden agony. "I must inform you that I protest this premature disclosure of vital data!"

"The truth, Knefhausen!" shouted the President. It was the first time Knefhausen had ever heard him raise his voice. "It won't go out of this room, but you must tell them everything. Tell them why it is that the Russians are right and we are lying to the world! Tell them why we sent those human beings on a suicide mission, with orders to land on a planet that we have always known does not exist!"

6

Message received from Shef Jackman, Day 130.

It has been a long time, hasn't it? I'm sorry. Call me a lousy correspondent. There's so much to keep me busy, and I just don't get around. Like the last two days, I was playing a thirteen-game chess series with Eve Barstow—she was playing the Bobby Fischer games and I was playing in the style of Reshevsky—and it was going really well until Jim came to collect her for their weekend. "Give my regards to Kneffie," he said, and then I happened to think I owed you a report. So here it is—better late than never, ha-ha, right?

In my own defense, though, it isn't only that we've been busy with our things. It takes a lot of energy for these chatty little letters. Some of us aren't so sure they're worthwhile. Just this talking to you, you know, the way you people talk to each other, takes a lot more of my own personal energy than, gosh, I don't know, than the whole eisteddfod we had the other night, but there's the ship's reserve to be considered, too. The farther we get, the more power we need to accumulate for a transmission. Right now it's not really so bad yet, but, well, I might as well tell you the truth, right? Kneffie made us promise that. Always tell the truth, he said, because this is one grand damn experiment and you're a big part of it yourselves, and we need to know what you're doing, all of it. So we usually do tell just about everything. Well, almost just about, ha-ha.

Anyway, the truth in this case is that we were a little short of disposable power for a while because Jim Barstow needed quite a lot for research purposes. You will probably wonder what the research is, but I can't really answer. We have a rule that we don't criticize, or even talk about, what anyone else is doing until they're ready. And Jim isn't ready yet. I take the responsibility for the whole thing, not just the power drain but the damage to the ship. I said it was all right for Jim to go ahead with it. (On the other hand, Will Becklund had no business being there, so that part was his own fault.)

We're going pretty fast now, and to the naked eye the stars fore and aft have blue-shifted and red-shifted nearly out of sight. It's funny, but we haven't been able to observe Alpha-Aleph yet, even with the occulting disk in the spotting telescope to block out the star. Now, with the shift to the blue, we probably won't see it at all until we slow down. We can still see the Sun all right, but I guess what we're seeing is ultraviolet when it's home.

I don't know if all of you understand this "starbow" effect. I've just begun to, myself. It's like—oh, say, like you can only see one octave on a piano keyboard. Somebody slides the piano a couple of inches to the left. So what used to be the A-flat is now maybe the C-sharp, but it looks like the same A-flat. It sounds like A-flat; it's the same number of keys down from the upper limit of your vision.

Let me tackle it a different way. See, the way your eye perceives color is, photons hit the organic dyes in the retina. The photon has its own energy. *Ping* go the dye molecules sensitive to that much energy, and we say, aha, that one's blue. Another one comes by a little less energetic, and it excites some other molecules, and we say, ah, green. Okay? Now we get relativistic. Because we're moving away from the photon—or it's moving away from us, makes no difference—it loses a little energy. So that first one arrives a little tired out. Has a little less energy. It started out blue, but now it's weakened down to green, and that's what we see.

Or anyway, that's what we're supposed to see. Right now we're seeing more in front than I expected to and less behind. Behind, mostly just blackness. It started out like, I don't know what you'd call it, sort of a burnt-out fuzziness, and it's been spreading over the last few weeks. Actually in front it seems to be getting a little brighter. I don't know if you all remember, but there was some argument about whether we'd see the starbow at all, because some old guys ran computer simulations and said it wouldn't happen. Well, *something* is happening! It's like Kneffie always says, theory is one thing, evidence is better, so there! (Ha-ha.) Of course, all this relativistic frequency shifting means that every time we transmit we have to figure our velocity in and retune accordingly, which is another reason why, all in all, I don't think I'll be writing home every Sunday, between breakfast and the ball game, the way I ought to!

But don't worry. The mission's going fine. Well, almost fine. Well, I might as well tell the truth and say, yes, there are a few little things. Nothing big. The structural damage was really minimal, absolutely. A few sort of personal problems. Jim Barstow has a bee in his bonnet, and not just because of what happened to the ship. But all he's done is sort of hint about it. Well, more than hint. He and Ski had practically a big fight just before they tested out the power-plant modifications, and they wouldn't tell the rest of us what it was about until they were sure. I guess they're not sure yet. But if it was anything really urgent I'm sure they'd tell us.

No more of that. Let's talk about the good things. The "personal relationships" keep on being just great. We've done a little experimental research in that area too that wasn't on the program, but it's all okay. No problems. Worked out fine. I think maybe I'll leave out some of the details, but we found some groovy ways to do things. Oh, hell, I'll give you one hint. Dot Letski says I should tell you to get the boys at Mission Control to crack open two of the stripy pills and one of the Blue Devils, mix them with a quarter-teaspoon of black pepper and about 2 cc of the conditioner fluid from the recycling system. Serve over orange sherbet, and, oh, boy. After the first time we had it Flo made a crack about its being "seminal," which I thought was a private joke, but it broke everybody up. Dot figured it out for herself weeks ago. We wondered how she got so far so fast with *War and Peace* until she let us into the secret. Then we found out what it could do for you, both emotionally and intellectually: the creative over the arousing, as they say.

Ann and Jerry Letski used up their own recreational programs early—real early, they were supposed to last the whole voyage! So they swapped microfiches, on the grounds that each was interested in an aspect of causality and it was worth seeing what the other side had to offer. Now Ann is deep into people like Kant and Carnap, and Ski is sore as a boil because there's no *Achillea millefolium.* Needs the stalks for his researches, he says. He is making do with flipping his ruble to generate hexagrams. In fact, we all borrow it now and then, but it's not the right way. Honestly, Mission Control, he's right. Some more thought should have been given to our other needs, besides sex and number theory. We can't even use chop bones from the kitchen wastes, because there isn't any kitchen waste and besides all our frozen meats were cut off the bone to save mass. I wish they hadn't saved quite so much. I know you couldn't think of everything, but, after all, there's no Seven-Eleven on the corner to run to out here.

Anyway, we improvise. As best we can, and mostly well enough.

Let's see, what else?

Did I send you Jim Barstow's proof of Goldbach's Conjecture? Turned out to be very simple once he had devised his multiplex parity analysis idea. Mostly we don't fool with that sort of stuff anymore, though. We got tired of number theory after we'd worked out all the fun parts, and if there is any one thing that we all work on (apart from our private interests) it is probably the calculus of statement. We don't do it systematically, only as time permits from our other activities, but it's fun trying to use it to talk to each other. We're all pretty well convinced that a universal grammar is feasible, and it's easy enough to see what that leads to. Flo has done more than most of us. She asked me to put in that Boole, Venn, and all those old people were on the wrong track, but she thinks there might be something in Leibniz's "calculus ratiocinator" idea. There's a J. W. Swanson suggestion that she likes for multiplexing languages. (Jim took off from it to work out his parity analysis.) The idea is that you devise a double-vocabulary language. One set of meanings is conveyed, say, by phonemes, that is, by the shape of the words themselves. Another set is conveyed by pitch. It's like singing a message, half of it conveyed by the words, the other half by the tune. Like rock music. You get both sets of meanings at the same time. She's now working on third, fourth and nth dimensions, so as to convey many kinds of meanings at once, but it's not very fruitful so far. (Except for using sexual intercourse as one of the communications media. Ha-ha.) Most of the senses available are too limited to convey much, like body orientation, or are difficult to generate properly, like smell. By the way, we thought of checking out the existing "artificial languages," so we put Will Becklund under hypnotic regression to recapture the Esperanto he'd learned as a kid. Looks like a blind alley. Doesn't even convey as much as standard English or French. (But we'd like to investigate the others, so list appended of texts requested for Volapük, Interlingua, Latine sine flexione, and so on. And, listen, please don't be so chintzy with your transmissions, will you? You've got more power than we do!)

Medical readouts follow. We're all healthy. Eve Barstow gave us a medical check to make sure. Ann and Ski had little rough spots in a couple of molars, so she asked if she could fill them for the practice and they let her. I don't mean practice in filling teeth, I mean practice in using acupuncture instead of procaine. Worked fine.

We all have this writing-to-Daddy-and-Mommy-from-Camp-Tanglewood feeling, and we'd like to send you some samples of our handicrafts. The trouble is there's so much of them. Everybody has something he's personally pretty pleased with, like Barstow's proof of most of the classic math problems and my own multimedia adaptation of *Sur le pont d'Avignon*. It's hard to decide among them, especially when we have to watch our power drain a little bit for a while. So we took a vote and decided the best thing was Ann's verse retelling of *War and Peace*. As you can guess, it runs pretty long! I hope the power holds out. I'll transmit as much of it as I can . . .

7

IN THE "HONEYMOON HOTEL" OF THE STARSHIP CONSTITUTION Eve Barstow lay with her husband's arms around her, staring wide-eyed at the blank wall. They were not making love. They hadn't been, and it did not seem likely they would be.

Abruptly the lights went out, and then came on again in quick flashes as the ship's circuit breakers coped with an overload. "Shef's probably transmitting again," Eve guessed.

Her husband moved slightly in the cupped-spoons position behind her. "Uh-huh," he agreed, and yawned loudly. He sounded tired, but Eve knew that in fact he was simply bored.

The flickering of the lights was terribly annoying and, although neither Eve nor any other member of the crew was prone to such things as migraines, she could feel one coming on. Back on Earth she had *never* had headaches. Back on Earth she had never lain in her husband's arms and felt lonely, either.

Just outside the curtain that gave them all the privacy they had, Ann Becklund and Flo Jackman were disagreeing. Not just disagreeing. Eve could tell without seeing that they were facing each other across the dropline shaft, Ann with her hands on her hips, shouting, Flo with her arms outflung, shouting, the two of them almost drowning out the drone of the plasma generator. You got very few surprises when you lived on board the *Constitution*. Eve knew exactly how every member of the party stood, and spoke, and shaped his face, in every state of feeling of stimulus, because she had seen each one, again and again. The *Constitution* was pretty big, as spaceships go, but spaceships go rather many to the barrel, and the farthest any member of the party had been from any other in all the weeks and months since they took off was fifty-three feet. No, Eve thought, not true. Will and her husband had been three or four times that far away at least once—when they were outside the hull with the power cut off, studying the externalities of the drive. But she didn't want to think about that. She shifted uncomfortably on the rather hard foam mattress. Her husband didn't even notice. Honeymoon Hotel was a kind of special place for them—not just the way it had been for all the couples, of course. They'd practically built it. The curved couches themselves, one of which they were now lying on, had been vertical stress-bearing members for the extra bursts of acceleration when they rounded the Sun, before she and Jim had unshipped them and fitted them against the inner hull wall; the thin mattress had once been part of the protective foam for that same time . . . and when they fixed them up, what ribald jokes and squeezes and goosings went on. And how little since!

The flickering stopped and the diffused bead-lights resumed their steady glow. Jim stirred uncomfortably and raised his head to peer at her. "Blow your nose, sit up," he said. He wasn't giving orders. He was just describing what she would be doing for the next few minutes, and he was quite right, and she discovered he was right about needing to blow her nose, too; good heavens, had she been weeping?

She said bitterly, "I might as well, since nothing's happening here."

Jim rolled over and yawned. That was a sort of answer, signifying that he didn't care much one way or the other. As she pulled on the wraparound that she still usually wore he absentmindedly stroked her flank. That was the rest of the answer, meaning that they could make it some other time when she was feeling more cheerful.

When she exited Honeymoon Hotel, Flo and Ann were standing exactly as she had imagined them, and they neither stopped their discussion nor looked at her as she walked past to the shaft, tugged the line to make it rise, and put her foot in a stirrup. She envied them. She wished that someone on the ship cared enough about what she did or thought to argue with her about it.

8

AS KNEFHAUSEN WAS LEAVING HIS OFFICE, MRS. AMBROSE came running after him. Telephone? At this time? But it was urgent and from Goldstone; he took it, listened for a moment, slammed the phone down, and left, scowling. So! The telemetry had stopped! Really, those young people were almost no longer excusable! He barked at the driver of the scout car and scowled at the machine gunner until he moved over to make room in the back seat. At least now they gave him a driver again, and an armored helicopter even for the actual entry to the White House. But that was not really courtesy; it was simply the only way one could get there.

So. This new aggravation, should he tell the President about it? He thought not. There was no need to trouble the President with extraneous details. Perhaps even there was some simple explanation, perhaps technical, and by the time he got back to his office it would have been analyzed and corrected—a relay failure, some sort of radio interference from the solar wind, who could know?

He knew this was untrue. The telemetry did not matter for its overt purposes, for there was no need to go on reporting the same densities of H+ ions and the same blue-shift measurements, and if anything changed the young people would surely observe and report. That at least one could count on! But what the young people might not tell was the measurements of pheromones in the air, the scraps of their pillow talk, the hundred other little sampling snoops he had seen to. They had discovered this. Yes, that was the case. They had closed off his eyes and ears and nose in their ship. He now could know only what they chose to tell him of their states of sexual arousement, their private confidences, their developing interests and discoveries. And it did not matter if he liked this or loathed it, there was no help, it was done!

Well, other matters pressed. He throttled his indignation and entered the helicopter.

Under other circumstances it might have been a pleasant ride. Spring was well advanced, and along the Potomac the cherry blossoms were beginning to bud, and Rock Creek Park was all the pale green of new leaves. There were darker prospects. Even over the *whup, whup* of the helicopter rotor Knefhausen could hear an occasional rattle of small-arms fire from around Georgetown, and the Molotov cocktails and tear gas from the siege at the Kennedy Center were steaming the sky with smoke and fumes. They never stopped! For what reason should one try to help people like this?

And his children in the *Constitution*, were they any better? Such reports they were sending, hints where there should be only facts. He had had to get expert help in translating what the latest one was all about. He didn't like the need, and even less liked the results. What had gone wrong? They were his kids, handpicked! How had he missed the signs of this, this hippiness, this moral decay? There had been no suggestion of such a thing in any of their records, at least not past the age of twenty or so when one might forgive it, and even then only for Ann Becklund and Eve Barstow. So then! How had they got into this *I Ching* foolishness, and the stupid business with the *Achillea millefolium,* better known as the common yarrow? What "experiments" were these they spoke of? Who among them started this disgustingly unscientific thing of acupuncture? How dared they depart from their programmed power budget for "research purposes," and what were these purposes, then? Above all, what was the "damage to the ship"?

He pulled a pad out of his briefcase and scribbled a note:

With immediate effect, cut out the nonsense. I have the impression you are all acting like irresponsible children. You are letting down the whole ideals of the program.

Knefhausen

As soon as he had run the short distance from the chopper pad to the sandbagged White House entrance, he gave the slip to a page from the Message Center for immediate encoding and transmission to the *Constitution* via Goldstone, Lunar Orbiter, and Farside Base. All they needed was a reminder, he persuaded himself. Then they would settle down. But he was still worried as he allowed himself to be strip-searched and his crevices investigated, and worried as he dressed himself again under the eye of the guards. Still. What could one do? He peered into a mirror as he adjusted his tie, patted his hair down, smoothed his mustache with the tip of a finger, and presented himself to be led away.

This time they went down, not up. Knefhausen was going to the basement chamber that had been successively Franklin D. Roosevelt's swimming pool, the White House press lounge, a TV studio for taping jolly little two-shots of the President with Congressmen and Senators for the folks back home to see, and, now, the heavily armored bunker in which anyone trapped in the White House in the event of a successful attack from the city outside could hold out, could at least have some real hope of holding out, for several weeks, during which time the Fourth Armored would surely be able to retake the grounds from its bases in Maryland. It was not a comfortable room, but it was a safe one. Besides being armored against attack, it was as thoroughly soundproof, spyproof, and leakproof as any structure in the world, not excepting the Under-Kremlin or the Colorado NOROM base.

Knefhausen was not kept waiting at all. Once this would have been a good sign. Now it could only be bad. But all signs were bad when one knew what was coming.

There were no leather armchairs here. The room was set up as for a meeting of some social club or P.T.A., folding metal chairs arranged in rows. Most of them were occupied, no less than thirty-five people, perhaps more, many of them mere Congressmen or military officers. Several, Knefhausen noticed as they left off their whispering to each other to stare at him, wore bandages, one even a great cast on his upper arm and chest; a Congressman, perhaps, who had had the ill judgment to return to his district in Newark or Cleveland or San Francisco? It was distressing that Knefhausen did not even recognize some of these people! Internally he fumed. But he maintained his benign expression of polite dignity as he was seated in a chair by the door, with of course one of the Marine guards posted just behind him.

The President was standing in a corner, whispering with Murray Amos and someone with three-star general's stars. At length he broke off and made his way to the little cinder-block platform at the front of the room. (Cinder blocks, like steel chairs, could not be made to burn.) He drank from a crystal goblet of water on the table by his chair, looking wizened and weary, and disappointed at the way a boyhood dream had turned out: the Presidency was not what it had seemed to be from the farm outside Muncie, Indiana.

He raised his head and looked out over the room. "All right," he said. "We all know why we're here. The government of the United States has given out information which was untrue. It did so knowingly and wittingly, and we've been caught at it. Now we want you to know the background, so that you will all support us in maintaining this pretense for a time longer, and so Dr. Knefhausen is going to explain the Alpha-Aleph project. Go ahead, Knefhausen."

Even counting the teeth, the man had a certain dignity. Knefhausen rose and gave him a nod of respect before he walked unhurryingly to the little lectern set up for him, off to one side of the President. He opened his papers on the lectern, studied them thoughtfully for a moment with his lips pursed, and said:

"As the President has said, the Alpha-Aleph project is in fact a camouflage. A few of you learned this some months ago, and then you referred to it with other words. 'Fraud.' 'Fake.' Words like that. But if I may say it in French, it is not any of those words, it is a legitimate *ruse de guerre.* Not the *guerre* against our political enemies in other nations, or even against those crazy persons in the streets with their Molotov cocktails and bricks. I do not mean those wars, I mean the war against ignorance. For, you see, there were certain sings—certain *things* we had to know, for the sake of science and progress. Alpha-Aleph was designed to find some of them out for us, and for no other purpose at all. Especially not for the purposes for which we said it was intended, this is true.

"I will tell you the worst parts first," he said. "Number one, there is no such planet as Alpha-Aleph. The Russians were right. Number two, we knew this all along. Even the photographs we produced were fakes, and in the long run the world will find this out and they will know of our *ruse de guerre*. I can only hope that they will not find out too soon, for if we are lucky and keep the secret for a while, then I hope we will be able to produce good results to justify what we have done. As I believe," he went on, "you gentlemen and ladies who are present have had some suspicions that these things may be true, and so the President has authorized me to tell you all of this, so that you can see the importance.

"Number three," he said, "when the *Constitution* reaches its destination in the vicinity of the star Alpha Centauri there will be no place for them to land, no way to leave their spacecraft, no sources of raw materials which they might be able to use to make fuel to return, no nothing but the star and empty space. This fact has certain consequences. The *Constitution* was designed with enough hydrogen fuel reserve for a one-way flight, plus maneuvering reserve. There will not be enough for them to come back, and the source they had hoped to tap, namely the planet Alpha-Aleph, does not exist. So they will not come back. Consequently they will die there. Those are the bad things to which I must admit."

There was a murmurous sigh from the audience. The President was frowning to himself, his upper teeth nibbling his lower lip. Knefhausen waited patiently for the medicine to be swallowed, then went on.

"You ask, then, why we have done this thing? Condemning eight intelligent and courageous young people to their death? The answer is simple: knowledge. To put it with other words, we must have the basic scientific knowledge we need to protect the free world. You are all familiar, I si—I believe, with the known fact that basic scientific advances have been very few these past ten years and more. Much development of applications. But of basic knowledge? Not so much. There have been many peculiar discoveries and strange suggestions. Particles you cannot count within the atom, astronomical peculiarities which one can only catalogue, without comprehension. The grand, simplifying intuitive leaps, where are they? Very few, in the years since Einstein, or better still since Weizsäcker. Our science is drowning in quasars and quarks.

"But without these new basic understandings, the new technology must soon stop developing. It will run out of steam, you see. A Newton or a Kant discovers a new island, and then the R&D people can build on it; but unless someone is always discovering new islands, soon they have no place to build."

Knefhausen stepped back and laced his fingers across his chest. "Now I must tell you a story," he said. "It is a true scientific story, not a joke. I know you do not want jokes from me at this time. There was a man named de Bono, a Maltese, who wished to investigate the process of creative thinking. There is not much known about this process, but he had an idea how he could find something out. So he prepared for an experiment a room that was stripped of all furniture, with two doors, one across from the other. You go into one door, you walk through the room, you go out the other. He put at the door that was the entrance some materials for his experiment. Two flat boards. Some ropes. And he got as his subjects some young children. Now he said to the children, 'Now, this is a game we will play. You must go through this room and out the other door, that is all. If you do that, you win. But there is one rule. You must not touch the floor with your feet or your knees or with any part of your body or your clothing. We had here a boy,' he said, 'who was very athletic and walked across on his hands, but he was disqualified. You must not do that. Now go, and whoever does it fastest will win some chocolates.'

"So he took away all of the children but the first one and, one by one, they tried. There were ten or fifteen of them, and each of them did the same thing. Some it took longer to figure out, some figured it out right away, but it always was the same trick. They sat down on the floor, they took the boards and the ropes, and they tied one board to each foot and they walked across the room like on snowshoes. The fastest one thought of the trick right away and was across in a few seconds. The slowest took many minutes. But it was the same trick for all of them, and that was the first part of the experiment.

"Now this Maltese man, de Bono, performed the second part of the experiment. It was exactly like the first, with one difference. He did not give them two boards. He only gave them one board.

"And in the second part every child worked out the same trick, too, but it was of course a different trick. They tied the rope to the end of the single board. Then they stood on the board, and jumped up, tugging the rope to pull the board forward, hopping and tugging, moving a little bit at a time, and every one of them succeeded. But in the first experiment the average time to cross was maybe forty-five seconds. And in the second experiment the average time was maybe twenty seconds. With one board they did their job faster than with two.

"Perhaps now some of you see the point. Why did not any of the children in the first group think of this faster method of going across the room? It is simple. They looked at what they were given to use for materials and, they are like all of us, they wanted to use everything. But they did not need everything. They could do better with less, in a different way."

Knefhausen paused and looked around the room, savoring the moment. He had them now, he knew; even the Marine guards were hanging on his words. It was just as it had been with the President himself, three years before. They were beginning to comprehend the vastness and the necessity of the plan Dieter von Knefhausen had devised, and the pale, upturned faces were no longer as hostile, only perplexed and quite afraid.

He went on:

"So now you know what Project Alpha-Aleph is about, gentlemen and ladies. We have selected eight of the most intelligent human beings we could find—healthy, young, very adventurous. We played on them a nasty trick, to be sure. But we gave them in exchange an opportunity no one has ever had. The opportunity to *think*. To think for ten *years*. To think about basic questions. Out there they do not have the extra board to distract them. If they want to know something they cannot run to the library and look it up and find that somebody has said that what they were thinking could not work. They must think it out for themselves.

"So in order to make this possible we have practiced a deception on them, and it will cost them their lives. All right, that is tragic, yes. But if we take their lives we give them in exchange immortality.

"How do we do this? This is again trickery, gentlemen and ladies. I do not say to them, 'Here, your task is to achieve new basic organizing understandings and report them to us.' I camouflage the purpose of the experiment, so that the subjects will not be distracted even by that. We have told them that all of this is recreational, a way to help them pass the time. This too is a *ruse de guerre*. The 'recreation' is not an expedient to make the long trip tolerable. It is the central fact of the experiment, without which the trip would not have been undertaken.

"So we start them with the basic tools of science. With numbers, that is with magnitudes and quantification, with all that scientific observations are about. With 'grammar.' This is not the grammar you learned from Miss Mulholland in your composition class when you were thirteen years old, it is a technical term. It means with the calculus of statement and the basic rules of communication, and this is so that they can learn to think clearly by communicating fully and without fuzzy ambiguities. We give them very little else, only the opportunity to mix these two basic ingredients and come up with new forms of knowledge.

"What will come of these things? That is a fair question. Unfortunately there is no answer. Not yet. If we knew the answer in advance we would not have to perform the experiment. So we do not know what will be the end result of this, but already they have accomplished very much. Old questions that have puzzled the wisest of scientists for hundreds of years they have solved already! I will give you one example. You will say, 'Yes, but what does it *mean*?' I will answer, 'I do not know'; I only know that it is so hard a question that no one else has been able to answer it since it was first asked, for hundreds of years. It is a proof of a thing which is called Goldbach's Conjecture. Only a conjecture; you could call it a guess. A guess by an eminent mathematician some many years ago, that every even number can be written as the sum of two prime numbers. This is one of those simple problems in mathematics that everyone can understand and no one can solve. You can say 'Certainly, sixteen is the sum of eleven and five, both of which are prime numbers, and thirty is the sum of twenty-three and seven, which also are both prime, and I can give you such numbers for any even number you care to name.' Yes, you can do this; but can you prove that for *every* even number it will *always* be possible to do this? No. You cannot. No one has been able to, but our friends on the *Constitution* have done it, and this was in the first few months. They have yet more than nine years. I cannot say what they will do in that time, but it is foolish to imagine that it will be anything less than very much indeed. A new relativity, a new universal gravitation—I don't know, I am only saying words. But much."

He paused again. No one was making a sound. Even the President was no longer staring straight ahead without expression but was looking directly at him—one could not say with kindness, certainly, but without loathing at least.

"It is not too late to spoil the experiment. It therefore follows that it is necessary to keep the secret a bit longer, as long as possible in fact. But there you have it, gentlemen and ladies. That is the true protocol for the Alpha-Aleph experiment." He dreaded what would come next, postponed it for a second by consulting his papers, shrugged, faced them, and said: "Now, are there any questions?"

Oh, yes, there were certainly questions! *Herr Omnes* was dazzled for a moment, stunned a little, took a few breaths to overcome the spell of the simple and beautiful truths he had heard. But then first one piped up, then another, then two or three shouting at once. There were questions of all sorts. Questions beyond answering. Questions Knefhausen did not have time to hear, much less answer, before the next question was on him. Questions to which he did not know the answers. Questions, worst of all, to which the answers were like pepper in the eyes, enraging, blinding the people to sense. But he had to face them, and he tried to answer them. Even when they shouted so that, outside the thick double doors, the Marines in the machine-gun post looked at each other uneasily and wondered what made the dull rumble that penetrated the very good soundproofing of the room. "What I want to know, who put you up to this?" "Mr. Chairman, nobody; it is as I have said." "But see now, Knefhausen, do you mean to tell us you're murderin' these good people for the sake of some Goldberg's theory?" "No, Senator, not for Goldbach's Conjecture, but for all that great advances in science will mean in the struggle to keep the Free World free." "You're confessing that you've dragged the United States of America into committing a palpable fraud?" "A legitimate ruse of war, Mr. Secretary, because there was no other way." "The photographs, Knefhausen?" "Faked, General, as I have told you. I accept full responsibility." And so on and so on, the words "murder" and "fraud" and even "treason" coming faster and faster.

Until at last the President stood up and raised his hand. Order was a long time coming, but at last they quieted down.

"Whether we like it or not, we're in it," he said simply. "There is nothing else to say. You have come to me, many of you, with rumors you have heard, and asked for the truth. Now you have the truth, and it's classified Top Secret and must not be divulged. You all know what this means. I will only add that in this matter there are to be no leaks whatsoever. I personally propose to see that any breach of this security is investigated with all the resources of the government and punished with the full penalty of the law. I declare this a matter of national emergency, and remind you that the penalty includes the death sentence when appropriate—and I say that in this case it is appropriate." He nibbled at his lower lip as though something tasted bad in his mouth, looking older than his years. He allowed no further discussion, and dismissed the meeting.

Half an hour later, in his private office, it was just Knefhausen and the President. Although presumably it was still broad daylight outside, all the Oval Office's lights were on; the steel plates on the windows kept out the sun, if not the distant sounds of the troubled city. "All right," said the President, "it's hit the fan. The next thing is the world will know it. I can postpone that a few weeks, maybe even a few months. I can't prevent it."

"I am grateful to you, Mr. President, for—"

"Shut up, Knefhausen. When I agreed to do this I took the risk of impeachment knowingly. Now I think the stakes are higher than that."

"Mr. President! I must point out that at that time only three people knew the secret. It was not my decision that there should be more."

"I don't want speeches from you, and I won't accept recriminations. There is one thing I want from you, and that is an explanation. What the hell is this about mixing up narcotics and free love and so on?"

"Ah," said Knefhausen, "yes, you refer to the most recent communication from the *Constitution*. I agree completely. I have already dispatched, Mr. President, a strongly worded order. Because of the communications lag it will not be received for some months, but I assure you the matter will be corrected."

The President said bitterly, "I don't want any assurances, either. Do you watch television? I don't mean 'I Love Lucy' and ball games, I mean news. Do you know what sort of shape this country is in? The bonus marches in 1932, the race riots in 1967—they were nothing. Time was when we could call out the National Guard to put down disorder. Last week I had to call out the Army to use against three companies of the Guard. One more scandal and we're finished, Knefhausen, and this is a big one."

"The purposes are beyond reproach—"

"Your purposes may be. Mine are, I hope, or at least I try to tell myself that it was for the good of science and humanity I did this, and not so I would be in the history books as the President who contributed a major breakthrough. But what are the purposes of your friends on the *Constitution*? I agreed to eight martyrs, Knefhausen. I didn't agree to forty billion dollars out of the nation's pockets to give your eight young friends ten years of gang bangs and dope."

"Mr. President, I assure you this is only a temporary phase. I have instructed them to behave responsibly."

"And if they don't, what are you going to do about it?" The President, who never smoked, stripped a cigar, bit off the end and lit it. "My *God,*" he said, shaking his head, "it's politicians who are supposed to be the manipulators, not scientists. You're acting like a tinpot Jehovah! You use human beings like laboratory rats, tricking them and in the end killing them."

It is not an easy thing to challenge a President in his Oval Office, but Knefhausen faced him stoutly. "All of that, yes," he agreed. "For a good end. You yourself, Mr. President, agreed that the end in this case justifies the, I will admit, not pleasant means, and in any case for such questions as this it is too late for you and me. Our ruse must be continued as long as possible."

"And when the people on the *Constitution* find out?"

"That is impossible," Knefhausen declared. "I give you my word on that. Not for a long time."

"And when they do?"

Knefhausen shrugged. "Then the experiment passes beyond our control," he said.

9

THERE WAS NOT ACTUALLY A HYDROPONICS "ROOM" ON the *Constitution*. There were hydroponics trays and hydroponics clusters. The designers of the ship had meant them to be fitted into crannies and alcoves all over the vessel, but the occupants had redesigned the designers' work here, as in much else. Plants were still in unlikely places, but the fourth "level" (it wasn't really level, anymore) above the plasma shields was now stuffed with growing things. An orangerie, a hothouse, a place that smelled of vines and damp.

Everybody liked it. They liked it too much to suit Eve Barstow, who was spending more and more of her time there. The plants did not particularly need tending, because they grew well by themselves with the automatic trickle-drips and drains that fed them; even the experiments could get along quite well without Eve, because Flo Jackman did most of that. But it was a nice place. It was a place for Eve Barstow to be, and there weren't many like that on the ship. Thinning seedlings, picking ripening fruit, loosening the soil (or the sort-of soil, partly quartz pebbles, partly what you didn't really want to think about)—that was a form of solitaire for Eve, a self-imposed task to conceal the fact that she had very few real ones.

It was astonishing to Eve to find how quickly she had grasped hard subjects when she had nothing to do but study them. But it was distressing to find how far beyond the hardest of them some of the other people on the ship had gone. She could rely on the fact that the plants would not surpass her. And they smelled good, and there was a jungly, exotic feel in the hothouse air. With Flo's concurrence and no one's objection, she had encouraged the tomato vines to curl across the gaps between the stacks of trays, and the beans to climb along hooks set in the wall. It made the tending and the picking a little harder, but it created a wild prettiness among all the steel and plastic. She was put out by the fact that the others liked it, too, and so she was not left undisturbed very much of the time. But sometimes, sometimes it was all hers. Apart from wishing she were somewhere else . . . or wishing her husband would try a little harder to communicate . . . or wishing she were as tall as Ann Becklund or as well-breasted as Dot Letski . . . or wishing she would get laid a little more often or could get to a garage sale now and then . . . apart from wishing, being in the hydroponics room was her favorite thing to do.

Like a watermelon seed from someone's lips, she was, she felt, being squeezed out. She thought she recognized the signs. When Eve was younger she had served her term in the counterculture—nothing bad, none of the hardest stuff. Just a time to rebel and fool around. She had observed or experienced almost every known form of interpersonal relationship, from quickies to the communes. For a time she had been enthralled by the notion of plural marriage. Three or four husbands, a batch of sharing wives—what a nice thing! How marvelous to have tenderness there for you whenever you wanted it, and how more marvelous still to be allowed to go off by yourself when you chose, without depriving someone else. But she had observed that something always went wrong. In the sturdiest of the four-way, six-way, multiple-way marriages she had seen, sooner or later one of the equal partners stopped being equal. The group expelled the individual. Within the shared joy was individual misery.

The crew of the *Constitution* had not begun the practice of multiple mating, or at any rate had not institutionalized it. But Eve could feel the forces pressing against her. The balanced atom had been ionized, and one electron, named Eve Barstow, had been flung out. She circled the nucleus wistfully, at no great distance, but she could no longer join the dance.

Since Eve was a sensible person she knew that the case was not as bad as she pictured it to herself. Of course there were problems! There had to be. This was certainly a stressful situation, and the shrinks had briefed them thoroughly. They had dinned into each of the voyagers that, however relaxed any of them might seem on the surface, there would be fear and anger and hysteria bubbling underneath. Of course, they hadn't explained just how great the stress would be. Because how could they have known?

And Eve was not wholly neglected. Shef still played chess with her, although he was as likely as not to be both reading and carrying on a conversation with someone else at the same time. Her husband, every now and then, remembered to invite her to bed. And there was Ann Becklund. Ann was also a sensible person, and even kind. Sometimes kind—actually, most of the time she was kind, when she wasn't fighting back some internal shit-storm of her own. They talked together. Sometimes about the ship; sometimes girl talk, what kinds of kids they would like to have if ever there were any chance of having any, what they remembered of their different, but similar, youths.

But there was a poison in the air. Ann stopped talking, or annoyedly allowed Eve to talk *to* her once in a while. She threw the toe bones over and over, her lips tightening, whispering to herself and clamming up when Eve came near her.

There was a lot of whispering going on in which Eve was not included. And a lot of silences. And a lot of absences. Eve's own husband was spending more and more of his time up in the lookout bubble, peering through the spotter scope or sometimes just with the unaided eye. What was he watching? As far as Eve could see, nothing. It was astonishing to her how interesting nothing was to her husband.

The trip was turning sour in Eve's mouth. But she did not know how sour, or what the spreading sickness was, until Jerry Letski woke her out of a sound sleep. She had curled up on a nest of blankets under the broccoli trays, dreaming of multiple fornications with unbelievably handsome men, and her name was called. Ski spotted her and came racing and flying between the carrots and the mint patch. "Come on, for Christ's sake, there's a meeting. Where've you been?" He caught her by the arm, his gentle, triangular face working with fury. At her? she wondered. No, not at her. But it was not until she got to the common room that she understood to whom the rage belonged, and how terribly it changed everything.

They were all there, and all upset. They showed it in their own individual ways, Dot Letski with her knees folded and eyes closed, communing with who knew what; Shef cursing to himself as he punched out programs on his calculator and fumed at the results. He had been letting his hair grow, Eve saw; it made him look gaunt and wild.

But they all looked wild. Flo Jackman grabbed her by the shoulder as she came in and pushed her face into Eve's. "Well? Shall we do it?" she shouted, spraying Eve's cheek.

Eve pulled away, as much frightened by the intensity in the group as thrilled by the experience of someone asking her advice or consent to anything, for the first time in weeks. "Shall we do what?" she asked, and then they all began talking at once—Shef without looking up, Dot without opening her eyes, even Will Becklund, in his rustly, hoarse whisper, from whatever corner he was hiding in. Ann cast the bones at Eve's feet and cried, "Don't you see? We're screwed!"

Eve gazed at the bones, but the hexagram she could not read. Nor did she have time to try to figure it out because Flo was shouting in her ear. "Dot can write a grammar," she shouted, "in which the whole planet Earth stops rotating. Ski says—"

"Ski says it's too big an investment of our resources," Letski yelled, from Eve's other side. "No way! Now Shef says—"

Shef turned from his calculator to take up his part: "Shef says we go back and beat the piss out of them."

"We can't do that," Eve objected, startled out of her mute confusion.

"Almost! Maybe not quite. We're blowing seven fifty centimeters per second squared against the relativistic mass increase; we can decelerate to zero, turn around, build up to point zero four *c*, coast, and still have enough to decelerate and maneuver. Of course the time's bad, thirty-three years. On the other hand—"

"And then what?" Letski shouted. "Go back and live among *them* again?"

And then everyone stopped talking for a moment, considering what it would be like to return to the familiar life of Earth. Shef started to speak, scratched his stubbly beard, shook his head, and subsided. Ann gathered up her toe bones, stared at them, then shook her blond head wildly and threw them against the wall. "Any way you look at it," she said, "we're screwed."

"We might as well just keep on going," said Letski, and, one by one, the others began to nod. All but Eve.

"I don't understand!" she cried. "Has something happened I don't know about?"

Ann stared at her, combing her long hair through her fingers. "I thought you knew," she said.

"Knew what? Please! What's it all about?"

Ann's expression softened. "I forgot you haven't been involved," she said apologetically. "It's confirmed. We've all double-checked it. It's been in the hexagrams for weeks, Shef worked it out from a personality analysis of Knefhausen, Jim verified it by direct observation. There's no planet around Alpha Centauri. We have no place to go!"

10

THE THIRD WORST THING IN DIETER VON KNEFHAUSEN'S LIFE was that conditions in Washington had continued to worsen. There were ominous rumblings of tank treads at night, and now and then a flight of low-flying jets overhead that made one ask whom they might belong to. Knefhausen slept now on a cot in the little office next to his own; some days even his secretary could not make it in to the office, though one would expect she was protected by the badge of her skin color. And the food he had to eat! Such food the Army even turned up its nose at, desiccated hash and gummy fruit bars that defied recognition.

The second worst thing was that the President had put him in the doghouse again. Back in the isolation ward, where there were no armored helicopters and no favors offered. He could not ask the President for any, even, because the President was "traveling." Traveling where? One could not be told, because of security. Perhaps he was orbiting in Air Force One, out of the range of any possible heat-seeking missiles in the hands of black insurrectionists or campus rowdies. Perhaps in the rabbit warrens under Camp David. Perhaps, most likely of all, simply cowering in the White House and refusing to be seen.

But it was almost better that the President did not see him and he could go nowhere; because there was the worst thing of all. From the *Constitution*, nothing! No telemetry. No regular reports. Not even one word, not even a bad one! There had been ample time for his scolding order to reach them and a response to return. No response. One could not even say that they were angered by the curtness of his tone, because they must have stopped transmitting long before that was received.

So, then, what? Some terrible accident? A collision with some misplaced asteroid or comet body in the Oort cloud?

It would almost be better if that were the case, Knefhausen grieved. The alternative was worse. The alternative was that, no matter what assurances he had given the President, the ruse had been discovered, heaven could only guess how. And so the experiment was out of control; and worse than that, his participation in it was at an end.

So much had been risked! So much already lost! But that was not important to Knefhausen; he would wager more than that and accept a losing roll of the dice—gladly!—if only he could see the end of his work.

So he pored over the old reports, and dispatched messages —wheedling, pleading, begging—that might never reach the spacecraft, much less be answered. And if he had known how to pray he would have prayed for a message, any message at all! Anything would be better than this!

Or so he thought until, at last, a message came.

11

THIS IS SHEF AGAIN AND IT'S OH, LET ME SEE, MAYBE ABOUT day two hundred and fifty? Three hundred? No, I don't think it can be that much. Look, I'm sorry about the ship date, but I honestly don't think much in those terms anymore. I've been thinking about other things. Also I'm still a little upset. We've all calmed down a lot (you can tell that by the fact that you're getting this!), but when I tossed the ruble the hexagram was K'an, which is danger, over Li, the Sun. That's a crappy modality to be communicating in—with you, I mean. "Danger" is too close to true to be funny. We aren't vengeful types, but the fact is that some of us were pretty sore when we found out what you'd done. For God's sake, why did you do it? Didn't you know it would piss us off transcendentally? I don't *think* you need to worry about what's going to happen, because we've decided to take no action for the present; but I wish I'd got a better hexagram.

I don't really know how to talk to you now, either. You're so rotten it's embarrassing. It's like if the bride farts at the altar. There isn't any social provision for dealing with that sort of thing, so the best you can do is everybody proceed with the wedding as if nothing had happened. So I'll try that, but you know what I'm thinking! (Ha-ha.)

Let me tell you the good parts first. Our velocity is pushing point four oh *c* now. The scenery is beginning to get interesting, but not exactly as advertised. (Like anything else you can think of about this cruise?) For several weeks now the stars have been drifting around, as the ones up front get up into the ultraviolet and the ones behind sink into the infrared. When we first noticed this starcreep Letski sent back for the original papers, Einstein and Sänger and all those other people, and he got with them an old one by two fellows named McKinley and Doherty that said we'd never get a starbow because as the spectrum shifts the other parts of the EMF bands would come into the visible range. Well, I guess they do, but stars peak in certain frequencies, and most of them seem to do it in the visible frequencies, so the effect is that they disappear. Of course, we know they're there. We can detect them fairly well with phase-shift equipment, just as we can transmit and receive with you folks by shifting the frequencies.

But what we see with the naked eye (not counting what Jim Barstow sees, or says he sees, because he's practicing his farsight on the stars) is—well—scary. We do get a kind of a starbow, or at least we get a band of stars that run from a sort of dull purplish color through bright blue and a sort of leafy green and yellow to the bands nearest the black patch behind us, which are orange shading to a nasty dark red.

But in front of us, my God, you wouldn't believe how bright it's getting! Not as bright as the Sun used to be, maybe. But a hell of a lot brighter than anything else I've ever seen in the sky, and getting brighter. It's actually kind of scary. It looks as though we're heading right into a supernova or a quasar, and, dear friends (not counting Knefhausen), that is a scary thought. But it's beautiful. It's worth the trip. (Though not worth the way it's going to turn out!) Flo was learning oil painting so she could make a picture of it to send you for your wall, if we could figure out a way of sending it, but when she found out what you'd been up to she thought of booby-trapping it with a fusion bomb. But she's over that now. (I think.)

So we're not really so mad at you anymore, although there

was a time when, if I'd been communicating with you at exactly that moment, I would have said some bad things. I don't know how long this placidity will last, though.

. . . I just played this back, and it sounds pretty jumbled and confused. I'm sorry about that. It's hard for me to do this. I don't mean hard like intellectually difficult (the way chess problems and tensor analysis used to be), but hard like shoveling sand with a coke spoon. I'm just not used to constricting my thoughts in this straitjacket any more. I tried to get one of the others to communicate this time instead of me but, no surprise, there were no takers. I did get a lot of free advice. Dot says (I'll leave out the hostility; you can figure that out for yourself) that I shouldn't waste my time remembering how we used to talk. She wanted to write an eidetic account in simplified notation, mostly for the fun of it, but she would have let me transmit it, which she estimated a crash program could translate for you in reasonable time, a decade or two, and would give you an absolutely full account of everything. I objected because of the practical difficulties. Not in preparing the account, I don't mean. Shucks, any of us could do that now. I don't forget anything, except irrelevant things like the standard-reckoning date that I don't want to remember in the first place. Neither does anybody else. But the length of transmission would be excessive. We don't have power to waste on all those groups, especially since the incident with the plasma chamber. Dot said we could Gödelize it. Will Becklund said (I think he said; it's a little hard to tell with Will these days) that you were too dumb to de-Gödelize it. Dot said it would be good practice for you.

Well, she's right about that, and it's time you all learned how to communicate in a sensible way, so if the power holds out I'll include Flo's eidetic account in Dot's Gödelized form at the end. Lots of luck. I won't honestly be surprised if you miss a digit or something and it all turns into *Rebecca of Sunnybrook Farm* or some missing books of apocrypha. Or, more likely of course, just gibberish. Ski says it won't do you any good in any case, because Henle was right. I pass that on without comment.

Sex. You always want to hear about sex.

Well, it's great. Now that we don't have to fool with the

pills anymore we've been having some marvelous times. Flo and Jim Barstow began making it as part of a multiplexed communications system that you have to see to believe. Sometimes when they're going to do it we all knock off and just sit around and watch them, cracking jokes and singing and helping with the auxiliary computations. When we had that little bit of minor surgery the other day (we've got the bones seasoning now), Ann and Ski decided to ball instead of using anesthesia. They said it was better than acupuncture. It didn't block the sensation. They were aware of their little toes being lopped off, but they didn't perceive it as pain. So then when it was Jim's turn he had an idea and he tried going through the amputation without any anesthesia at all, in the expectation that he and Flo would go to bed together a little later, and that worked well too. He was all het up about it: claimed that it showed a reverse causality that his theories predicted but that had not been demonstrated before. Said he was at last over the cause-preceding-the-effect hangup. It's like the Red Queen and the White Queen, quite puzzling until you get the hang of it. I'm not sure I've gotten the hang of it yet. Suppose he hadn't balled Flo after the operation? Would his toe have hurt retroactively? I'm a little mixed up on this, Dot says because I simply don't understand phenomenology in general, and I think I'll have to take Ann's advice and work my way through Carnap, although the linguistics are so poor that it's hard to stay with it. Come to think of it, I don't have to. It's all in the Gödelized eidetic statement, after all. So I'll transmit the statement to you, and while I'm doing that it will be a sort of review for me and maybe I'll get my head right on causality.

Listen, let me give you a tip. The statement will also contain Ski's trick of containing plasma for up to 500K milliseconds, so when you figure it out you'll know how to build those fusion power reactors you've been bullshitting about all these years. That's the carrot before your nose. So get busy on de-Gödelizing. The plasma dodge works fine, although of course we were sorry about what happened when we converted the drive. The explosion killed Will Becklund outright, and it looked hairy for all of us. But Will doesn't hold a grudge.

Well, anyway, I have to cut this short because power's running a little low and I don't want to chance messing up the statement. It follows herewith:

$(3.875 \times 12^{26})! + 1973^{854} + 331^{852} + 17^{2008} + 3^{9606} + 2^{88}$ take away 78.

Lots of luck, fellows!

12

KNEFHAUSEN LIFTED HIS HEAD FROM THE LITTER OF PAPERS on his desk. He rubbed his eyes, sighing. He had given up smoking loyally at the same time as the President, but, like the President, he had taken it up again. It could kill you, yes. But it was a tension reducer, and he needed that. And what was wrong with something killing you? There were worse things than being killed, he thought as he lit his twenty-fifth cigarette of the day.

Looking at it any way you could, he told himself objectively, the past two or three years had been hard on him. It was wrong that this should be so. They should have been his very best! And indeed they had started so well, before they went so bad. Not as bad as those distant memories of childhood when everybody was so poor and Berlin was so cold and what warm clothes he had came from the *Winterhilfe*. By no means as hard as the end of the war. Nothing like as bad as those first years in South America, and then in the Middle East, in the time when even the lucky and famous ones, the von Brauns and the Ehrickes, were having trouble getting what was due them and a young calf like Knefhausen had to peel potatoes and run elevators to live. But harder and worse, surely, than a man at the summit of what one could not deny was a glorious career had any reason to expect.

And so unfair! The Alpha-Aleph project, fundamentally, was sound! He ground his teeth, thinking about it. It would work—no, by the Lord God, it *was* working, and it would make the world a different place. Future generations would see!

But the future generations were not here yet, and in the present things were going not so well.

Reminded, he picked up the phone and buzzed his secretary. "Have you got through to the President yet?" he demanded.

"I'm sorry, Dr. Knefhausen. I've tried every ten minutes, just as you said."

"Ah," he grunted. "Yes, I see. No, wait. What calls have there been?"

Rustle of paper. "The news services, of course, asking about the rumors again. The man from CBS."

"No, no, I will not talk to press. Anyone else?"

"Senator Copley called, asking when you were going to answer the list of questions his committee sent you."

"I will give him an answer. I will give him the answer Götz von Berlichingen gave to the Bishop of Bamberg."

"I'm sorry, Dr. Knefhausen, I didn't quite catch—"

"It does not matter. Anything else?"

"Just a long-distance call, from a Mr. Hauptmann. I have his number."

"Hauptmann?" The name was puzzlingly familiar. After a moment Knefhausen placed it. To be sure, the radio astronomer who had cooperated in the faked pictures from Briareus Twelve. Well, he had his orders to stay out of sight in Alabama and shut up. "No, that is not important. None of them are, and I do not wish to be disturbed for such nonsense. Continue as you were, Mrs. Ambrose. If the President is reached you are to put me on at once, but no other calls."

He hung up and returned to his desk.

He looked sadly and fondly at the papers. He had them all out of the locked file. The reports from the *Constitution*. His own messages to them, including the one in which he had confessed everything and begged them to continue—without, confound them, even a response. His drafts of interpretation and comment, and more than a hundred footnoted items compiled by CapCom, his own staff, and half a dozen other agencies of government, to help untangle the meanings and implications of those ah, so cryptic sometimes! reports from space:

"*Henle*. Apparently refers to Paul Henle (note appended); probably the citation intended is his statement, 'There are certain symbolisms in which certain things cannot be said.' Conjecture that what is meant is that the English language is one of those symbolisms.

"*Orange sherbet sundae.* A classified experimental study was made of the material in Document Ref. No. CON-130, Para. 4. Chemical analysis and experimental testing have indicated that the recommended mixture of pharmaceuticals and other ingredients produce a hallucinogen-related substance of considerable strength and not wholly known properties. 100 subjects ingested the product or a placebo in a double-blind controlled test. Subjects receiving the actual substance report reactions significantly different from the placebo. Effects reported include feelings of immense competence and deepened understanding, as well as euphoria and sexual stimulation. However, data is entirely subjective. Attempts were made to verify claims by standard IQ, manipulative, and other tests, but the subjects did not cooperate well, and several have since absented themselves without leave from the testing establishment.

"*Gödelized language.* A system of encoding any message of any kind as a single very large number. The message is first written out in clear language and then encoded as a product of prime bases and exponents. Each letter of the message is represented in order by the natural order of prime numbers—that is, the first letter is represented by the base 2, the second by the base 3, the third by the base 5, then by 7, 11, 13, 17, etc. The identity of the letter occupying that position in the message is given by the exponent, simply: the exponent 1 meaning that the letter in that position is an A, the exponent 2 meaning that it is a B, 3 a C, 4 a D, up to 26 as the exponent for a Z. The message as a whole is then rendered as the product of all the bases and exponents. *Examples.* The word 'cab' can thus be represented as $2^3 \times 3^1 \times 5^2$, or 600. $(=8\times3\times25.)$ The name 'Abe' would be represented by the number 56,250, or $2^1 \times 3^2 \times 5^5$. $(=2\times9\times3125.)$ A sentence like 'John lives.' would be represented by the product of the following terms: $2^{10} \times 3^{15} \times 5^8 \times 7^{14} \times 11^0 \times 13^{12} \times 17^9 \times 19^{22} \times 23^5 \times 29^{19} \times 31^{27}$ (in which the exponent 0 has been reserved for a space and the exponent 27 has been arbitrarily assigned to indicated a full stop). As can be seen, the Gödelized form of even a very short message involves a large number, although such numbers may be transmitted quite compactly in the form of a sum of bases and exponents. The quantity of information in the example transmitted by the crew of the *Constitution* is estimated to exceed that contained in a standard encyclopedia; no upward limit has yet been assigned.

"*Farsight.* The subject James Madison Barstow is known to have suffered from some nearsightedness in his early school years, apparently brought on by excessive reading, which he attempted to cure through eye exercises similar to the 'Bates method' (note appended). His vision at time of testing for the Alpha-Aleph project was optimal. Interviews with former associates indicate his continuing interest in increased visual acuity. *Alternative explanation.* There is some indication that the subject was also interested in paranormal phenomena, such as clairvoyance or prevision, and it is possible, though at present deemed unlikely, that his use of the term refers to 'looking ahead' in time."

And so on, and on.

Knefhausen gazed at the litter of papers lovingly and hopelessly, and passed his hand over his forehead. These kids! They were so marvelous . . . but so unruly . . . and so hard to understand. How wicked of them to have concealed their true accomplishments. The secret of hydrogen fusion! That alone would justify, more than justify, the entire project. But where was it? Locked in that number-jumber gibberish! Knefhausen was not without appreciation of the elegance of the method. He, too, was capable of taking seriously a device of such luminous simplicity. Once the number was written out you had only to start by dividing it by 2 as many times as possible, and the number of times would give you the first letter. Then divide by the next prime, 3, and that number of times would give you the second letter. But the practical difficulties! The numbers became so quickly so large! Of course, they had at once started decrypting it. They were already up to such prime bases as 23,753 and now at each time the computers were taking longer and longer to print out a single character; soon it would be several minutes for each character, even hours, ultimately no doubt days! And what had they so far to show? A message of less than two thousand words in which this Flo Jackman was discussing chattily with herself where to begin! IBM's experts had undertaken to decrypt all of it, yes, to be sure, but would not commit themselves to a delivery time of less than twenty-five years. *Twenty-five years.* And meanwhile in that number was hidden probably the secret of hydrogen fusion (no doubt at the very end!), possibly many greater secrets, most certainly the key to Knefhausen's own well-being over the next few weeks. . . .

His phone rang.

He grabbed it and shouted into it at once: "Yes, Mr. President!"

He had been too quick. It was only his secretary. Her voice was shaking but determined.

"It's not the President, Dr. Knefhausen, but Senator Copley is on the wire and he says it is urgent. He says—"

"No!" shouted Knefhausen, and banged down the phone. He regretted the action even as he was doing it. Copley was very high, chairman of the Armed Forces Committee. He was not a man Knefhausen wished to have as an enemy, and he had indeed been very careful to make the Senator a friend over years of patient fence-building. But he could not speak to him, or to anyone else, while the President was not answering his calls. Copley's rank was high, but he was not in the direct hierarchical line over Knefhausen. When the top of that line refused to talk to him, Knefhausen was cut off from the world.

Fretfully Knefhausen pushed all these irritations aside and tried to concentrate on the daily state-of-the-nation briefing documents which, probably through some oversight, continued to reach him by guarded messenger every morning. The pressures on the President just now: They were enormous. It was not merely the *Constitution* matter which was troublesome, all the world was troublesome. The military position worsened every day, the cities were crippled with strikes, paralyzed by power blackouts and transportation breakdowns, and, always, each month the curve of violent crime and property damage writhed toward new highs. The world was on the point of explosion. And how terribly unfair! If only his project were allowed to come to its proper conclusion, what a new vista would open for all of mankind! But the President could not deal with all of this, and also with the terror of the cities, and also with the political conventions which were coming up. There was the need to get elected for a third term, and the need to get the law amended to make that possible. And was that possible with all these troubles? And if the President were not reelected, what?

And yes, Knefhausen admitted to himself, the worst political problem the President faced was the imminent loss of security on the *Constitution*. The rumors were growing. He had warned the President. It was unfortunate the President had not listened. He had said that a secret known to two people is compromised, and a secret known to more than two is no secret. But the President had insisted on disclosure to that ever-widening circle of high officials—sworn, of course, to secrecy, but what good was that?—and, of course, in spite of everything, there had been leaks. Fewer than one might have feared. More than one could stand.

It was terrible that the crew of the *Constitution* had discovered the deception so early, but that was bound to come. For the world to know it, that was a terribleness that threatened not only Knefhausen's position but also his very life! For what would become of him if the President withdrew even the limited protection he still enjoyed? A vagrant in the streets of the District of Columbia, a new convict in the seething hell of a federal prison?

He sighed, lit another cigarette, and touched the reports from the *Constitution* caressingly. Those beautiful kids! They could still make everything right, so wonderful . . .

Wonderful because it was he who had made them wonderful, he confessed to himself. He had invented the project. He had selected them as personnel from all the world. He had done things which he did not quite even yet reconcile himself to, to make sure that it was they and not some others who were on the crew. He had, above all, made assurance doubly sure by ensuring their loyalty in every way possible. Training. Discipline. Ties of affection and friendship—how many rock concerts he had sat through, with his teeth grinding while his face wore a sleepy smile, to make sure that they would regard him as a comrade! More reliable ties: loading their food supplies, their entertainment tapes, their programmed activities with every sort of advertising inducement, B-mod compulsion, psychological reinforcement he could invent or find, so that whatever else they did they would not fail to report back to Earth. Whatever else happened, there was that. Their reports were sparse and cryptic and even unwilling, but they still came. The data might be hard to untangle, but it would be there. For they could not help themselves! His commandments were stronger than God's; like Martin Luther, they must say *Ich kann nicht anders,* and come Pope or inquisition, they must stand by it. They would learn, and tell what they learned, and thus the investment would surely be repaid. . . .

The telephone!

He was talking before he had it even to his mouth. "Yes, yes! This is Dr. Knefhausen, yes!" he gabbled. Surely it must be the President now—

It was not.

"Knefhausen!" shouted the man on the other end. "Now, listen, I'll tell you what I told that bitch pig girl of yours, if I don't talk to you on the phone *right now* I'll have the Fourth Armored in there to arrest you and bring you to me in twenty minutes. So listen!"

Knefhausen recognized both the voice and the style. He drew a deep breath and forced himself to be calm. "Very well, Senator Copley," he said, "what is it?"

"The game is blown, boy! That's what it is! That boy of yours in Huntsville, what's his name, the astronomer, photographer, whatever—"

"Hauptmann?"

"That's him! Would you like to know where he is now, you dumb Kraut bastard?"

"Why, I suppose—I should think in Huntsville—"

"Wrong, boy! Your Kraut bastard friend claimed he didn't feel good and took some accrued sick time. Intelligence kept an eye on him up to a point, didn't stop him, wanted to see what he'd do. Well, they saw. They saw him leaving De Gaulle airport an hour ago in an Aeroflot plane. Put your big Kraut brain to work on that one, Knefhausen! He's defected. Now start figuring out what you're going to do about it, and it better be good!"

Knefhausen said something, he did not know what, and hung up the phone, he did not remember when. He stared glassily into space for a time.

Then he flicked the switch for his secretary and said, not listening to her stammering apologies, "That long-distance call that came from Hauptmann before, Mrs. Ambrose. You didn't say where it was from."

"It was an overseas call, Dr. Knefhausen. From Paris. You didn't give me a chance to—"

"Yes, yes. I understand. Thank you. Never mind." He hung up and sat back. He felt almost relieved. He had given Hauptmann a splendid position back on Earth with no duties, really, but what he chose for himself; it had not been enough. Very well. It was over. If Hauptmann had gone to Russia it could only be to tell them that the picture was faked and not only was there no planet for the astronauts to land on but it was not a mistake, even, actually a total fraud. So now it was all out of his hands. History would judge him now. The die was cast. The Rubicon was crossed.

So many literary allusions, he thought deprecatingly. Actually it was not the judgment of history that was immediately important but the judgment of certain real persons now alive and likely to respond badly. And they would judge him not so much by what might be or what should have been as by what was. He shivered in the chill of that judgment and reached for the telephone to try once more to call the President. But he was quite sure the President would not answer, then or ever again.

13

OLD RELIABLE PEED-OFF SHEF HERE. LOOK, WE GOT YOUR message. You know, you're not in very close touch with reality. I don't want to discuss what you said, except to say you've got a humongous nerve. Don't take your bad moods out on us, unless you want us to do the same, all right? If you can't say something nice, don't say anything at all. We do the best we can. That's not bad. If we don't do exactly what you want us to, maybe it's because you don't deserve it. Not to mention that, really, we all know quite a lot more about the world than you did when you fired us off at that blob of moonshine you call Alpha-Aleph. Well, thanks a lot for nothing!

On the other hand, thanks a little bit for what little you did do for us, which at least worked out to get us where we are, and I don't mean spatially. So I'm not going to yell at you. I just don't want to talk to you at all. I'll let the others speak for themselves.

Dot Letski speaking. This is important. Pass it on. I have three things to tell you that I do not want you to forget. *One: Most problems have grammatical solutions.* The problem of transporting people from the Earth to another planet does not get solved by putting pieces of steel together one at a time at random, and happening to find out that by accident you've built the *Constitution.* It gets solved by constructing a model (=equation (=grammar)) which describes the necessary circumstances under which the transportation occurs. Once you have the grammatical model all you have to do is hang the metal around it, and then it goes like gangbusters.

When you have understood this you will be ready for: *Two: There is no such thing as causality.* What a waste of time it has been, trying to assign "causes" to "events"! You say things like, "Striking a match causes it to burn." True statement? No. False statement. You find yourself in a whole waffle about whether the "act" of "striking" is "necessary" and/or "sufficient" and you get lost in words. Pragmatically useful grammars are without tenses. In a decent grammar (which this English-language one, of course, is not, but I'll do the best I can) you can make a statement like "There exists a conjunction of forms of matter (specified) which combine with the release of energy at a certain temperature (specified) (which may be the temperature associated with heat of friction)." Where's the causality? "Cause" and "effect" are in the same timeless statement. So, *Three: There are no such things as empirical laws.* When Ski came to understand that, he was able to contain the plasma in our jet indefinitely, not by pushing particles around in brute-force magnetic squeezes but by encouraging them to stay together. There are other ways of saying what he does (="creates an environment in which centripetal exceed centrifugal forces"), but the way I said it is better because it tells you all something you really need to know about your personalities. Bullies, all of you. Why can't you be nice to things if you want them to be nice to you? Be sure to pass this on to T'in Fa at Tientsin, Professor Morris at All Soul's, and whoever holds the Carnap chair at UCLA.

Flo's turn. My mother would have loved my garden. I have drumsticks and daffodils growing side by side in the sludgy sand. They do so please us, and we them. I will probably transmit a full horticultural handbook at a future date, but meanwhile be aware that it is shameful to eat a radish. Carrots, on the other hand, enjoy it.

A statement of Willis Becklund, deceased. I emerged into the world between feces and urine, learned, grew, ate, worked, moved, and died. Alternatively, I emerged from the hydrogen flare, shrank, disgorged, and reentered the womb one misses so. You may approach it from either end, it makes no difference at all which way you look at it.

Observational datum, Letski. At time *t*, a Dirac number incommensurable with GMT, the following phenomenon is observed: Bolometric analysis indicates that the bright spot ahead of us, occupying approximately one minute of arc, is in fact the fossil 2.7 K blackbody radiation left over from the Big Bang, blue-shifted up to a perceived temperature of 3.7×10^4 K, with a visual magnitude of approximately $m_v = 24.5$. We are aiming at the womb of the universe. Harvard–Smithsonian notification service, please copy.

"Starbow," a preliminary study for a rendering into English of a poem by James Barstow:

> Gaggle of goslings but pick of our race
> We wander through relativistic space,
> Out of the evil unspeakable Night
> Into the awful unknowable Bright.
> Dilated, discounted, despondent we scan:
> But vacant the sign of the Horse and the Man,
> Vacant the sign of the Man and the Horse,
> And now we conjecture the goal of our course.
> Tricked, trapped, and cozened, we ruefully run
> After the child of the bachelor sun.

The trick is revealed and the trap is confessed
And we are the butts of the dim-witted jest.
O Gander who made us, O Goose who laid us,
How lewdly and twistedly you betrayed us!
We owe you a debt. We won't forget.
With fortune and firmness we'll pay you yet.
Give us some luck and we'll timely send
Your pot of gold from the starbow's end.

Ann Becklund: I think it was Stanley Weinbaum who said that from three facts a truly superior mind should be able to deduce the whole universe. (Ski thinks the feat is possible with a finite number, but one which is considerably larger than three.) We are so very far from being truly superior minds by those standards, or even by our own. Yet we have a much larger number of facts to work with than three, or even three thousand, and so we have deduced a good deal.

This is not as valuable to you as you might have hoped, dear old bastardly Kneffie and all you bastardly others, because one of the things that we have deduced is that we can't tell you everything, because you wouldn't understand. We would be willing to help you along, some of you, if you were here—and what a tribute to our essential decency that is! And then in time you would be able to do what we do easily enough; but not at remote control.

But all is not lost, folks! Cheer up! You don't deduce like we deduce, but on the other hand there are an awful lot more of you. So try. Get smart. You can do it if you want to. Set your person at rest, compose your mind before you speak, make your relations firm before you ask for something. Don't be like the fellow in the Changes. "He brings increase to no one. Indeed, someone even strikes him."

We've all grown our toes back now, even Will, although it was particularly difficult for him after he was killed, and we've inscribed the bones and used them with very good effect in generating the hexagrams. I hope you see the point of what we did. We could have gone on with tossing coins or throwing the yarrow stalks, or at least with the closest Flo could breed to yarrow stalks. We didn't want to do that because it's not the optimal way.

The person who doesn't keep his heart constantly steady might say, "Well, what's the difference?" That's a poor sort of question to ask. It implies a deterministic answer. A better question is, "Does it make a difference?" and the answer to that is, "Yes, probably, because in order to do something right you must do it right." That is the law of identity, in any language.

Another question you might ask is, "Well, what source of knowledge are you actually tapping when you consult the hexagrams?" That's a better kind of question in that it doesn't *force* a wrong answer, but the answer is, again, indeterminate. You might view the *I Ching* as a sort of Rorschach bundle of squiggles that has no innate meaning but is useful because your own mind interprets it and puts sense into it. Feel free! You might think of it as a sort of memory bank of encoded lore. Why not? You might skip it entirely and come to knowledge in some other tao, any tao you like. ("The superior man understands the transitory in the light of the eternity of the end.") That's fine, too!

But whatever way you do it, you should *do* it that way. We needed inscribed bones to generate hexagrams, because that was the right way, and so it was no particular sacrifice to lop off a toe each for the purpose. It's working out nicely, except for one thing. The big hangup now is that the translations in the only book we have are so degraded, Chinese to German, German to English, and error seeping in at every step, and you bastards wouldn't transmit us the originals. Never mind. We'll make out.

Perhaps I will tell you more at another time. Not now. Not very soon. Eve will tell you all about that.

Eve Barstow, the Dummy, comes last and, I'm afraid, least.

When I was a little girl I used to play chess, badly, with very good players, and that's the story of my life. I'm a chronic overachiever. I can't stand people who aren't smarter and better than I am, but the result is that I'm the runt of the litter every time. They are all pretty nice to me here most of the time, even Jim, but they know what the score is and so do I.

So I keep busy, and applaud in them what I can't do myself. It isn't a bad life. I have everything I need, not counting pride.

Let me tell you what a typical day is like here between Sol and Centaurus. We wake up (if we have been sleeping, which most of us still do) and eat (if we are still eating, as all but Ski and, of course, Will Becklund do). The food is delicious and Florence has induced it to grow cooked and seasoned where that is desirable, so it's no trouble to go over and pick yourself a nice poached egg or a clutch of French fries. (I really prefer brioche in the mornings, but Flo can't manage them for, I think, some kind of sentimental reasons.) Sometimes we ball a little or sing old campfire songs. Ski comes down for that, but not for long, and then he goes back to looking at the universe. I don't see how he stands it. It almost burns out your eyes. The starburst is magnificent and appalling. One can always look in the other frequencies and see ghost stars before us and behind us, but in the birthright bands the view is just about dead black, and then that beautiful powdery ring of colored stars—and then the starburst. It will of course disappear when we slow down again, but right now it is exactly like plummeting right into the hottest pit of Hell.

Sometimes we write plays or have a little music. Shef deduced four lost Bach harpsichord concerti, very reminiscent of Corelli and Vivaldi, with everything going at once in the tuttis, and we've all adapted them for performance. I did mine on the Moog, but Ann and Shef synthesized whole orchestras. Shef's is particularly cute. You can tell that the flautist has early emphysema and two people in the violin section have been drinking, and he's got Toscanini conducting like a *risorgimento* metronome. Flo's oldest daughter made up words and now she sings a sort of nursery-rhyme adaptation of some Buxtehude chorales; oh, I didn't tell you about the kids. We have eleven of them now. Ann, Dot, and I have one apiece, and Florence has eight. (But they're going to let me have quadruplets next week.) They let me take care of them pretty much for the first few weeks, while they're little, and they're *so* darling.

So mostly I spend my time taking care of the kids and working out tensor equations that Ski kindly gives me to do for him and, I must confess it, feeling a little lonely. I *would* like to watch a TV quiz show over a cup of coffee with a friend! It's not what you'd call cozy around here. Though they do let me do over the interior of our mobile home now and then. The other day I redid it in Pittsburgh suburban just as a joke. Would you believe French windows in interstellar space? We can't open them, of course, but they look real pretty with the chintz curtains and lace tiebacks. And we've added several new rooms for the children and their pets. (Flo grew them the cutest little bunnies in the hydroponics plot; they're warm and they sort of breathe, but of course they don't hop or anything.)

Well, I've enjoyed this chance to gossip, but I'd better get to the point. I don't know why I'm the one who has to give you the bad news, but anyway let's get it over with.

None of the others are going to see what I'm transmitting to you. They simply aren't that interested anymore. There's a lot of other things they simply aren't, anymore, and, dear friends back home, I'm not a bit sure that one of those things isn't "human." I don't want to talk about it. But I don't like it, either, and you all should understand that the Will Becklund and the Sheffield Jackman and even the Eve Barstow you used to know simply do not exist anymore, and any assumptions you may make about what any of them, or us, will do are wholly at your own risk. More than that. You've been quite annoying. There's a lot of free-floating hostility around here that belongs to you.

For some time now the vibrations here have been pretty sour. You know how it is around the Cape when there's a hold, and then a slipback, and you don't know if the mission's scrubbed or not, and if it isn't you don't know if the damn bird's going to blow up on the pad, and the prime crews are missing sleep, and the backups are getting hopeful and grouchy and mostly all raw nerves, and the wives are yelling at the kids and locking themselves in the bedroom for a cry two or three times a day and wondering if a divorce would be, after all, all that much of a bad thing? I don't mean it was like that. I mean it was a million times worse than that. I mean, when something like that comes down at the Cape it's just your average all-American Joes and Sallys that are jumping out of their skins. We're not like that anymore. I mean, not even am I sweet little Eve anymore. And if any of us had any sweetness left, it sure dried up when we found out you were murdering us.

Oh, we're not dead—not counting Will, I mean. But that doesn't make all of you any less a pack of murderers.

So we found it out; and, oh, my dears, what a meeting we had after that! I'm not going to tell you some of the things we talked about doing. You don't want to know. And I don't think we're really going to do them, or anyway the worst of them, at least not right now. Probably.

But there's something we are going to do. Folks, you're all in Coventry. No talking anymore. The others have decided we don't want to get any more messages from you. They don't like the way you try to work on our subconsciouses and all (not that you succeed, of course, but you can see that it's still a little annoying), and so in future the dial will be set at six-six-oh, all right, but the switch will be in the "off" position. It wasn't my idea, but I was glad to go along. I *would* like some slightly less demanding company from time to time, although not, of course, yours.

14

ONCE UPON A TIME THE BUILDING THAT WAS NOW KNOWN as DoD Temp Restraining Quarters 7—you might as well call it with the right word, "jail," Knefhausen thought—had been a luxury hotel in the Hilton chain. He had once addressed a General Assembly of the World Future Society in its Grand Ballroom, not twenty yards from where he sat—such days! Such grand prospects! In those days the future was something one could contemplate with awe and joy. But now the rooms below the ground level, which had been for meetings and other frolicking, had become maximum security cells. There were no doors or windows to the outside. If you did storm out of the door of your own room in some way, you had then a flight of stairs to get up before you were at ground level, and then the guards to break through to get to the open streets, and then what? One had gained very little. Even if there happened not to be an active siege going on at the moment, one took one's chances with the roaming addicts and activists outside.

Knefhausen did not concern himself with thoughts of

escape, or at least didn't after the first few panicky moments when he realized he was under arrest. He stopped demanding to see the President after the first few days. There was no point in appealing to the White House for help when it was the White House that had put him there. He was still sure that if he could only talk to the President privately for a few moments he could clear everything up. But as a realist he had faced the fact that the President would never talk to him privately again; and then, as time wore on, more painful doubts occurred to him. Was the President even still alive? There were hints that he was no longer ever seen; orders were issued in his name, but was there still a living being behind the orders?

And, in any case, did it matter?

So he counted his blessings. First, it was comfortable here. His bed was good. His room was warm. His food came still from the banquet kitchen of the hotel, and though it was simple it was quite often edible. For jailhouse fare, excellent.

Second, the kids were still in space and still doing some things, even if they did not report what. His ultimate vindication could still be hoped for.

Third, the jailers let him have writing materials and occasionally a book, although they would not bring him newspapers or a television set.

He missed his own books, but nothing else. He didn't need TV to tell him what was going on outside. He didn't even need the newspapers, ragged, thin, and censored as they were. He could hear all the news that mattered for himself. Every day there was a rattle of small-arms fire, mostly far-off and sporadic, but once or twice sustained and heavy and almost overhead. M-60s against AK-74s, it sounded like, and now and then the slap and smash of grenade launchers. Sometimes he heard sirens hooting through the streets, punctuated by clanging bells, and wondered that there was still a civilian fire department left to bother. (Or was it still civilian?) Sometimes he heard the grinding of heavy motors that had to be tanks. When he became curious he would sometimes press his ear to the door and listen for chance remarks from the patrols in the corridors outside; they said little to fill in the details, but Knefhausen was good at reading between the lines. The Administration was still in some sort of control, at least of part of the country, but it was holed up somewhere—Camp David or the Florida Keys, no one was saying where. The cities were all in red revolt. *Herr Omnes* had taken over. At least there had not been, as far as he knew, a major war or an invasion from some other country; perhaps their own cities were to be thanked for that.

For any part in these disasters Knefhausen felt unjustly blamed. No one had, in so many words, accused him. Nevertheless, in the early days he composed endless letters to the President, pointing out that the serious troubles of the administration had nothing to do with Alpha-Aleph. The cities had been increasingly lawless for most of a generation, the dollar had been each year more ludicrous ever since the Indochinese wars. Some letters he destroyed, some were taken from him, a few he managed to dispatch—and got no answers.

Once or twice a week a man from the Justice Department came to ask him the same thousand pointless questions once again. It was a self-sustaining bureaucratic phenomenon, Knefhausen was sure; it had been begun, perhaps in the attempt to build up a dossier to prove that it was all his fault, and no one had remembered to terminate it. Well, let it be. Knefhausen would defend himself if charges were ever laid. Or history would defend him. The record was clear. With respect to moral issues, not wholly clear, he conceded; there were certain deceptions and quite difficult acts he had performed even within the grand deception itself, but no matter. One could not speak of moral issues in an area so vital to the search for knowledge as this. The dispatches from the *Constitution,* when the *Constitution* was still reporting to its masters on Earth, had already produced so much! Although, admittedly, not so much as one would like of a practical value. Some of the most significant parts were hard to understand, and that great Gödel message, which would surely unlock so much, remained mostly unscrambled. The computers had slogged on through primes of five and six digits, each day producing a little less than the day before, and then something never explained had happened—an attack of some sort on the decrypting facilities in Langley, Knefhausen was sure—and it had all stopped. The last bits had seemed to deal with reconciling the tuning of a piano keyboard to the true frequencies of the harmonic scale! The hints of its greater contents remained only hints.

So unruly, those young heroes!

Sometimes Knefhausen dozed and dreamed of projecting himself somehow to join them on the *Constitution*. It had been a year or more since the last message, and that received nearly a year after they transmitted it because of the slow crawl of radio waves. He tried to imagine what they might be doing now. They would be well past the midpoint now, no doubt decelerating. The starbow would be broadening and diffusing every day. The circles of blackness before and behind them would be shrinking. Soon they would see Alpha Centauri as no man had ever seen it. To be sure, they would then see with even the naked eye that there was no planet that could be called Aleph circling the primary, but they had discovered that in some unguessable fashion long since.

Brave, wonderful kids! Even so, they had decided to go on. This foolishness with drugs and sex that had so disturbed the President, making him bite at his lip with those rabbit teeth, what of it? Such misplaced prudery! One opposed such goings-on when they occurred in the common run of humanity, and indeed punished them severely; that was for the orderly running of the state. But it had always been so that those who excelled and stood out from the herd could make their own rules. As a child he had learned that the plump, proud air leader frequently sniffed cocaine, that the great warriors took their sexual pleasure sometimes with each other. And of what importance was that? An intelligent man did not concern himself with such questions, which was one more indication that the man from the Justice Department, with his constant hinting and prying into Knefhausen's own sexual interests, was not really very intelligent.

The good thing about the visits of the man from the Justice Department was that one could sometimes deduce things from his questions, and rarely—oh, very rarely—he would sometimes answer a question himself. "Has there been a message from the *Constitution?*" "No, of course not, Dr. Knefhausen; now, tell me again, who suggested this fraudulent scheme to you in the first place?"

Those were the highlights of his days. Mostly the days passed unmarked.

He did not even scratch them off on the wall of his cell, like the prisoner in the Chateau d'If. It would have been a pity to mar the hardwood paneling. Also, he had other clocks and calendars. There was the ticking of the arriving meals, the turning of the season as the man from the Justice Department paid his visits. Each of these was like a holiday—a holy day, not joyous but solemn. First there would be a visit from the captain of the guards, with two armed soldiers standing in the door. They would search his person and his cell on the chance that he had been able to smuggle in a—a what? A nuclear bomb, maybe. Or a pound of pepper to throw in the Justice man's eyes. They would find nothing, because there was nothing to find. And then they would go away, and for a long time there would be nothing. Not even a meal, even if a mealtime then happened to be due. Nothing at all, until an hour or three hours later the Justice man would come in with his own guard squad at the door, equally vigilant inside and out, and his engineer manning the tape recorders, and the questions.

And—once in a very great while—his answers. Knefhausen had lost track of the days; on one visit he asked, then begged, to be told the date. The Justice Department man refused curtly, but on the next visit relented. Some superior had decided, no doubt, that after all such information could not cause harm. Knefhausen thanked him profusely and then, after he had left and Knefhausen was greedily eating his long-delayed breakfast, he realized what the date was. It was his birthday! He was sixty-five years old that day!

Surely a significant age for one to attain, he thought; the traditional age of retirement, an age at which a man should be able to look back on a career and count up its prides and failures. How frustrating that in his own case neither the world nor he himself could yet be sure what those were.

It was an age, too, only five years short of the Biblical three score and ten. Knefhausen's life would in no great time be over.

He put down his spoon and regarded the rest of his oatmeal with loathing. Those ruffians on the *Constitution!* How dare they not report? To close out the ledgers of his own life with proper accounting of credits and losses they must render their statement! For months now, even years, he had thought of them with jealous sorrow, but now it was only rage. Let them come to him now, and he would wring their impudent, ruffianly necks!

15

TWO HUNDRED THOUSAND ASTRONOMICAL UNITS AWAY IT was the birthday for another human being, whose name was Jeron. It was his first. Although he was too small to know it, he was not having a happy infancy.

By the time Jeron was born, in the same, most unusual way as the rest of his cohort, his parents (all of them) had learned of their sentence of death. They did not recover quickly. Although there were times when they seemed able to screen off that knowledge, there were other times when it colored every word and action. Jeron was a fast learner even before he was weaned. He took in attitudes with his mothers' milk, and words with his first spoonsful of what he would later learn to call "squacipro." Jeron was a healthy and strong baby, who emerged into the world without that boiled-lobster look of every generation before him. He was also, of course, inordinately intelligent. He was speaking before his first birthday. He responded to words like "eat" and "bed" and "wet?" without knowing that they were words, or that words were a part of language. Since his infant brain was not greatly more competent than a dog's, he learned as a dog might: the words were cues, like a tone of voice or the rattle of a leash. Some words and phrases he took in without processing at all. "Goddam Kneffie" and "Kraut bastard" were stored as single concepts, he heard them so often.

He heard them a lot, in raging tones or despairing, in his first months, because then the terror and the outrage had not yet worn off for his parents. The dollops of baby food Aunt Eve steered past his tiny new teeth were sometimes salted with her tears. She was the one hit hardest, for reasons Jeron would learn as he grew older; and the other parents were tender with her, sometimes, as she was with the babies she cared for. When they remembered, they would stop to soothe her. Even Uncle Will (who was dead) whispered kindly to her, "We can live in the *Constitution* for a long, long time." He used their birthright English language, and that was another kindness. Most of the grown-ups spoke English around Eve, pretending that it was for the children's sake rather than hers. It would be a long time before Jeron understood how hurtful all that kindness was.

Eve wiped a clot of baby food off the corner of Jeron's chubby mouth with a fingertip, then pushed the food through his lips and spun the lazy Eve to bring the next baby into reach. By the large brown eyes Eve knew this one was Forina. She smoothed the little girl's tufty black hair before dipping the spoon again into the puree of squash (citrus/protein). "Oh, sure," she muttered, "we can hang on until we run out of something. But what about *them*?"

Although Uncle Will was kind, or meant to be, Eve and the others had concerns that he was no longer equipped to share. "It will be all right," he whispered, drifting off on one of his unfathomable errands.

Eve spun the wheel to the next child. "Easy for you to say!" she called after him. "You don't have to worry about dying anymore!" She sighed, finished feeding the last child, touched each diaper to make sure none had yet turned damp, and then, for the first time, smiled. "All right, you kids," she said softly. "Now comes the nice part. You're all going to get your presents as soon as I finish singing! Happy birthday to you, happy birthday to you . . ."

Although Jeron did not know it, his home changed rapidly all through his first year of life. The *Constitution* was slowing down, though still moving at nearly 40 percent of the speed of light. Outside—though he rarely saw it, and did not know what he was seeing when he did—the narrow rainbow ring of stars had widened, become less intense, and the circles of blackness fore and aft were shrinking. In each second they traveled a distance ten times as great as the diameter of the Earth they had left behind. In not much over a quarter of an hour they could have plunged from the Earth into the Sun—and might as well have, for all the hope of long-range survival they could realistically entertain.

But they were no longer realists; they had broken through that cage as well as others.

It was not only in its position in space that the starship *Constitution* was changing. Its appearance changed, too. It no longer looked the same, inside or out, as when it left low-Earth orbit, and it kept on looking different. The ship that had pulled slowly away from its assembly orbiter two thousand and some days before was simple and clean, inside and out. As the *Constitution* had been put together in space, it did not need to be streamlined. But it was as easy to make it radially symmetrical as not, and moreover the surface/volume relationship made the roundest shape the cheapest.

So as it first moved under its own power it looked like a football with sections of pipe strapped to its side. By the time it rounded perihelion and used up its gravity gain from the Sun the side boosters were jettisoned. It was plain football, then, all the way out to Pluto's orbit and a long way beyond.

Then the nest-building began, and the alterations to the ship's basic drive, and the accident.

Will Becklund died in that accident, or at least his body did. A great tragedy. Especially to Will. The accident need not have happened if they had all been more skilled, but they were still learning.

By then all of the original crew of the *Constitution*, or all but sweet, slow Eve, were no longer patient with the clumsy, primitive work of the ship's designers. Restructuring the plasma drive was only one step, although it was the hardest; they had not yet got used to brute-force manipulation of refractory metals. The rest was comparatively easy. Outside the smooth hull shedlike extrusions and willowy towers grew. Jim Barstow opened a glassy seam all down the length of the ship, so that he could watch the starbow more beautifully. Inside, each of the eight astronauts—or of the seven, after Will Becklund passed beyond that sort of concern—shaped himself a living space, and all of them joined to expand the greeneries and sweeten the common chambers. After Jim Barstow rebuilt the drive it became simple to control the ship's acceleration. Some thrust was useful, so that they would know which way was down; very much thrust was wasted, because they were pushing against relativistic mass increase. They compromised on three-quarters of a G, then on half, then on about a tenth of a gravity for a long time, gentle enough so that walls supported little weight and partitions need not be strong. Their home was not much more than tissue and foil, as easy to change to suit their changing moods as a Japanese dwelling before the firestorms of World War II.

Jeron was lucky. He was not one of the first-born. He was in the third cohort. The infancy of the twenty-one babies in the earlier cohorts was less athletic, but a great deal more chancy, because none of the parents involved really knew what they were doing. By the time Jeron was well and truly toilet-trained, his main task had been decided for him: it was staying out of the way. Or, actually, just staying alive.

What made Jeron's childhood athletic was his spooky Uncle Ski, whose specialty back home had been astrophysics and who now devoted himself to the attainment of satori through child-rearing. Uncle Ski wasn't dead, like Uncle Will Becklund; but he sure was spooky. Aunt Eve was given the physical care of the babies. Uncle Ski took charge of their spiritual growth, which involved a great deal of running and slashing and hiding. Between times, when he was not being taught how to hold a spoon by Aunt Eve or being challenged by one of Uncle Ski's grow-up-quick stratagems, Jeron practiced talking on anyone who would stay still long enough, adult or child.

There were not as many of either to be stayed as one might think. It was a cranky, fretful environment he grew up in. Even the children were quirky; and the adults were mostly terrifying.

They were the only adults Jeron had ever known and he had no basis for comparison, but even his tiny infant mind thought they were bizarre. Aunt Mommy (he had not yet learned to call her Aunt Eve Barstow) was always fussing and fluttering over an unblown nose or a wet sleeping bag, but she was cuddly nice. As she was nearly always lactating, she smelled heavenly of warm milk. The others—well, they *fought*. Jeron did not understand the word "obsession," but he recognized in each of them an internal drive that nearly blinded them to other concerns. Each one had a burning compulsion to know and to do—*his* thing, or hers—and when they communicated with each other, or with one of the children, it was nearly always at a high pitch of emotion. They seemed to range between fury and black despair, and were almost always frightening to be around. The only male tiny Jeron felt close to at all was Uncle Will. It was Uncle Will who monitored the displays over his sleeping bag, pretty patterns of bunnies and toddlers displayed on the liquid crystal panels, with simple words to name them enunciated clearly from the speaker under Jeron's swaddling-bag. It was Uncle Will who taught him to distinguish between k's and t's, and to pronounce his final g's. Jeron seldom saw Uncle Will, but then most people never saw him at all. He was a whispering disembodied voice, a shimmering haze like the air over a hot highway, or, when he remembered to make a hologram, an intangible glassy form of light like the outline of a human figure. What he looked like more precisely was a Thom optical catastrophe, but Jeron was not yet two and would not learn catastrophe theory for at least another year. First he had to learn to speak and read, and he did that from Uncle Ghost's bedside displays. They were not electric. They came in ripe fruit colors, banana yellow, peach, apple red, grass green. They were created by some of Uncle Ghost's magic. Jeron didn't know how. It did not occur to him to ask how dead Will Becklund created the pretty pictures for him, or, for that matter, how he had created himself. He took Uncle Ghost as he found him; although he seldom called him that, as the other children did. Jeron did not think of Will Becklund as a ghost, in spite of the fact that Uncle Will Becklund by then had been dead for nearly four years.

The years of the young are very long; it is a relativistic time-dilation effect like accelerating toward the velocity of light. Jeron's years were longer than most. In this third year he already spoke quite well and was beginning to read.

He was a strong young child by then, and quite handsome. Before he was born, in fact almost as soon as he was conceived, his mother had allowed Aunt Flo to select among the paired genes for muscles and blue eyes and quickness.

Eve would not allow any other tampering, such as the addition of genes from other sources, but she saw no objection to improving the luck of the draw, and so Jeron was strong and quick. He was also quite smart, but no special selection was needed for that. All the possible parents on board the *Constitution* were smart as hell to begin with, or else they wouldn't have been there. He had a full-time job by then, helping Aunt Flo and then Aunt Eve in the painstaking breeding and rearranging in the hydroponics flats. He was more than a helper. There were long periods when he was the only person in charge, alone among the rows of curious growing things, because the aunts were busy elsewhere.

A decision was being made; it was part of the reason why the atmosphere in the ship was growing more and more frantic and upsetting.

Uncle Will took time to explain the decision to the child, rehearsing every word until he was sure Jeron understood. "You know we were all tricked, Jeron," he whispered out of a shadow under the ledge for Jeron's sleeping sack. "We were tricked in a very mean way. We were all sent to a place that does not exist, and we were meant to die there."

"I a'ready know all that, Unca Will," Jeron lisped.

"Ung-*kull*. Say your L's, Jeron. Well, we are going to that place anyway. And, although there is no place for us to live there, we are going to make a place."

Jeron leaned over the edge of his bunk to peer into the shadow. As he had thought, there was nothing to see down there. Uncle Will had not chosen to make himself visible. "Will that be hard for us to do, Ung-kull Will?" he asked.

"It will be very hard. I am not sure how we can do it. But we don't have any choice."

"All right, Uncle Will," said Jeron, and, half an hour later, when his tutor had quizzed and corrected him until comprehension was complete, he drifted comfortably to sleep. One concept he found hard to grasp: "another" place; what could another place than the *Constitution* possibly be like? Anything like the stories Aunt Flo told him (which he had taken to be fairy tales) about "home"?

But he was not disturbed. He had known about the treachery of human beings on Earth as long as he had known anything at all. The very primers that Will programmed to teach him his alphabet, glowing gently over his sleeping sack, told the story:

A's for America, that sent us out to die.
B's for all the bastards who did us in the eye.
C's for Centaurus. We'll reach it all the same.
D's for bad old Dieter. He plays a dirty game.

What Jeron did not have was any very realistic picture of Dieter von Knefhausen. Horns and a tail? Scaly or furry? Would he sit on a hill of skulls, farting sulfoxides and belching soot, gnawing a haunch of human child?

So his dreams were often troubled. So are the dreams of all children, everywhere, at all times, as their small subconscious minds try to map the terrors of Hell or the mad onslaught of werewolves or whatever other terrifying fantasy grownups have been feeding them against the tiny wickednesses for which they are sent to bed or deprived of a toy. But when he woke he had his work, and his pets, and his peers, and his parents . . . and the others.

Although Aunt Flo's skills were extreme, she had not succeeded in breeding really satisfactory tame animals. Not real ones. The cottony-downy bunny plants were soft and cuddly, and as good as any Teddy bear for a little kid to sleep with. But they were no better than that. They did not eat, sleep, wet, or move. The place that a kitten might have filled for him if he had been born on Earth was taken by the others. There were times when he drifted off to sleep with another presence beside him, and sometimes when he and the other three children of his cohort sang their lesson songs it seemed that there were five voices raised, or even more, more whispery even than Uncle Ghost, even harder to see. They were not very satisfactory either. So mostly Jeron's companionship was infant human, like himself, or—whatever the original eight had become.

In his third year Jeron was mature enough for more adult responsibilities, so Aunt Ann began teaching him elementary Chinese and Uncle Shef put him to work.

He was not alone. Sheffield Jackman, who no longer was addressed by that name and certainly never by the title "colonel," drafted everybody too weak to resist to his project. He wanted a better telescope. What he really needed was a ten-meter mirror, but he did not have ten years to cast it and cool it and figure it. So he elected to make ten thousand ten-centimeter mirrors instead. The light-gathering capacity would be the same, it was only a matter of so arranging them that each would contribute its share of photons to the same point. Difficult, to be sure. Not impossible, especially as they could stop the thruster for observations and so excuse themselves from the troublesome effects of sagging or twisting. It was necessary, in any case, because Uncle Shef was going to have to locate every object with a magnitude of plus-25 or better through a large section of the heavens, and sort out the ones that moved. He would have to scan more than two hundred astronomical units from the primary Alpha Centauri, and locate everything with a diameter of more than one hundred kilometers; and it was even harder than it seemed. The brightest ones would be easy, but they were not the ones he wanted to find. What was the use of finding a comet core of frozen gases and clathrates when what he needed was structural steel? It was the low-albedo objects that he wanted most, which were by definition the hardest to see.

Intelligence replaced brute force. The ten thousand tiny shells cooled quickly and easily, especially as there was no reason not to cast them of pure aluminum instead of quartz. The first crude sculpting of each took only a week, and then each of the first batches of mirrors was within a millimeter of its figure at all points. But then there was nothing to replace the pads and the rouge and the constant testing with knife edge and beam of light; and that was where Jeron and his cohort and the older kids came in. They had to work under nitrogen, because of the aluminum, their hands inside sealed hoods; they had to use what Aunt Flo had grown for an abrasive, because no jewelers' supply store was nearby; and they had to get it right. At first it took each of them the better part of a week, spoiling half a dozen blanks in the process, to do one mirror. But they learned. They learned enough to do five or six apiece in each day's work, because Uncle Shef made them. Long before the last mirror was in place and collimated Uncle Shef had begun stopping the ship's thrust to begin his primary observations, and by the time they were finished he had mapped more than eighteen hundred chunks of matter.

After each shift Aunt Eve rubbed their sore forearms and hugged their weary bodies, and Uncle Will tried to comfort their fatigued minds. "It's how we're going to make a home," he whispered to Jeron out of the shrouded cherry-fruit vines that grew over his bed. "It will all be worth it, you'll see."

"I never doubted it, Uncle Will," yawned Jeron, rubbing his eyes. "Please, now go talk to some other kid. I want to go to sleep."

And actually, none of the children minded at all; it was a great communal effort, and they were part of it. After Uncle Shef finished his sky map there was even more work, but not quite as satisfying because much of it involved brute force and therefore adult bodies. They helped when they could. The problem was the delta-V forces involved in deceleration. Before deceleration could even start a great deal had to be done—or, rather, undone. Fully three-quarters of the mirrors they had so painfully ground had to be brought back in and remelted and replaced as structural members to strengthen the ship's interior. All of the grown-ups were fussing and tidying around the ship, lashing things down, stowing things, undoing the careless alterations they had made over the years when the thrusters were working at fractional strength because relativity made further acceleration fairly pointless. The inside was a lot of work, but the kids could help. The outside was worse, and the kids could do nothing there. Most of it fell on Uncle Shef and Uncle Ski and Uncle Jim, who were outside the hull in their EVA suits more often than in, cutting away all the extrusions and annexes that had been tacked on so unconsideringly over the years. Uncle Jim was in charge of that project. He drove the others, muttering and cursing. He drove himself even harder.

What brought him to profanity was the recollection of the jettisoned side boosters and the blown-away sections of the hull from the time they rebuilt the drive. "Chrome steel and magnesium!" he shouted into his suit radio. "And where are we going to get that kind of stuff again?" Every gram his torch severed was cherishingly brought back aboard. He did not trouble to remove every last strut and stub, only the ones that might cause trouble if there were violent decelerations as they rounded Alpha Centauri to slow down. When at last he pronounced the *Constitution*'s hull integral once more he came back to the hydroponics gardens, where Jeron had taken over the grownup chores to relieve adult muscles, and lay a whole day between the bright lemon-smelling squash vines on one side and the vegetable porks on the other, refusing to move.

By the time Jeron was four they were approaching the bright yellow star, now recognizably a sun.

It would be bigger, later, when they took up a proper orbit and began their presumptuous construction project of a permanent home. But already it was bigger than anything Jeron had ever seen. In his short lifetime it had grown immensely.

The spectacle had a terribly high price for Jeron and the other children, for now deceleration began in earnest. There were no more interludes of weightlessness for games and thrills. There was not even the steady slowing thrust they had grown up with; the plasma burned hotter and hotter, and the pressure on everybody increased. The adults hated it, but it was what they had been born to. For the children it was new and terrible. Jeron had weighed ten kilos, more or less; now he weighed twenty, then twenty-five. Half a dozen of the littlest kids fractured bones in one week, and then Aunt Eve began making them drink nasty messes that she said were rich in calcium and they added vomiting to their miseries. One G, then one point two, then one point four, and even the grownups were wheezing and falling down; and then they jockeyed around the immense terrifying star for the final shedding of surplus *v*; no one's navigation had been quite good enough for that delicate operation, and so there were bursts of two-G and even three-G acceleration that left the babies too weak to whimper and even Jeron blacked out twice.

But then it was over, and Aunt Eve was cuddling the littlest ones and Uncle Ghost trying to reassure the others, and the real work was about to begin.

Alpha Centauri had no proper planets. Perhaps the nearness of its companion had something to do with that fact.

But it did have a girdle or two of rubble where otherwise planets might have formed, and wandering cometary lumps scattered all through nearby space. "We're going to mine them," whispered Uncle Ghost from the shadows behind Jeron's cohort as they peered out into the starry sky. "We're going to show that bastard what we can do!"

"Damn bastard Knefhausen," Jeron responded automatically, wondering what it would be like to be in one place and not to be eternally traveling toward it.

The *Constitution* was ready for the asteroids long before its orbit was stable. Pinpoint lasers stabbed at every tumbling rock in the asteroid belts. Photon counters trapped and diagnosed the returns. The useful worldlets were indexed and followed, and Uncle Ski cast soft nets of magnetic force that swept the useful objects together into clusters sorted by analysis. Carbonaceous bodies went here, pure iron there, heavy metals in another place. The element abundances were not very satisfactory, because they reflected cosmic, not planetary, proportions; Alpha Centauri had never had a planet. That did not matter. There was plenty of mass to waste, and soon Alpha Centauri would.

They did find one small cinder of a planetoid very near the star, but decided moving and cooling it was more than it was worth; the dozen-kilometer-sized bodies were the most useful. When they had finished collecting and sorting them the really hard work began. By then *Constitution* was locked in a nearly circular orbit one and a half A.U. from the central star, out of the plane of its ecliptic in a path that nibbled at the edges of the first and largest asteroid belt. And they started to build.

It was around this time that young Jeron, having reached that stage of sitting in judgment on adults that on Earth was called adolescence—he was four and a half—realized that his Uncle Shef was going insane.

Of course, with Uncle Shef, how could you tell? Or how could you tell with any of the people on the *Constitution*, including the kids? What struck Jeron as strange would have seemed baseline normal anywhere in the world they had left behind: Uncle Shef appeared to be lusting after the body of Aunt Ann.

Jeron's knowledge of what was baseline normal was at

best sketchy. It was made up of casual remarks and bedtime stories, full of concepts that had no tangible reference to anything around him. Freeways. Singles bars. Expense accounts. Resort hotels. VD. Soap operas. Air raids and guided missiles; school busing and Christmas vacations; mumps; toothaches; runny noses—none of that ever happened or existed in the world he lived in and, although Uncle Ghost was always willing to explain everything, some things merely got more confusing. In this particular area Jeron was particularly handicapped. He was intellectually quite mature, sexually not at all. What the grownups did with each other he had observed, but why they did it escaped him. Also there was the observed fact that they all made use of each other's bodies quite casually, and why was this sudden interest so uncasual? Jeron watched Aunt Ann at every opportunity to try to unravel the mystery. From comparative analysis of photographs in the tattered old magazines he perceived that she had begun to return to the "pinup" norms—had lost weight after blimping up for several years; had combed and cut her long blond hair after letting it spill ragged.

That sort of change could be quantified and understood well enough; but there were other changes. Aunt Ann had returned to her Chinese period. She had dug out the old toe bones. She cast them, with Shef hovering over her shoulder, whenever the two of them could find a moment from the incessant work of readying the ship for its new destiny; and after they had scanned the bones and looked up the hexagrams and muttered to each other they usually made love. No one else seemed to mind, or even notice. When Jeron mentioned it to Uncle Will the shadowy outlines would flicker for a while in indecision before the whisper would come: "They are not hurting anyone, Jeron, why should they be disturbed?" But even Uncle Ghost had observed that the closer the intimacy between Ann and Shef became the more Shef's cheeks sank and the more furiously he raged at everyone else around. It was Shef who mostly controlled the complex webs of forces that were seeking and tugging at all Alpha Centauri's family of useful rocks, and as the task was only partly physical, he was certainly draining his energies.

So Jeron wondered, and spied on them, not knowing what

to expect to see; and when he did see something quite beyond belief he did not know it. Not until he was much older.

16

THERE WAS A GREAT GRINDING OF TANK MOTORS OUTSIDE the detention center. It was unusually loud and persistent; it woke Knefhausen up, although for several years at least he had been hearing such things as part of his interminably dull life.

He had no idea of the time. They had not allowed him a watch for—how long?—half a lifetime it seemed! And one did not ever see sunlight in this foxes' lair underground. Knefhausen was sure it was the middle of the night, though. And, as the ragged firing of weapons was to be heard even above the noise of gears and treads, there was something up, beyond doubt. He rose and dressed quickly in the dark. When the door opened and blinded him with the hall light he was ready for whatever might come.

Yet what came was a considerable surprise. It was the man from the Justice Department, yes, the familiar face of the fourth or fifth of that line who had been interrogating him forever. But there had been no preliminary search this time. And the man was not alone. No! Even with a mob, this time! The armed guard was at least a dozen soldiers now, one of them with a bloody bandage on his head instead of a helmet, all of them looking as though they had fought their way through hell to get there. But most astonishing of all was that with them was the President's secretary, Murray Amos! Knefhausen had not even known Amos was still alive—had not been sure, really, that the President was still alive, or still President, since surely his terms would have expired by now, if not his life. Knefhausen gaped and blinked, and then realization struck home.

How treacherous is the human heart! When it has given up hope, how little it takes to make it hope again!

"Murray!" cried Knefhausen, almost weeping, "it's so

good to see you once again! The President, is he well? What can I do for you? Have there been developments?"

Murray Amos paused in the doorway. He was much older than when Knefhausen had seen him last, and much gaunter. He looked at Dieter von Knefhausen and said bitterly, "Oh, yes, there have been developments. Plenty of them. The Fourth Armored has just changed sides again, so we have to evacuate Washington. And the President wants you out of here at once."

"No, no! That is not what I mean—although, yes, of course, it is good that the President is concerned about my welfare, although it is bad about the Fourth Armored. But what I would wish to know, Murray, is this: Has there been a message from the *Constitution*?"

Murray Amos and the Justice Department man looked at each other. "Tell me, Knefhausen," said Amos silkily, "how did you manage to find that out?"

"Find it out? How could I find it out? No, I only asked because my heart hoped. There has been a message, yes? In spite of what they threatened? They have communicated again?"

"As a matter of fact, they have," said Amos thoughtfully. The Justice Department man whispered piercingly in his ear, but he shook his head. "Don't worry, we'll be coming in a second. The convoy won't go without us. . . . Yes, Knefhausen, the message came in a few hours ago. They have it at the decoding room now."

"Good, oh, so very good!" cried Knefhausen. "You will see! They will justify all! But what do they say? Have you good scientific men to interpret it? Can you understand the contents?"

"Not exactly," Amos began; but he got no farther. Running unceremoniously into the room a tank officer shouted:

"They're running over us, sir! Let's get out of here while we still can!" And Amos whirled and was gone, leaving the soldiers to hustle Knefhausen after. No chance to pick up his papers! Not even to look around his room and see what he had forgot! It was out the door, down the hall, up some stairs, out into a wide circular driveway with looming main battle tanks all around and a fireworks display of white and red bursting in the heavens. Knefhausen was astonished to discover it was summer again; when had that happened? But there were no answers for trivial questions, not even for serious ones. He was crammed down the hatch of an MB-4 quite roughly—quite painfully, because his head scraped against the side of the hatch and he could feel blood running into his pajama collar. Amos was not with him. There was not room for more than one passenger in this small and uncomfortable space; the tank was battle-ready. And battle-active. It spun and heaved across the sidewalk, crunching aside some long-abandoned car, and the main gunner was firing at something down the hill, the two machine gunners apparently trying to ward off infantry—or terrorists—or figments of their own scared imaginations; they were teenage boys in uniforms that did not fit, and what had become of the disciplined troops Knefhausen remembered? They were not local, either. Knefhausen could smell apples in the exhaust fumes, which meant New York State alcohol in the tank.

They fought a running engagement for nearly two hours, and then the firing dwindled away behind them. The tank stopped.

Either they had outrun the enemy or outfought them, whoever the enemy was, because Knefhausen was hustled out of the tank and into a half-track personnel carrier, which set off across what Knefhausen recognized with indignation as Arlington National Cemetery. It was nearly dawn now. The modest marble grave markers showed pearly white, where they were not overturned and half buried in some other vehicle's wake. Knefhausen was not alone in the vehicle. But he might as well have been. Apart from the guard who clung to the rear gate, all the others were casualties, most of them unconscious or raving, the rest dead. By the time they came to a stop Knefhausen's will was ebbing away and his courage was long gone. He was only glad to be alive and out of that prison.

But as soon as they had stopped his spirits began to rise again, as he was hurried across a motel parking lot, as he was conducted to a room with a pool of spilled blood on the floor and an unmade bed—as the door closed behind him.

And then, as the door remained closed, he realized he had only moved prisons. At one time he would have shouted and raged against the awful injustice of keeping him here without giving him, at once!, the message that would make all well again.

But that time was over. Knefhausen had lost track of birthdays again, but he didn't need a calendar to know that, without observing it happen, he had somehow grown very old.

17

JERON NEVER FORGOT WHAT HE HAD SEEN, AND DARED NOT speak of it, either. He was afraid. Shef, chuckling through his whiskers, peering through the lookout port; Ann, her body locked with his in some sort of sexual embrace—oh, yes, they had been doing something! They were celebrating it. Or perhaps they were repenting it. Jeron could not tell; they were communicating, but not in words.

He would not have known they had been doing anything if they had not reacted so violently when they caught him watching. Shef moved like lightning. He shouted wordlessly, dived across the chamber and had Jeron by the hair in an instant; he must have untangled himself from Ann in the process, but so quickly that Jeron didn't see it happen. Ann shrieked after him—one word, "Don't!", and simultaneously her thumb-tip ripped across her throat. Jeron understood the message. It was his good fortune that so did Uncle Shef.

Shef did not release the boy, but the arm that had whipped across his throat relaxed. The two adults grunted and shrugged at each other over the terrified Jeron's head, and then Shef took him firmly by the two shoulders and stared into his eyes. He was trying to remember how to say what he wanted. His lips moved silently for a moment, and then he got out: "Don't . . . tell." And, a moment later, "Anything. No. Any*one*."

"I promise, Uncle Shef," Jeron whined, and was allowed to struggle free. It was not over yet. There was something in Shef's eyes that was mad even by the flaky standards of the *Constitution*. Jeron moved cautiously away, inch by inch, far from sure that this terrifying adult would not grab him again. As Jeron was about to turn and dive for the downshaft, Shef managed to get out one more word:

"Ever!"

For the next few days, Uncle Shef and Aunt Ann seemed to be popping up all the time. It didn't matter where Jeron went. Working at his job on the hydroponics flats, he would look up and there would be Uncle Shef's eyes burning at him through the tangles of vines and raggedy hair. Taking his turn at KP, Aunt Ann's face would appear over the steaming vats of stew. He even fled to the communications room, where the printers spat out the latest budget of disaster and contradictions from Earth whenever anyone on Earth remembered to transmit—whenever anyone on the *Constitution* bothered to turn them on. And there was one of them, pausing in the descent tube to give him a cold-eyed stare.

A "promise" was not particularly binding in Jeron's view. He had rarely been asked for one by a grownup, and what passed between him and the other kids was not significant. But he was too scared to talk. Uncle Ghost at once noticed something was wrong. So, a little later, did Aunt Eve and Uncle Ski. He told them all he was upset by the changes in gravity, in domestic arrangements, in prospects, which was true even if not relevant; so Jeron learned to lie. And a week or two later Aunt Ann came to the hydroponics room. Births had been postponed until there was room to house them, so the vegetable wombs lay empty. The milk plants were stored as seeds, and now Jeron was uprooting the squacipro that even the youngest had outgrown to put in some new venture of Aunt Flo's. Aunt Ann stood over him without speaking for a time.

She should have looked quite nonthreatening, really. Her long blond hair was well brushed and pulled back in a silky tail. She was wearing the black pajama suit that went with the Chinese life-style she had been affecting again, but the pajamas, this time, were clean. By normal human standards, she had never looked more the model of an all-American woman of an interesting age. Jeron's standards were different. He thought she looked scary. He retreated from the bare flats and tried to busy himself with picking sweetbeans, nipping off the fleshy cinnamon-colored pods with his thumbnail and depositing them in a bowl, but she followed him with her eyes. He was aware she was rehearsing things to say to him in children's English.

At length she hopped a row of vines and smiled down at him. "Jeron," she said seriously, "I tell you a story. When Emperor K'ang-hsi in boat at Hangkow, petitioner swam out, letter in teeth. Petitioner said, 'Please use imperial power help punish my enemy, who is wickedest man in world.' You know what K'ang-hsi say?"

He looked up at her and nibbled a raw sweetbean. "Not really, Aunt Ann," he said.

She thought for a moment, then brought it out: "Say, 'Who then is second wickedest?' And tear up petition; so I tell Shef this. You understand?"

"Well, not exactly," Jeron admitted. She scowled at him in disappointment, then shrugged. When Ann Becklund shrugged her whole body was involved, like a soldier who has just received a bullet in the chest; a spasm. She said angrily, "Must understand! Shef very unhappy! Needed to do this thing! Knefhausen wickedest of men!"

Jeron wriggled under her gaze, a finger in his mouth. He had no idea what sort of response she wanted from him until she made it clear by repeating what Shef had said: "Don't tell anyone, ever!"

"Oh, I won't, Aunt Ann." He would have promised far more than that to get her eyes off him.

"Good . . . uh, boy," she said, patting his young genitals. He exhaled a sigh of relief as she turned away, but the relief did not last long. She stopped, then faced him again, scowling in the effort to remember the children's-English words for what she wanted to say:

"I warn them, you understand. You understand? Sent warning. Late a little. But radio faster than kaons, get there first." She stared at him, her face clouding again. "Good boy," she said again, and strolled thoughtfully away.

Although Jeron had understood almost nothing of the exchange, he understood that it was over. He dumped the sweetbeans back into the gravelly substrate they were growing in and headed in the other direction. It was a worrying position for a four-year-old to be in, especially if he wanted to live to reach five.

"Wait, Jeron," whispered Uncle Will from the tangle of citrus at the entrance. "What was that all about?"

Jeron jumped. "You scared me, Uncle Will," he accused, peering around until he located the glassy shadow behind the rich fruit.

"I'm sorry," said Uncle Will, waiting for the answer Jeron wanted mightily to give, but did not dare.

"Oh," the boy said, "she was telling me Chinese stories again. And all that other stuff all you grownups say, that I'm acting funny. Damn sick of hearing it," he added shrewdly.

"Is that all?" whispered Uncle Ghost.

"All I understood." There was silence from among the oranges while Uncle Will pondered. If he had really wanted to know, Jeron reflected, he would have come up and listened; but even Uncle Will did not like interfering with his widow's private matters.

If Will had pressed any harder Jeron would have told him the whole thing, or as much of it as he understood, but Will didn't press and the boy didn't dare. It wasn't that he didn't trust Will. Will would have kept his confidence. Would even have tried to protect him, but how much protection could you expect from a ghost?

To build a planet they needed structural materials. To forge the materials from raw spaceborne rubble they needed heat. Alpha Centauri gave them the heat—once they had rolled out the foil to cup it and pour it into their furnaces—once they had built the tools to roll the foil—once they had captured the ores to make the metals to build the tools to roll the foil. They were in orbit a year, and Jeron was five years old, before the first artifact not made out of original ship's stores was ready. It was a thirty-ton roller. From then on progress was exponential. Everyone was working, all eight adults (even shadowy Will) and all fifty-two of the children. The youngest cohort was now nearly four, and thus of laboring age. There was no room now for anyone not working, and the six-year-olds were kept occupied holding the webby edge of a shell section or overseeing an automatic welder, the fives like Jeron did more adult but less physical tasks, and even the fours toted meals to the grownups. It was not enough, of course. The job was too big for human beings. So no person from the starship, not even a child, ever did anything that a machine could do instead . . . after they had achieved the machines.

In all that time Jeron kept locked the ununderstood event he had been forbidden to disclose. All through his studies, all through his games and maturation rites with the other kids, all through the slow growth of their new home, he remembered that one subject was not to be talked about. Uncle Will Ghost worried at him about it for months, but Jeron was too scared at first to open up and, anyway, learned how to be more clever about concealing the fact of concealment as time went on. Finally even Uncle Ghost let it drop. There was an exponentially growing inventory of secrets among them anyway. With all the modes of communication the grownups had invented, there was still an increasing corpus of information each retained. Partly for privacy. Mostly because few of them were, really, very interested in what any of the others was doing any more.

There is no trip like a knowledge trip, no hallucinogen more potent than an area of knowledge no one else shares. All eight of them were constantly stoned out of their minds with revelatory insights. Occasionally they offered to discuss them with each other, and found few listeners. Now and then they thought to try to pass them on to the children—and failed; there were not enough points of common experience for communication at these rarefied levels. It would have been as easy to teach eschatology to a cat. The only area which all of them shared was the building of the habitat, and that occupied most of everyone's time anyway. In thirty-one months from the first orbital approximation, the machines they built were building the machines that did the work, and Alpha-Aleph was growing. Ring on ring the O'Neill habitat took form. When the third ring locked on it became their home.

Even though he was now seven Jeron still worked in the fields, no longer because he was not good enough for anything else but because he had become very good at that. He was transplanting a seedling, patting the damp made soil with one hand while the other held the plastic film to put over it, when he realized someone was near.

"Hai!" shouted a voice over his shoulder. But before that he had already begun to rise and turn, his right hand grasping out for the trowel.

"Hai!" he shouted in return, ready for attack. But it was only Jemolio, a full sister from his own cohort, holding a grain stalk as though it were a sword.

He relaxed from the ready position, scowling, and put the trowel down. They eyed each other warily, both bare and glistening with sweat, only their cache-sexes marring the shiny tanned skins. "You lost that one," he said, "and you're not supposed to pull up the plants."

She tossed the stalk onto the compost heap. "It was one of Uncle Ghost's failures anyway. There's a cohort meeting. Uncle Ski wants us all there. Twenty minutes. I think the grownups are fighting again."

"Oh, Jesus."

"Sure, but be there."

"All right," he said, turning away—and then quickly twisted, catching up the trowel and lunging at her belly, shouting, *"Hai!"*

She was ready for him. They were always ready for each other, or for spooky Uncle Ski, in all of these Zen stimulations; by the time they were three they had each been challenged a thousand times. They rolled lazily about in the light gravity. It did not matter how quickly you moved when you weighed just a few kilos, everything turned out to be slow motion anyway. And there was the heat. They were gasping by the time they separated, and Jemolio had wound up on top. She was as strong as Jeron and a little faster. It was not uncommon for her to win the one-on-ones with him, and also not important. Winning was not important. Being always ready—being always accepting of what might come, never surprised, never at a loss—that was what Uncle Ski called important. "Twenty minutes, Jeron," she panted, scratching at her belly. In the heat and terribly low humidity sweat vanished as fast as it formed, but seared mucous membranes and parched skin paid for exertion.

"All right. Don't ever pull up any of my plants again. You don't know which are failures."

She stuck out her tongue and turned away. He had been half tensed for one more pseudoattack, but she simply left. It was a good thing Uncle Ski wasn't there. He would have seen that Jeron was tensed. Punishment would have followed.

The boy finished packing the earth around the seedling and carefully sealed down the vapor shield. The hydroponics were all his now. The grownups were too busy for more than occasional visits. Day by day Jeron was in charge.

Jeron had a knack for plant development. He did not have dead Will Becklund's skill. None of the children did. None were willing to do what Will had done to acquire it.

But Jeron was good. And sometimes he would set out his pots of seedlings and spooky Will would come by in the night and make his magic. And then, out of a row of ten identical sprouts, one might develop soft jelly-fleshed fronds, and another might flower with blooms bigger than hibiscus —and most of the rest die. Will's tricks did not always work.

What they had started with was no more than a hundred plant varieties. A few had been ornamentals. Most had been food. All had been selected because they were really good at soaking up carbon dioxide and exhaling oxygen into the air. There were no trees. There was nothing like kelp; there were no water plants at all, except for a few microscopic ones. And that was all they had to work with.

Aunt Flo had changed that a lot and, after his accident, so did Uncle Will. Flo's efforts were mostly rudimentary Luther-Burbankian crosses and selections. Will went deeper. The same patient submicroscopic coaxing that had tripled the thrust of their fusion reactor could switch amino acids within the genes as readily as Flo had urged genes to move about the chromosomes. Plants that started as, mostly, carrots became indistinguishable, nearly, from sweet potatoes. An allele from a volunteer milkweed seed turned sweet corn into cottony-downy pear-shaped fruits that, with a few other tamperings, tasted (nearly) like lamb chops. Out of the frozen and stored meat supplies Uncle Will had salvaged a few viable structural parts from animal chromosomes to add to their basic resources, but they were not really necessary. Long before Alpha-Aleph had begun to fill with their manufactured air Jeron could produce something very close to mahogany veneer—or strawberries, or Gorgonzola at will —out of the materials at hand.

Jeron looked around the gentle sweep of the hydroponics

plot and was content. Far at the other side of the ring was another plot, sterile and empty until they made enough water to give it life, to balance the spin of the three joined rings. Someday they would have ground enough rock into sand and squeezed enough organics for loam and the whole habitat would be soil-covered and growing things; but not yet. He left the plot and, hand over hand, pulled himself up the shinnying cable to what was left of the *Constitution* at the hub. Later on, when they accelerated the habitat to full spin, that would be hard work. But by then there would be more moisture to soak the air, and the temperature of the shell would not have to be kept so high. Jeron could feel the salt drying on his skin as the parched air sucked away his sweat. It itched terribly. He paused to reach down to scratch, and something caught his ankle.

"Hai!" shouted Uncle Ski from beneath him, tugging furiously at his leg. Jeron reacted without thought. He did not pull away. He shifted position and kicked. The foot broke free as Uncle Ski scrambled for a better hold, and Jeron pulled himself a meter or two higher, peering down, ready to place the next kick between Ski's eyes.

"Good enough," said Uncle Ski, panting. "Where are your sibs?" His voice was high and hoarse, because of the air, but he was relaxed as he swung below Jeron, gazing up at the boy.

"Ammarin and Jemolio are there already, I think, Uncle Ski. Forina and Famine are supposed to be with Aunt Mommy. I don't know about the others."

"Aunt Eve Barstow," Ski corrected. "They're not there now. Everybody's supposed to be at the meeting. Get a move on."

Jeron nodded courteously and swarmed up the cable, careful to keep above Uncle Ski's lunging distance. There was something in the old man's eyes that made Jeron think this meeting was special. That would not prevent Uncle Ski from assaulting him again, or a dozen times more; it was the fundamental of his lessons that one must be ready for challenge when one expected it least.

But not this time.

They emerged into the old *Constitution* and the last one in slammed the locks behind them. The air was noticeably cooler and more comfortable even before that, and the heat pumps and humidifiers quickly made it optimal. It was sheer bliss to feel normal beads of perspiration trickle down his nose before the temperature dropped, but it was not a good sign. Something was going on. And Jeron saw at once that it centered around the grownups, and the hologram of the Earth in the middle of *Constitution*'s main compartment.

Jeron had three siblings in his cohort, two female and one other male, but he also had three full sibs in the fourth cohort, born so soon after his own that they had grown up almost as a unit. They were still into having children by marital partners when the cohort was conceived. But Ann Becklund wanted children, of course, and of course Uncle Will Becklund was temporarily not able to sire them because of his death. So Uncle Dad—Jim Barstow—donated sperm for Ann's litters. By the time of the fifth cohort the problem of Uncle Will had been solved. They were the largest cohort of all, and the youngest—more than a year younger than Jeron's, just babies!

But now that there was room for real babies again the fifth was admitted to the meetings too. It made a considerable crush in the little *Constitution*. Jeron crowded through the littler kids and took his place with the medium-sized ones, peering through the tallest at the scene in the middle of the room.

There was the hologram of Earth, basketball-sized and brightly glowing in green and blue and white, and there were a handful of the grownups, chattering and screeching around it. Jeron counted quickly. It was not easy, because they were chattering and screeching and, some of them, leaping about, but there were Uncle Shef and Aunt Ann on one side of the globe, Shef clutching at any of the others who came in reach, Ann serene and silent; there were Aunt Flo and Aunt Eve, whispering savagely to each other; Uncle Jim was shouting at nothing at all, which on closer examination turned out to be Uncle Will Ghost; and there came Uncle Ski, burrowing through the children and sending them flying, as he struggled to get into the cockpit. It was rare for all eight of the grownups to be present in the same place. That they were at each other's throats was not rare at all, for the eight adults were often that way, though not usually as badly as this. The noise was deafening, and, of course, the audible quick-speech words were only a minor fraction of the arguments. Uncle Ski grabbed Aunt Dot's hand, tapping out pulsed finger pressures to supplement his facial expressions and shrugging shoulders. He was not talking to her with his voice; that was reserved for the other conversation he was carrying on, with Aunt Eve and Uncle Shef, who were now arm in arm, but not in affection. Aunt Dot was trying to pull her hand free because, stripped nude, she was anointing herself with skin cream to take advantage of the comfortable humidity, and Ski was causing her to smear the shiny stars she had grown on her shoulders. At the same time she talked and grimaced to most of the other adults, and they to her. Even Uncle Will flickered in and out of visibility, an unstable shimmer over the globe itself, and his harsh whisper penetrated the yelling.

Like all of the children, Jeron understood a little quick-speech. It would not have sufficed, except for Aunt Dot. She had elected to take seriously—or jokingly, but the joke had been going on for more than a year now—the orders that had come in from Earth ludicrously promoting her to general's rank; and so she practiced speaking in approved West Point English. "Ten-hut!" she shouted, and at least the children reluctantly fell silent. Into the dwindling din she rapped out: "At oh five hundred hours this date Willis NMI Becklund, civilian, discorporeal, informed this officer that he had obtained evidence indicating that Lt Col Sheffield H Jackman, 0-328770, of this command, had been screwing around retributively with the kaons. Date of offense approximately three years ten months fifteen days prior to present. As senior officer commanding I have convened this court-martial."

Uncle Shef combed the dreadlocks out of his eyes and spat a long, incomprehensible sentence at her; he seemed about to follow with a lunge, but Uncle Ski leaped between them in full unarmed-combat stance. "Knock it off, you two!" Aunt Eve cried furiously. "What are you talking about, Dot?"

Dot merely looked at her frostily; it was Uncle Ghost who replied. "Shef sent a burst of kaons toward the Earth," he whispered. "Pure revenge. Shameful. Jeron! Was that it, boy? Was that what you wouldn't tell me about?"

Aunt Ann flashed, "Not his fault. Anyway, warned them. Message there now, kaons not yet."

"That is verified," nodded Aunt Dot, rubbing her general's stars. "Session is apprised that velocity of kaon stream is approximately point nine nine three light. Subject kaons will therefore arrive approximately nine days twenty-one plus hours after message, less time of delay between dispatch of kaon stream and message." She was making an effort to sit at attention, not easy in the almost gravityless core of the habitat.

Aunt Eve's eyes flashed. "You monsters!" she cried. "What have you done?"

"Revenge!" cried Aunt Ann, and then subsided, folding her hands and making an attempt to regain detachment.

"Revenge," repeated Eve, weeping. "What kind of animals have we become? What possible crime could justify wiping out every nation in the world?"

18

A SINGLE KAON, WHICH CARRIES ONE UNIT OF "STRANGENESS" and not much else, is not very significant, but trillions of trillions of them were spearing through space between Alpha Centauri and Sol. They moved in an orderly train twenty billion miles long to their calculated rendezvous, and for the first few years of their journey they had little to do. It was not until they reached the Solar System that they found suitable targets. It was heavy elements they sought: a few pockets of mineral on a satellite or two, a handful of exceptionally dense and far-ranging asteroids, the surviving nuclear power systems of some forgotten exploratory spacecraft in orbit around Jupiter and floating between Earth and Mars. Each was bathed in the gentle kaon stream. Each kaon found a neutron of the proper resonance deep inside a radioactive nucleus, turned it into a lambda particle, threw out a pion, and settled down to separating the nucleus into less troublesome fractions. The radionucleides began to melt, and the bulk of the stream continued inward, toward the Earth, where Dieter von Knefhausen, among others, was puzzling over the announcement of their coming.

The message was clear enough in its way, which is to say it wasn't in code. But the language was Chinese.

It had been translated, of course, but to Dieter von Knefhausen, shaking his head over the twentieth rereading, it was still Chinese:

Ref.: CONSIX T51/11055/*7

CLASSIFIED MOST SECRET

Subject: Transmission from U.S. Starship *Constitution*.

The following message was received and processed by the decrypt section according to standard directives. Because of its special nature, an investigation was carried out to determine its provenance. Radio-direction data received from Farside Base indicate its origin along a line of sight consistent with the present predicted location of the *Constitution*. Strength of signal was high but within appropriate limits, and degradation of frequency separation was consistent with relativistic shifts and scattering due to impact with particle and gas clouds.

Although available data do not prove beyond doubt that this transmission originated with the starship, no contraindications were found.

On examination, the text proved to be a phonetic transcription of what appears to be a dialect of Middle Kingdom Mandarin. Only a partial translation has been completed. (See note appended to text.) The translation presented unusual difficulties for two reasons: One, the difficulty of finding a translator of sufficient skill who could be granted appropriate security status; two, because (conjecturally) the language used may not correspond exactly to any dialect but may be an artifact of the *Constitution*'s personnel. (See PARA EIGHT, Lines 46-54 below, in this connection.)

This text is PROVISIONAL AND NOT AUTHENTICATED and is furnished only as a first attempt to translate the contents of the message into English. Efforts are being continued to translate the full message, and to produce a less corrupt text for the section herewith. Later versions and emendations will be forwarded when available.

TEXT FOLLOWS:

1 PARA ONE. The one who speaks for all *(Lt-Col*
2 *Sheffield H Jackman?)* rests. With righteous
3 action comes surcease from care. I *(identity*
4 *not certain, but probably Mrs Annette Marin*

Becklund, less probably one of the other three female personnel aboard, or one of their descendants) come in his place, moved by charity and regret.

PARA TWO. It is not enough to study or to do deeds which make the people frown and bow their heads. It is not enough to comprehend the nature of the sky or the sea. Only through the understanding of all can one approach wisdom, and only through wisdom can one act rightly.

PARA THREE. These are the precepts as it is given us to see them.

PARA FOUR. The one who imposes his will by force lacks justice. Let him be thrust from a cliff.

PARA FIVE. The one who causes another to lust for a trifle of carved wood or a sweetmeat lacks courtesy. Let him be restrained from the carrying out of wrong practices.

PARA SIX. The one who ties a knot and says, "I do not care who must untie it," lacks foresight. Let him wash the ulcers of the poor and carry night soil for all until he learns to see the day to come as brother to the day that is.

PARA SEVEN. We who are in this here should not impose our wills on you who are in that here by force. Understanding comes late. We regret the incident of next week, for it was done in haste and in error. The one who speaks for all acted without thinking. We who are in this here were sorry for it afterward.

PARA EIGHT. You may wonder *(literally: ask thoughtless questions of the hexagrams)* why we are communicating in this language. The reason is in part recreational, in part heuristic *(literally: because on the staff hand one becomes able to strike a blow more ably when blows are struck repeatedly)*, but the nature of the process is such that you must go through it before you can be told what it is. Our steps have trodden this path. In order to reconstruct the Chinese of the *I Ching* it was first necessary to reconstruct the German of the translation from which the English was made. Error lurks at every turn. *(Literally: false apparitions*

51 *shout at one each time the path winds.)* Many
52 flaws mark our carving. Observe it in silence
53 for hours and days until the flaws become part
54 of the work.
55 PARA NINE. It is said that you have eight days
56 before the heavier particles arrive. The dead
57 and broken will be few. It will be better if all
58 airborne nuclear reactors are grounded until
59 the incident is over.
60 PARA TEN. When you have completed rebuild-
61 ing send us a message, directed to the planet
62 Alpha-Aleph. Our home should be prepared
63 by then. We will send a ferry to help colonists
64 cross the stream when we are ready.

The above text comprises the first 852 groups of the transmission. The remainder of the text, comprising approximately 7500 groups, has not been satisfactorily translated. In the opinion of a consultant from the Oriental Languages Department at Johns Hopkins, it may be a poem.

/s/ Durward S Richter
Durward S Richter
Maj Gen USMC
Chief Cryptographer
Commanding

Distribution: X X X BY HAND ONLY

Knefhausen had almost read the spots off the blue-bound flimsy when his jailors came for him and escorted him, no, rushed him to the room where Murray Amos was waiting for him. "Explain that garbage!" Amos commanded.

In spite of everything, one had one's pride. Although he was shaking with fatigue, and perhaps with more than fatigue, Knefhausen moved precisely to the center of the room, peering down at the President's assistant as he sat behind a steel Army desk. "My duty is to the President," he said steadfastly. "I wish to see him at once."

Murray Amos had fatigue of his own, and perhaps it had made him more reasonable. He sighed. "Oh, Knefhausen," he said, "do you think I don't know that? The President is—not very well. I am carrying out his instructions." He glanced up curiously and frowned, for the lights were flickering. "I do not have much time," he said to Knefhausen, "so come on, boy! Give us a break."

Knefhausen hesitated, but what choice did one after all have? "Very well. I can of course tell you little that is not apparent. Have you complied with the instructions and grounded all nuclear aircraft?"

Amos's eyes narrowed. "Not questions, Knefhausen. Answers!"

"Very well. But what is there to say? 'Heavier particles' no doubt refers to some sort of nucleides, for what purpose I cannot conjecture, although from the reference to 'dead and broken' one may suspect—"

"And I don't want to hear what you suspect, either! I want you to tell me—oh, damn the lights!" They had gone out completely, and only a faint sunset glow through the shuttered windows let them see each other.

In the old heart of Dieter von Knefhausen a thrill of both fear and excitement struck. He watched Amos stab at buttons on his desk, and swear when there was no response; and then, howling with surprise and pain, wrench his wristwatch off his arm and hurl it to the floor, rubbing the scorched skin.

Knefhausen could not know just what had happened; he had no instruments; he had been through too much for his wits to be entirely about him; he was too tired and perhaps too old. But he could observe the results as the kaons struck, and could guess that it was the end of radioactivity on the surface of the Earth.

Fortunately the kaons did not penetrate very deep. If the nucleides at the core had broken apart the planet could not have survived it. But he could see that much had broken apart already, of what little in the world he had known had managed to survive.

There was a noise at the door, and an Army doctor burst in. "The President!" she cried. "The life-support system isn't working! His signs are flat!"

Knefhausen nodded thoughtfully and walked over to a chair. "I think," he said, "there is now no longer a need to speculate at what it is that is coming to us, for it has arrived."

19

SINCE I DON'T HAVE ANYONE MUCH TO TALK TO, I TALK TO myself. I look in my mirror, at that ugly old face that's really only about thirty-eight years old, well, maybe forty or so but certainly not much over, and I say: "Hello, Eve Barstow. Let me introduce myself. I'm Evelyn Clarissa Letterman. You used to be me, you know, before you married that good-looking Jim Barstow. Heaven knows who you are now." And heaven does know, I hope, because I am not sure I always do. Mostly I am called Aunt Eve, and mostly by the kids. The grownups seldom call me at all. And what I mostly do is tend the truck garden and the cabbage patch.

It isn't just that my fellow pioneers don't much want to talk to me. I'm not thrilled to be talking to any of them, either. Their conversation never did much to raise my spirits, even when I could understand what they said.

I used the word "said" very loosely, for they have evolved their own quicker, preciser ways of communicating. Old married couples rub together for half a century before they understand that his yawn means he doesn't agree and she signifies depression by sewing curtains. My dears didn't take that long. They didn't confine it to their true spouses, either. My God, no. Jim said so little to me over the years that, without the kids, I would surely have lost the power of speech while he was smacking his lips and snapping his fingers and twitching his toes and his nose and, I swear, his ears and his scalp to Flo and Ski and Dot and even now and then to some of the kids. But never, ever, to me. All right. I'm the dummy. I don't care. I don't want to hear what they're saying anyway. I do sometimes want *them* to hear *me*, to be sure. That's mostly when I think they're doing something wrong, which is a lot of the time. They don't listen to that, either. They didn't even listen to me when we found out what Shef and Ann had been doing. They don't care if I oppose them, and they don't even care if I approve. (Do you care if a daisy approves when you pluck its petals?)

Sometimes I wonder what has happened to us. I pull out the family album I have meticulously hung onto through all these years. There are our prelaunch pictures, with the King of England kissing Dot Letski's hand, and the President of the United States, looking like Bugs Bunny in a morning coat, pinning a ribbon on Shef. The grownups won't even look. Even the older kids are pretty tired of Aunt Eve's photographs, although the littlest ones are generally thrilled with them. Or pretend to be.

We have all changed so very much since those pictures. Shef is a stick figure of himself, less than a hundred pounds, his Ruggero the Gnome King whiskers flying all around his head. I think he starches them. Or perhaps it is only willpower that stretches them taut. Flo has become grossly fat. She says it has to be that way so she can accommodate two uterine lobes working at once, since she is a frequent mommy. But it is also from eating too much. As to the late Will Becklund—well, Will is what he chooses to be, and mostly he chooses to be nearly invisible. So we are rather an odd-looking lot, skeletal Shef, gross Flo, pyknic Dot, bent Ski, willowy Ann—not to mention my lord and master Jim, who seems to have sagged all of his innards into a potbelly you cannot imagine. I am the only mesomorph in the bunch and even I, I must confess, no longer trim my nails or blow-dry my hair. Add in the scuttling littlest kids and the half-civilized older ones and, if you want to know what we all look like, go to any swamp and tip over a rock.

I will not speak of the other sensory impressions you might get of the lot of us, or at least not of the smells.

As to the sounds, ah, my God, how strange! Back when the U. S. of A. really cared about us they used to transmit cheer-up tapes. I have one of all of us on "Meet the Press" —steam radio, not TV—broadcast over the American propaganda network so that all the world could hear what delicious middle-American types we all were. And we really were. Shef's Tulsa, Ann's Bryn Mawr, just a hint of Brooklyn in Ski. Now, my heavens! None of the grownups speak English anymore, or at least not if they can help it. Except to me, and there they try when they have to but don't always succeed. Shef has completely lost the knack, and uses a computer translator to convert those majestic thoughts of his into words I can understand, but I would not say that it works at all well. The children speak pretty good English, it's true. But for some reason or other they'd rather talk to each other than to any of us. You've heard of a generation gap? No. You just think you have. Here on the old *Constitution* we've raised a race of enemies. I don't know why. Except that we original eight have ourselves become quite inimical people, or seven-eighths of us have.

The Holocaust was Jim's fault, originally. For all I know they were all in it, but it was James Madison Barstow, my dear whilom All-American hubby, who was our resident nuclear wizard, custodian of quarks, basher with the big stick. Way back in circumsolar space he began tinkering with the ship's fusion drive. Along about midpoint he rebuilt it. Well, that produced both good news and bad news. The good news was that it worked a lot better. The bad news, not counting that it killed old Will, was that he got Shef interested in his hadron hatchery, and, oh, how I wish that had not happened!

So what Shef wound up with was one of those marvels of technological sophistication from the space program we used to hear about all the time. Only this one wasn't a frying pan. It was a way of frying Dieter von Knefhausen. Shef's miracle of better living through science gifted him with a whole new litter of feisty little nuclear particles that just loved fat atoms. When any one of them came near a big one it screwed right into it, and all that superheavy fission energy just oozed out as great gooey glops of heat.

I'm not sure why. Or how. After I cooled down I kept after them until they explained it to me, but there were gaps. Jim gave it a good try but, whatever he was saying, what I heard was:

"All he had to do was   , modulate a   of
            for baryon–baryon interactions with   .
Then he just   ,   and   and every
heavy actinide on Earth had to   ." And that's when
I began to scream, but they'd done it anyway.

On the next morning, which was the morning of Day 3841, I woke up not really wanting to wake up at all, because it was so nice to be dreaming of home and Mom and Dad and all the heads I used to hang out with in Southern California.

Of course, the home I had now wasn't so bad. The architect for our little world was a fellow named Tsiolkowsky, or maybe O'Neill; my nearly eidetic memory tosses up both names and I've long since tired of arguing which. I didn't have a personal room anymore. I had a personal *house*. Or maybe you would call it a hut, because it surely wasn't fancy, but at least it had a kitchen and a bathroom and a plot of herbs and flowering plants around it. And a lock on the door. And when I opened the door to go out and see if this day, finally, was going to be worth living, I found something tucked under my door-knocker. It was a vegetable. Or a fruit, or a flower; I couldn't really tell what, so I reached out and caught the arm of one of Flo's two-year-olds as she bounded past. "Modany, do you know who put this here?"

Her eyes widened politely. "Wower, Aunt Eve! Doesn't that smell sweet!" But she didn't know. I patted her bottom and let her run on to the cookies and milk and took the thing out of the knocker.

It was something like a large carrot, heart-shaped in cross section, the color of honey. It was not anything I had grown, or even seen growing. Since I was the woman of all work in the hydroponics department, that meant somebody had been deliberately keeping it secret. When I bit a piece off, it tasted the way it smelled, chocolaty-mint. I didn't observe until I lifted it for a second bite that inside, on the fracture surface, it bore a message:

HAPPY BIRTHDAY
DEAR AUNT EVE BARSTOW

The lettering went all the way through the length of the stalk, like a stick of Brighton rock. It was unsigned. But who needed a signature to recognize the work of her first-born and maybe best-born son?

Jeron's personal room was only two north and four east of mine, but he wasn't in it to be thanked. Or scolded, if that was what I was going to decide to do. As I was breakfasting I decided that it would be thanked because, although in my simple old-fashioned heart I did not approve of his courting his own mother, he had at least taken my mind off Uncle Shef's villainy. I was able to make myself go to work. No matter what, someone has to till the cotton and someone has to hoe the corn, and that's me.

While I was stewing up the morning's protoplasts Molomy came flying back through the fruit vines, giggling and shrieking, along with half a dozen others of her cohort. They raced like bunnies being chased by a friendly fox, and the fox was the very son I was looking for, Jeron. As they came in sight he paused, yelled something after the prey good-naturedly, and let them escape. "Hello, Aunt Mommy," he said in his sweet, pure soprano.

I decanted the bright green soup and handed him the flask. "Hold this while I get some filter paper. What are you doing to those kids?"

He grinned. "Uncle Ski told me to struggle them while he works on the fifth cohort, but they're okay. Happy birthing day."

Jeron's simple English was pretty good, like most of the kids, but not perfect. "That's birthday, dear." I counted up. "My God. I'm thirty-nine years old today. And feel like ninety."

He steadied the flask while I repoured the decoction through the filter. "Don't be upset on your birthing day—birthday," he wheedled. "It's all over."

Jeron is a very handsome boy, not tall, complexion darker than either his father's or mine, a little portly for a seven-year-old. When he scowled he looked much older, and he was scowling now. "I know, Jeron. Thanks."

He rubbed his downy chin, nodding, then helped me put away the filtrate and knelt gracefully with me to snip shoot tips for the next enzyme stew. He was watching me out of the corner of his eye, and I knew I was in for some cheering up. "Aunt Mommy? If you were home on your birthday now, what would you be doing?"

"Oh, Jeron, you don't want to hear all that stuff again." But I could feel myself cheering. He persisted.

"Please, Aunt Mom. You would have a cake with candles?"

"Most likely, uh-huh. Of course, that kind of a party is really for children. If your father and I were still in our old apartment in Houston we'd probably ask a few friends over, maybe for dinner. You remember how we used to eat our meals, getting together in kinship or friend groups, all at about the same time? I told you about it."

"Parents and children, yes. And everybody eating the same thing."

"Well, that's because preparing meals was a lot harder, and it was pretty inefficient, yes. But it made a meal a kind of ceremonial. Especially if there was a real occasion, like Christmas or a birthday, or everybody getting together after the family had been all over."

"So that's what you would do for your birthday?"

"Oh, maybe more than that. After dinner perhaps we would all go to a play, or out dancing—to a public place, with a bar and a live band. There might be four or five hundred people all together in a place like that."

"Will you teach me how to dance, Aunt Eve?"

"Why, Jeron! Of course I will. If you're sure you really want to learn. I don't want you just being kind to me."

He frowned to look older. "Aunt Mom? I hate your logical inconsistencies. You praise me for being kind, and now you tell me you don't want to do it."

I said humbly, "You're right, Jeron, and of course I'll teach you how to dance and it doesn't matter what your reasons are."

"Now?"

"Well. I should be getting the crops in right now—"

"Not now," he decided. "Not because of your crops, though. Because I want to show you something."

There was no arguing with Jeron when he had his mind made up. He took my hand and tugged me through the quarter-acre I was supposed to be tending, and would not say why.

That didn't surprise. What would have surprised about Jeron would have been an occasion when he didn't go out of his way to be surprising. I tried to slow him down when I saw that he was dragging me into the unfinished sections of the shell. I didn't like going there. Outside of the microclimate of my little garden patch the air was too thin and too dry and generally too uncomfortable still, though not nearly as bad as it had been. But he wouldn't stop, not until he clattered across a bare strip of structural steel, nothing between us and the vacuum outside but a fingernail's width of asteroidal iron, and jerked me to a stop. "There!" he cried.

I looked.

It was Ann Becklund. Not one of my favorite sights. "She's meditating again," I said. "Now I'm going back—"

"Look!" He darted over and touched her; she didn't move. "Full padmasana! She's been there all day!"

"She does that all the time, Jeron," I said scornfully.

"Touch her!" he said angrily. "Stupid!"

The time for teaching manners to my son was unfortunately long past, so I decided to ignore his rudeness. I touched her.

Ann didn't seem to be breathing, but I was pretty sure she was, somehow—there was a trick of breathing in one nostril and out the other that went with the full-lotus pretzel she had bent herself into. She looked strange. Not just her padmasana position. I have mentioned that Ann's slim figure and long blond hair were a source of constant aggravation to me. They looked fine. In fact, she looked as perfectly well groomed as she ever had . . . except for one thing.

When I got close I noticed that there was a faint patina of dust on her hair and skin.

Jeron was hopping with excitement. "You see? All day today, just like that. And all day yesterday, and all day the day before, and—"

"That's impossible. After all, she had to eat—drink water, at least."

He stopped short, his nostrils flaring furiously. "It is not impossible, since I have said it was so!"

"I only meant it was hard to believe, dear. I wonder if there's something wrong with her. Maybe we should try to wake her up."

"Yes? Yes!" he crowed. "Please do!"

Well, I know a dare when it is offered, but I didn't like

looking cowardly in the eyes of my oldest son. I touched her again, harder, and called her name.

There was no response, at first. Then the rolled-back eyes came slowly down to focus on me, and the lacquered face cracked into an expression of rage.

I said shakily, "I'm sorry to bother you, but I was worried about you, Ann." She made a sound—I wouldn't say she spoke. "I didn't understand that, dear," I said, full of tenderness and sympathy.

Her mouth moved slowly for a moment, rehearsing the nearly forgotten skill of speaking. "No," she croaked. And then, "You don't." And then she hit me.

I don't mean she made a fist and punched me with it. It wasn't like that. I didn't know what she hit me with, but I felt it, all right; it was like an explosion in the air before me, and I went flying.

The shock must have dazed me, because the next thing I remember was hearing Jeron whimpering, and feeling his hands under my armpits as he was tugging me away. "You got her mad, Aunt Eve! How stupid!"

"Let go of me!" I pulled myself to my feet, holding onto Jeron's shoulder to keep from wobbling in the light gravity. "She's saying something."

"That does not matter. Let's leave her alone, Aunt Eve!"

"I want to hear!" I moved back toward her, though keeping a fringe of high-bush rhubarb between us. The expression on her face showed how hard it was for her to say English words, but she finally forced them out:

"*Not again.*"

Jeron was tugging at my arm. "She doesn't want you to bother her again," he said accusingly. "Now let's go!"

"Wait a minute, there's more!"

She was bawling something at us. It was more complicated and she forced the words out twice, but I could not understand them till Jeron translated for me: "She's saying 'Chandrasekhar's other limit,' Aunt Eve, whatever that means, and now can we get the hell out of here?"

On the morning of Day 4104 Jeron woke me up by stroking my ear. He was lying stretched out next to me, but on top of the flower comforter. "Jeron," I said sternly, coughing to get the hoarseness out of my throat—it had been a rough night—"cut that out. Your mother is not an appropriate sex object for you."

"I know that. I just like your bed." He was sulking, of course.

I have developed the bed myself, out of honeysuckle and milkweed mostly, but with flower scents bred in. "Do you want me to grow one for you?"

"If I *wanted* one, I would *grow* one, and it would be better than this." But he wasn't really angry, because he reached behind him and handed me a steaming cup of coffee—well, as near as we had come to coffee. It wasn't bad.

"God bless you." I swallowed as much as I could gratefully. "That's very sweet of you, Jeron."

"I know. You told me your mother used to do that for you in the mornings, and I wanted to surprise you. Don't worry, I made sure Uncle Ski was gone before I came in." He tasted the coffee to confirm that he still didn't like it, made a face, and handed it back to me. "Did he tell you what Aunt Ann meant about Chandrasekhar?"

"Now, just a minute, Jeron! How did you know what I asked Uncle Ski?"

"I wasn't listening at the door," he said indignantly. "Everybody knows everything you're going to do long before you do it, don't you know that? You're the easiest to figure out!"

I took another sip of the coffee and decided to let that pass. Actually, I had asked Ski, when there was time for talking, but of course he hadn't really been able to answer. Most of the grownups could talk to me, somewhat, if they wanted to, but not easily. And seldom wanted to. "I want to get cleaned up, Jeron," I said.

He grinned. "You mean you want me to leave. You are so *very* strange, Aunt Eve." But he was being courteous enough to grant me my idiosyncrasies; only, to make sure I understood he was going out of his way to be courteous, he took his time about it. He paused at the door to stroke his small, thin, dark mustache. "Do you like it?" he demanded.

He had been working on it for months, so I knew what he wanted to hear. "It makes you look older," I said, and I said it as though it were a compliment. Wholly pleased, he left me to my privacy and my unusual habits. Shower, eat, get to work: I was probably the only adult person within four light-years with so fixed a morning ritual.

It kept me going. It did not give me comfort. As I rinsed myself clean of sweat and Ski, and replenished my blood-sugar level at one end of me and replenished the hydroponics cultures at the other . . . as I tugged a comb through my very uncoiffed hair and studied the jagged ruins of my fingernails, as I headed across the fields of seedling trees and fabric plants to where my ten little helpers had already begun the day's work . . . I wondered why, really, I bothered.

But there was one good reason, always. I bothered because of the kids. I loved them every one. All of us had children—frequently and multiply—but I had more than anyone else, because I had theirs as well as my own. I was the only one of the crew, I think, who actually wanted children; what the others wanted was only subjects.

My work crew was unusually silent, all ten tiny little toddlers of them, and I instantly saw why. There was Aunt Flo, perched on a dewpole, silent as dusty Ann. She was wearing one of those red muumuus that were all the trouble she would go to to dress and, fat as she was, she looked like a candy apple on a stick. A mean one.

Under that wicked, wordless gaze my crew were busier than they had ever been for me, skinning plant cells to make protoplasts, challenging tip-of-the-shoot meristems with the witches' brew I had left for them. Actually, the recipe was Flo's in the first place. Flo was the one who started all those new models coming off the hydroponic assembly line, way back to the beets that tasted like lamb chops and even the exothermic vegetable womb, and so you might think she was just there to supervise our carrying out her project. I doubted that. All the supervision she ever did took one quick glance. Then either she went away ("Pass") or whopped you with a trowel ("Fail"), and that was the way you got your grades. Or you might think she was just being motherly, since all but three of my helpers were her own identical septuplet girls. Wrong again. Flo was often a mother but *never* motherly.

All of which left the problem of just what she was doing there.

Since it was not a problem I could solve, I ignored it. "Modany! Take Thruway and Ringo to the cabbage patch," I ordered—God, what strange names Flo gave her kids! "Check to see that all the babies are warm. Fry and Tudeasy, come with me." And I set about tweezering tiny calli onto a flat, and letting the children poke them into seedbeds.

The work was pleasant after a hard night. What I do makes no demands on the intelligence; I just have to do what any housewife does in the kitchen. Strain it, and stew it, and mix it, and set it out to ripen. You mince up the right parts of your plants. Then you make protoplasts; these are just naked cells, and the way you get the cell to take its clothes off is to stew it with an enzyme. In two weeks your protoplasts grow back their skins and they're cells again. A couple of days later they clump together and form calli, and they've begun to grow.

Of course, that's no good. You don't want them to spread into lumps like mold. You want them to specialize into stems and leaves and roots and fruits and so on, so you challenge them with some brew or other, and you watch your osmotic pressures like a hawk, and, next thing you know, the little callus turns emerald green and it's ready to be set out.

Most of what you get's no good at all, and at least half of it just dies. But the rest—well, that's where it all comes from, you see. Ski and Flo do stranger things than that, but they've never shown me how. You have to be pretty careful, too. Any time Shef comes near a new batch he's ruined it; he sweats too heavily. My husband, one morning when he stopped by and forgot what it was he wanted of me, ruined one whole crop because he kept sneezing. But it's still no more than cookery. If you can put a perfect chocolate souffle on the table two minutes after the last guest has finished his steak, you can do what I was allowed to do.

By the time I had the whole batch set out I noticed that Flo had moved. She was still on the dewpole, but she had turned around; she was looking toward where Ann Becklund still sat, and what she was looking at was Dot Letski.

I drifted over. Dot was studying Ann as carefully as I had, or somewhat more carefully, because she had the intelligence not to touch her.

I *never* start a conversation with any of my age cohort, but this time I broke my rule. I said, "She's been like that for days, Dot, and yesterday she said something like 'Chandrasekhar's other limit.' Also she hit me with something."

I have some very good rules, and every time I break them I realize how good they are. Dot didn't say anything. She was peering into Ann's nostrils from an eyelash length away; but she must have given some indication, because I heard a noise from behind me and when I turned Flo was leaping toward us. Behind her the dewpole was still vibrating, and the little foil streamers that catch the moisture in the air and drip it onto the plants were shaking like pennons in a breeze. She wasn't looking at Dot or Ann. She was looking at me. She stopped in the middle of her rush, poised daintily on one foot—Did you ever see the Walt Disney dance of the hippopotamuses? That was Flo—and said several English words. They were, in order, "Dragonfly. Barrier. Roll the bones."

I did not of course understand her any more than I'd understood Ann after she hit me, and I liked this just as little because I had started an argument between my two dear friends. Freely translated, the conversation went like this:

Dot: "Why are you confusing the dummy?"

Flo: "She doesn't understand what Ann's doing."

I mean, that was the first two seconds, if that, and only a tiny fraction of it, and it wasn't in words. It had to be seen to be understood, like dance mime. It went like this:

Why—eyebrows up—*you*—chin thrust at Flo—*confuse*—eyes crossed, jaw dropped—*dummy?*—contemptuous twitch of the shoulder toward me.

And then Flo replying: *She*—same twitch toward me, less contemptuous, maybe, but no more affectionate—*not comprehend*—same idiot eyes and jaw—*Ann*—jerk of the head toward the screening rhubarb.

And then Dot laughed, and stabbed her chin, tongue out and fluttering, toward Flo, shaking her head: The image of fast chatter, with a sort of wrinkle of the nose to suggest that not only did I not understand Flo, either, but perhaps all that Flo had to say was not very important anyway. But you must not think that was all of it. Or even much. Because at the same time they were talking, in clipped, run-together, sketchy words, to each other and perhaps to me or even to distant unhearing Ann. Not in sequence, like the dialogue in a play. Simultaneously. Maybe even interactively, so that the sentence one was saying was modified before it finished by the input from the other. What a catfight! They *sounded* like cats. They spoke so fast that, even when they used language, the words flew by in growls and yowls and screams.

I couldn't follow what they said after the first few seconds, but it appeared that Dot was taking my side—or at least opposing Flo's—on the grounds of an outmoded adherence to causality. Was I grateful? Oh, was I ever *not*! For to have Dot best Flo over me made Flo my enemy, and she was bad enough as my gene-splicing guru. I tried to look uninvolved. Now and then a single word lay in my ear long enough to be heard, sometimes even a phrase. I caught a few epithets: "Stochastic bitch!" "Aleatory asshole!" "Serendipitous slob!"—for there were times when even the efficiency of quick-speech had to be sacrificed for the solid English-language impact of an insult in words. But whether the names were aimed at me, or at unhearing Ann, or at each other, I did not know. Or care. These same fights had been going on for a decade or more, and my greatest concern was to stay out of them. I didn't care to be in the middle, like the family dog with his head on his paws, looking from Him to Her as they bickered, with no hope but somewhere to catch an "Eat" or a "Come!" or, dream of Heaven!, an "Out?"

So when Dot, still jabbering away at the jabbering Flo, jerked her head to signify "Let's move on," and Flo shrugged "All right," I was not at all displeased. The jabber kept up unchecked until Flo and Dot were ten meters away, and then it stopped like the throwing of a switch. Dot kept on; Flo turned back to me.

All my little helpers had been standing slack-jawed and grinning, enjoying the fireworks that were not aimed at them. When Flo faced back they all instantly resumed their occupations, but it was me she was approaching.

She did not seem to be angry, exactly, or at least not exactly at me. She scowled and scratched her immense belly and wrinkled her face. She was making an effort to find words, and it took her some time. And at last she failed, for what she finally produced was one explosive sentence:

"Forget it," she snapped, and was gone, lumbering lightly up the slope of the shell, over the planted fields.

I slept not very well that night, and alone, which may have been the reason I did not sleep very well.

But when I woke, on the morning of Day 4243, I still had the feeling that I had had visitors in the night. It felt as though some child of my own, lost but loving, had crept into my bed in the middle of the night, but of course when I stretched out my hand there was nothing there. Sometimes waking to find that a pet had snuggled in beside me was comforting. Mostly it was principally sad. Even guilty, in a way, because to some extent it was my fault that Will had made the first pet. I could not accept that Ann's first little girl had died, and pleaded with Will to do for her what he had done for himself—and he did try, but there was not enough there to save, really. Or on that later time, when I came to the vegetable womb to touch and fuss over my own, and found the cabbage soft and cold. I could not accept that, either.

It left me pensive, though, and the always difficult task of getting myself going in the morning took even longer than usual. When I got out of the shower there actually was someone in my bed. I mean someone live. I could not see who; he had the flowerlets pulled over his head, and all I could see was the lump of flesh under the blanket of roses.

It was too big to be one of the work team, and too small to be one of my regular gentleman callers. "If that's you, Jeron," I warned, "you're going to be in big trouble."

But it wasn't he. It wasn't any he, it was six-year-old Molomy, one of Flo's numerous children and, I had always thought, about the sweetest of them. She popped her head out of the coverlet, grinning, as pretty a poppet as Flo had ever pupped. "S'prise, Aunt Eve!" she cried. "Can I come back and work for you some more?"

I pulled my shorts on under my robe (how they laughed at Aunt Eve's robe!), dropped a blouse over my head, and sat down beside her. "Well, sure you can, honey," I said, extremely pleased. Molomy had been one of my very favorites, and it was quite a blow when, at four and a half or so, she had decided farming was too dumb for her to stay with and switched over to Shef and orbital dynamics. "I'm a little surprised, though," I added.

"I'm pregnant!" she said proudly. "So I want to tend my own baby the first time—isn't that the way you all used to do it, back on Earth?"

By the time I had explained to her that, yes, we all used to tend our own babies before they were born, but not exactly in the same way, I had got some more information out of her. She wasn't shy about it. She prattled gaily all the way to the farm plots. She just wasn't sure. She *thought* Jeron was the father, but of course she couldn't be positive until Aunt Flo or Uncle Ski removed the embryo and put it in the cabbage patch, when they would test it and let her know—and change it around any way she wanted, if she wanted, but she didn't really think she wanted to edit it, did I agree?, except of course to make sure that it had her aptitude for navigation and maybe a handful of other useful traits, because your first baby always ought to be kind of natural, as much as possible, didn't I agree?

I agreed. I put her to work, in charge of all ten of the other little girls, to keep them busy while I thought things out.

Actually Molomy was not the first of the girls to come up pregnant, or even the twentieth. Some of the others had been younger at the time than she. It wasn't Molomy I was worried about. Eight weeks after conception someone would take the fetus and implant it in a vegetable womb, and Molomy would be none the worse. What I was worried about was Jeron. He was so awfully young to be a father!

I was not getting much work out of my team that morning; Molomy's news was too exciting. They were all patting her belly and listening to her navel, and I could see the jealousy growing behind their pretty, bright, two-year-old eyes. I could even feel a little jealousy growing behind my own.

Maybe not really *jealousy*. I certainly didn't want to change places with them! But something unwelcome.

Was it because I felt threatened—because I was not ready to be a grandmother? (But actually I had been at least twice before that—but not with Jeron as the father.) Was it just that I was sorry for them, losing their childhood so early?

Only none of them were really children. They began to talk at six months, to read at two, to write legibly at two and a half—to make love at six or seven, sometimes earlier than that.

Early sexual maturity was bred into almost all the kids, from the fifth cohort on. Back in the early days when we were all primaparas and the simple common miracle of a child was excitement enough, we took what came. But then Flo and my quirky husband decided to play a more complicated game. They spliced and blended and turned out fifteen identical sibs from four mothers and three fathers. It was an experiment, Jim said (he was still talking in those days), to see if tailored genes could indeed produce absolute genetic clones, and so they did. I could not tell my own babies from the other twelve, and all fifteen were cross-tolerant of implants and transfusions. After that we got all sorts of things, but one of the designed traits for almost everybody was rapid maturation.

Which Ringo now proved—two years old, remember! Her nose was out of joint with Molomy's news, and she stood up and walked toward me: "I can't work anymore, Eve," she piped in her clear, sweet voice, bending her neck to look up at me, "because I have to go pick a tampon. I decided to menstruate today."

"Me too!" cried Odd, delighted by the idea, and so did two or three of the others, crowding around me and all chirping at once.

I started to give them my little menarche speech, about how it was all a natural function and they shouldn't worry (but who could think they were *worrying*?), and it should not interfere with most of their normal activities, especially including doing their work (but they had other ideas than that!) . . . and discovered none of them were listening.

So I dismissed them all for the day, my temper ragged. I had a small new agricultural experiment of my own that had looked as though it was ripening nicely, and I decided it was as good a time as any to test it out.

We had four sections added onto the habitat by then—nearly a mile along its axis—and the internal diameter was fifteen hundred feet. After the tenement squalor of the *Constitution* even the first section we moved into seemed like the endless plains of Iowa; by now every one of us, kids and all, had about seven acres to play with. So I hadn't had any trouble finding a section, a quarter of the way around the swell of the third section, where soil was laid and dewposts were moistening it from the water in the air (we didn't have much rain, you see, so we had to trick the water out another way)—and nobody usually came.

Nobody would have done anything to my crops, of course. But I do have this primitive need for privacy now and then, and some of my needs I am not proud of.

This particular patch was planted in a little invention of my own. It started out, basically, as watermelons; but I put a hard shell on them like coconuts, sweetened the pulp a little, injected each one with yeasts and a few other things—and, just the way I wanted it to come out, when I poked a hole in one end of the nuts, what came out was a really very satisfactory kind of beer.

I had planted rhubarb trees around for privacy, and they already made a sort of grove twice as tall as I was, and I lay back in the stripy sunlight from Alpha and tried another nut, and another, and with each one I felt a little better . . . up until the time I saw somebody sailing purposefully in my general direction, big, bounding leaps of ten yards at a time, and observed that it was Jeron.

I used the word "privacy," but in fact there's not a lot of it in Alpha-Aleph. Not counting the little bit that the old *Constitution* hid by being suspended at the center of the cylinder, there was hardly any part of the habitat that was not directly visible to every other part. I could see my own little house, with the blue and white honeysuckle growing over it, and the garden plots where the experimental plantings took place, and motionless Ann, still silent in her padmasana position; I could even see the bright red bounding dot that was Flo, pursuing some other bounding dot that I could not recognize for sure, but looked a lot like my husband; and the bad part of all that was that, if it were not for the rhubarb trees, they could all see me, too. Especially Jeron would, as soon as he got a little closer, and I didn't want to see Jeron. More accurately, I didn't want him to see his mother drunk.

Uncle Ghost saved me. Jeron brought up short, listening to what I could not see, scowling. "You sure?" he demanded. "I thought I saw her in her malt-nuts." He listened again, to a whisper I could not hear, said something annoyed and turned away.

I cracked another malt-nut and lay back, relaxing.

I was feeling grouchy, and even the malt-nuts were only blurring my discontent, not curing it. Discontent with what? With everything. With our habitat, with my work, with everyone around me. With myself. I was about as close to a hermit as a human being could get in Alpha-Aleph, and I was getting tired of it. If Shef and Ski, sometimes even Jim, had not come calling every once in a while at night, I would have had almost no contact with my own age group. And with Shef and Ski and Jim I rarely did much talking. I knew most of what was going on in our little community; we were too small for anything to be remote. But I knew it in the way I used to know what was happening in Washington by watching the network news. Most of it seemed no more relevant to personal me.

If the adults were remote, the children were elusive. I could love them, but I couldn't really understand them. I could be jealous of them easily enough. Especially of the little girls. Womanhood had become so very convenient! I'm not just talking about childbearing, because I got the benefit of that too—but that little trollop Molomy had got to me. Before us, I don't think the woman ever lived who took menstruating so easily—not for the first ten years of it, anyway. I don't think the woman ever lived who welcomed it, either—oh, maybe they were relieved sometimes, when they found they weren't knocked up, after all. But it had absolutely nothing else to recommend it. Especially when you were just starting. You'd be sitting in school, or in church, or in your boy friend's car, and you'd feel that warm damp spot growing, and, oh *God*, what shall you do? Get up and embarrass yourself? Stay there until you died? Ann Becklund could do that, in her damn padmasana, but not me—

"I did not know you hated her so," Uncle Will whispered from the rhubarbs.

"I didn't know I was talking out loud," I said, hiccoughing. "Sorry. Thanks for chasing Jeron away, though."

He didn't answer for a moment, and he had not chosen to make himself visible. Uncle Will makes me nervous. I said, as much to make sure he was still there as because I had anything to say, "She *hurt* me yesterday."

"I know. You disturbed her."

"I thought she was sick or something! And then she said something crazy about Chandrasekhar—you know, the astronomer, I guess—"

"About Chandrasekhar's other limit, yes."

"I don't even know what it is! Oh, of course, Chandrasekhar's limit is one point four solar masses, the mass range above which a star goes supernova; everybody knows that. But the other limit I never heard of."

Will did not exactly appear, but he let a shimmering sort of suggestion of himself appear among the rhubarbs. He sighed softly and whispered, "It is an old folk story he is supposed to have liked to tell, Evelyn. It is about dragonfly larvae. You see, if you are a dragonfly larva, swimming around in the water and getting ready to metamorphose, you don't know what will happen to you; you only know that from time to time your friends suddenly go to Heaven. That is, they go up through the surface of the water. What happens to them then? You don't know. What really happens, of course, is that they change into adult dragonflies; but you have no way of knowing that until you yourself become one, and then you can never come back to tell. No one ever does. Can't, because they can't penetrate the surface tension of the water, even if they had the desire to. So, being a stupid larva and not knowing this, you call all your friends around you and say, 'I will be different! I will come back, I promise! And I will tell you what lies beyond this shiny, wavery thing we see over our heads!' But you can't do it, when the time comes. It is an irreversible process."

I lay there staring at him in amazement. It was the longest speech I had heard from Will Becklund since he was alive. "And what has that to do with your dear widow, Ann?"

There was a hint of shadowy laughter, but all he said was, "That, too, is an irreversible process, Eve. And you interfered with it. She still had one tentacle on this side of the surface, so to speak, so she could communicate just a little.

But not anymore. She will pass Chandrasekhar's other limit, you see, and will never speak to a human being again."

I suppose it was the beer, but I suddenly felt that that was the saddest thing I had ever heard. "Oh, the poor thing!" I cried, forgiving her completely.

There was a pause. " 'Poor thing'?" Uncle Ghost whispered questioningly.

"To be cut off like that, forever! When will it happen?"

"It is already happening, Eve. It is what Jeron came to tell you about."

"Oh, my God! Where?" But I didn't have to ask, because I could see. I scrambled to my feet, staring at the place where Ann had sat so long and so silently, but she was not there anymore. She was still in the padmasana position, legs folded back on themselves, hands grasping her toes, head lowered to her breast, but instead of perching on a mound of undistributed soil she was floating in the air, a good hundred yards above the surface, moving slowly toward the end of the habitat. By the time she reached it she was too distant for me to see clearly, but I knew what was happening. That was where the exit lock was. It was open and waiting for her; it closed behind her, and she was gone.

"She'll die!" I cried.

"Why should she die?" whispered Uncle Ghost.

"But even if she lives—out there, all by herself! And you say she won't ever come back?"

"Never, Eve." There was a pause, and then his soft, despairing whisper: "Oh, how I wish I were she!"

20

MY NAME IS WILLIS BECKLUND, DECEASED. I AM AN ENGINEER, a soliton, an astronaut, and a ghost—depending on how you look at me, and providing you can see me at all. You can see me when I want you to, though, because unlike most of us dead I have a foot on either side of Chandrasekhar's other limit. Do you think that is an advantage? It is not. It means only that I am not wholly in either your here or that other here; I have no home anyhere, and so I wander.

This is what demonstrates that I am a ghost.

What demonstrates that I am an engineer is that I was trained that way, long ago when I was alive and young, and I'm still good at it. Better than all of them. Shef could never have deployed his dis-ray without me, not to mention building the O'Neill we all live in—no, make that reside in. Not to mention even the rebuilding of the drive long and long ago. None of this would have happened without me, although I do not usually claim credit. In some of those cases I am not sure there is any credit to claim.

What demonstrates that I am an astronaut, of course, is that dirty Dieter manipulated me into being one, and what demonstrates I am a soliton is that there is no other way to account for the fact that I am here. A standing wave. I don't dissipate. I just keep on being a wave.

Now, I know this is all very difficult for you. See, it is not what you don't know, it is what you think you do know that gets in the way. Take the dis-ray. That was very elementary. (Ha-ha. In the sense of elementary particles, do you see?) "Dis" doesn't mean disintegration. It's an acronym. The kaons break up atoms. They don't do it through fission in the normal way—they don't fiss—they do it through deep inelastic scattering, which we call DIS for short. The DIS weakens the bonds, and electrostatic repulsion breaks the heavy atoms up; could anything be more simple?

The best way to understand, really, is to roll the bones and absorb the hexagrams, but as most human beings are too lazy for that, let me simply say that your big problem is to avoid getting lost in the miasma of things like Einstein separability, which, when you come right down to it, I suspect is the single dumbest question Man has propounded to Man since the days of counting angels on a pin. Take the simplest case, that is, the question of spin in quantum mechanics, all right? Perform a simple experiment:

First steal two protons. Put them together in the singlet state, then break them up. Well, now, experiment will show you that every time one of them will turn out to have + spin and the other has – spin, whatever axis of the proton you measure spin on! Wow! How strange! How can that be? you demand. I mean, how can this proton over here, with a plus spin, know that that one over there has a minus, so it knows what to be?

See, that's your foggy thinking for you. It comes of using words like "spin" to mean rotation (my gosh, the little devils certainly don't rotate!), and even more it comes from using words like "there." There is no "there"! There are only a lot of different "heres"! So if you find that the Bell inequality is unequal, don't you see?, it is only because you are measuring it with two bent tools!

Now, with that basis for your understanding, I think I can tell you what it is that makes me sad. Then you can go back to listening to poor dumb little Eve. Eve has very little to recommend her, but she has an option open to her—the option of growing, and changing, and then of dying—which is no longer open to me. Someday, perhaps, she can do what Shef and Flo and the others have done; she may even be able to do what Ann has done. And I never can.

You know that when we arrived in the Alpha Centauri system we built ourselves a habitat out of bits and pieces of debris, and if you know anything at all you will know that we did not by any means use all the pieces. Even a loner like Alpha has quintillions of tons of matter floating around it. Ultimately we found that there were actually three asteroid belts, nearly an equal mass in comets, and about a Moon's worth of other trash, and some of us wanted to push them all together to make a real world. The wiser ones laughed. Building a world is not a matter of sticking bricks together with mortar, they said. There is a dynamic balance. The interior must be squeezed and heated into magma so that the oxygen and hydrogen can migrate to the surface. The surface must cool, so that the water can stay there and the rapid gas molecules will not spin off into space. Not hundreds of years, at least millions!

So causality doth capture us all . . . until we transcend it.

It had taken all this time for Ann to transcend it; and that was why I envied Ann Becklund, who was once my mortal wife.

21

On the morning of day 6354 Jeron was hurrying me—"Come and see something! Come on!"—and I didn't want to be hurried. "What's the matter, Aunt Mommy?" he demanded, bristling his little moustache at me. "You hung over again?"

I was not, or even close to it. The operative word was not "hangover" but "depression." But he was insistent: "You'll be really interested," he wheedled.

"I have to get to the cabbage patch."

"Do not! Aw. Come on. It won't take more than a minute."

Part of what he said was no doubt true—I didn't really have to get to the cabbage patch; Molomy had taken over the biggest part of keeping the crew in line. Part was false. It took a lot more than a minute, and I did not at first see what he was trying to show me.

Partly it was because he took me to the great viewing port with all the funny little wrinkles built into its glass, where I almost never go, and we were not alone there. Standing tall and strange was my dearly beloved Other Half.

"Hello, Jim," I said. It didn't matter. Jim is sometimes willing to talk to me, but he's got this speech impediment. He has forgotten how. He gets all sweating and stammering, trying to find the words, and then he's not good for much else. So we mostly don't talk at all anymore. He looked away from the viewer and at me, trying to remember who I was—maybe even *what* I was—and I patted him on the shoulder. "That's all right, Jim," I said. "Don't let us disturb you." He sighed rustily and turned back to whatever he was watching.

Which, it seemed, was what Jeron wanted me to watch too.

The viewing window is not a solid piece of glass, and I am not sure if it is glass at all. It is made of layers and clots of transparent material of many varieties and indices of refraction, so that if you move around you can magnify parts of what you are looking at. It helps to know what parts are of interest. The biggest thing outside the window at that moment was the factory, with its immense bright sails trapping the heat of Alpha and the structural parts of the next ring of the habitat, wandering out of the finished-products end until they brought up at the limits of their tethers. That did not interest me. It was not what interested Jeron, either, and he was quite irritable about it: "No, Eve, not there! Beyond! Toward the damn Dipper!"

Well, that was a part of the sky I knew pretty well, because in our Centaurian constellations it was not far from where the good old home Sun lay; there were only about half a dozen first-magnitude stars in that whole section.

But now there were seven. The new one was reddish-rusty-ugly, and I had never seen it before. I bobbed around before the port, trying to get the best look at it; and under the highest magnification I could find the damned thing displayed an actual disk.

"My God," I said. "What am I looking at?"

Jeron was crowing with excitement. "Aunt Ann!" he cried. "She's pulling a new planet around her!"

The reason I hadn't had a hangover was that I had been spending more and more time sleeping, just sleeping. And the reason I had been sleeping was that more and more I had preferred my dreams, or nothing at all, to the world around me; and among the things I liked least about it were notions such as Ann Becklund building a planet.

Molomy had all the gardening crew hard at work when at last I showed up, and she gave me a hard look. "There's something the matter, right?" she decided.

I certainly didn't want to talk about it, since I didn't even want to think about it. "Did you get the new rows in?" I asked—to change the subject, because I had already seen that she had. The ten tiny farmhands were already snipping off shoots for the next brew.

"Of course," she said, frowning, and stood up, rubbing gently at her small breasts. Now that Molomy had a child of her own in a vegetable cow she didn't trust the little kids to tend the cabbage patch anymore, and that was where

I had found her. "My boobs hurt, Aunt Eve," she complained. "It's just as though Albert was right in my belly, just like you used to have them in the old days."

I knelt down and felt the occupied pods myself. "I didn't really, Molomy," I said. "All the babies I had I had just the way you're having Albert—is that what you're going to call him?"

"Either that or Walter. Or Picklebick, or Bill. You mean you didn't ever get pregged with all that sex you were doing back on Earth?"

"Actually, no—well," I said, remembering, "I did get pregnant a couple of times when I was a kid. But I decided not to have them." That was in the Los Angeles days, and who wanted to have kids then? But no one knew about those old abortions, not even Kneffie; they were caught early and aspirated out, *schloop, ptooie,* and you weren't pregnant anymore.

"How very strange," Molomy said primly, and did not speak again for a while. We loosened the soil around the roots of the vegetable wombs and I thought about all that sex I had been doing back on Earth—although the sex had not been all of it. The most important part, maybe.

How long ago that seemed, and, from four light-years away, how pleasant! Especially compared to the scary thinking about what Ann was up to. It was an easy time. Los Angeles County paid for my root-canal work and doled out welfare checks, and the feds gave me food stamps, and for spending money all you had to do was hitch to Mexico to buy goods. I don't mean drugs. I was always too fearful to deal drugs. But in Tijuana you could buy cheap sleazy silver and cheap make-believe turquoise, and back home in Venice you could glue the turquoise to the silver, hitch down Santa Monica Boulevard (or take the bus) to the Century Plaza or one of the downtown hotels, and sell the stuff to the tourists. Easy money. Tax-free cash. And good friends! The loosest and coolest people I ever knew shared those beachfront houses. Don the Drunk, Harold the Head, sweet Lily, Marian the Marauder who could clean off any drugstore counter in the time it took the clerk to turn around for a pack of cigarettes. And studious old Jim.

Jim lived in the same lockless rooms as the rest of us, but

by day he went to engineering school and at night he tended bar in a beach joint; and, as soon as he asked me, we got married.

Why, if it wasn't for marrying Jim Barstow, how could I possibly have got to Alpha Centauri? He was the one who shamed me into going back to school, settling down, making careers for the two of us. I owe him a lot, damn his soul.

"Those kids!" cried Molomy in indignation, and stood up. "Ringo!" she screeched. "You break any more petri dishes and I'll pound you good!"

The two-year-old thumbed her nose and screeched back, "Up yours, Molomy!" Honor was satisfied; but there was less rattling of glassware as they worked in the stripy sunlight thereafter, so Molomy was satisfied too. Molomy was tired of working, if not of authority, so she decided to converse herself a rest. "I guess you've heard," she said confidingly, one grownup to another. "Crazy, isn't it?"

"You shouldn't say grownups are crazy," I said automatically, although of course I agreed with her. Crazy? Impossible would have been a better way to put it, if I hadn't seen the little worldlet growing with my own eyes. "It's quite an astonishing thing Aunt Ann is doing!"

"Oh, sure, but I meant the others. Flo wants more breeding stock, and Uncle Shef says it's too much trouble making chromium and iridium and all those things here, so he wants some shipped out—"

I stood up and faced her. "I don't know what you're talking about!"

She was triumphant; old Aunt Eve was always the last to know, but she hadn't been sure in this case. "Why, the plan to demand some new shipments from Earth, Eve. I thought you knew. *Everybody* knew, even the little kids." And tittering from the workbench confirmed it, until Molomy quelled them with a look.

And I hadn't known a thing about any of this!

I needed someone to talk to. When you came right down to it, there was only one logical candidate.

Jeron's personal house was in the middle of a cathedral grove of towering redwoods. Not *real* redwoods; the thirty-meter tallest of them was only six years old, and their chief ancestor had been rhubarb. But they looked quite fine.

They were my own grove, or had been, and you would think Jeron would have been a little grateful to the person who gave them to him.

Not he. He shrugged, and pointed out that I should not be surprised that Ann was making a new planet. She had, after all, said in the message to Knefhausen that she intended to.

"But that was just rhetoric! It's impossible—isn't it? The bits and pieces of matter have to take a long time to get together. Even longer to cool—"

He laughed. "Still trapped in the myth of causality," he observed. "If you don't understand, shall I show you?"

"Show me what?"

"Something." He led me proudly to his bedroom, a chamber I had been careful to stay out of for some years, and flung the door wide.

It was an Uncle Ghost production, and it looked like Fourth of July fireworks—only reversed fireworks, because they were going the wrong way. Not exploding. Imploding. It showed bits and pieces of matter spiraling into a central point, and that point becoming a world. It was rather pretty, like all of Will Becklund's toys for the kiddies, but it was not what I wanted to see. "Uncle Ghost made it for me personally," he said importantly, and unnecessarily.

"He doesn't like to be called Uncle Ghost."

"I don't like to be told what Uncle Ghost likes to be called," he said, "and anyway, you didn't come here to ask me about Ann's planet."

I hesitated. "Actually you're right. I'm concerned about this message to Earth."

He pushed me out of his room crossly and closed the door. "We want some things they have. What's wrong with that?"

"It's that word 'demand.' It just isn't the right way to do things, Jeron. I can understand wanting things from Earth—there are some I'd like too! Some decent coffee, a couple of recent issues of *Good Housekeeping*, a box of cordial cherries from Blum's. But I wouldn't *demand* them."

"We need templates," he said. "Anyway, it's not exactly a demand. More like a threat."

"A threat!"

"They send us what we want, Shef won't use the dis-ray on them again."

"Jeron! What we want can't be so much! That's like putting a pistol to somebody's head to ask him what time it is."

He shrugged. "What would you do?"

"I'd be more polite. We could exchange gifts! We've got all these wonderful new things we've grown—there's nothing like them back home! We could put together a sort of package of the best of them and send them off. Then, if we mentioned what kind of things we wanted, they'd send them to us. I'm sure they would."

He rubbed his velvet chin and scowled at me. "Mostly wouldn't work. Our stuff is adapted for light gravity. For Earth they'd need whole new stem and root systems, God knows what else."

"Oh, I could breed that in no time."

"Huh." He stood up and peered out at the habitat, thinking.

"Will you help me, Jeron?"

He shook his head irritably. "No, what you say is dumb, Eve. I don't like your idea. But I've got a better one."

22

THE PRESIDENT OF THE UNITED STATES (WASHINGTON, D.C.) opened the storm window of his study and leaned out to yell at his Chief Science Advisor. "Harry, get the lead out! We're waiting for you!"

Harry looked up and waved, then continued doggedly plowing through the dripping jungle that was the North Lawn. Between the overgrown weeds and the rain and the mud it was slow going, but the President had little sympathy. He slammed down the window and said, "Damn the man, he just goes out of his way to aggravate me. How long'm I supposed to wait for him so I can decide if we have to move the capital or not?"

The Vice President looked up from her knitting. "Jimbo, honey, why do you fuss yourself like that? Why don't we just move and get it over with?"

"Oh, woman! We can't do that. It would look so *bad*." The President threw himself into a chair despondently. He was a big man, and the old chair creaked warningly. "I was really looking forward to the Tenth Anniversary Parade," he complained. "Ten years, that's really something to brag about! And I don't want to hold it the hell out in the sticks, I want it right down Constitution Avenue just like the old days, with the people cheering and the reporters and the cameras all over and everything. Then let that son of a bitch in Omaha say I'm not the real President."

His wife said placidly, "Don't fuss yourself about him, honey. There's worse nearer."

"He wouldn't even send a delegation!"

"We got enough to feed right now, you know that. Jimbo? You know what I've been thinking, though? The parade might look a little skimpy on Constitution Avenue anyway. It would be real nice on a kind of littler street."

"Oh, what do you know? If Washington's under water, what makes you think Bethesda would be any better?"

His Secretary of State put down his solitaire cards and looked interested for the first time. "Doesn't have to be in Bethesda, Jimbo. I got some real nice land up near Dulles we could move to. It's high there."

"Why, sure. Lots of nice high land over to Virginia," the Vice President confirmed. "Remember when we went out on that picnic after your Second Inaugural? That was at Fairfax Station. There was hills there all around. Just beautiful."

The President slammed his fist on the coffee table and yelled, "I'm not the President of Fairfax Station, Virginia, I'm the President of the U. S. of A.! What's the capital of the U. S. of A.? It's Washington! Always has been. Always will be. And that's where the President stays! My God, don't you see how those jokers in Houston and Omaha and Salt Lake and all would laugh if they heard I had to move out of my own capital? 'Sides, there's all those delegations that's here already, the Amish and the New York and the Wheeling folks." He broke off and scowled suspiciously at his Vice President, who was also his wife. "Now, what are you looking that way for?"

She said placidly, "I didn't hear you mention that little fox from Puget."

" 'Specially her! I mean them. Look how far away they come!"

"Not so far they haven't been eating us out of house and home two weeks, over there to Blair House. I notice you spend a lot of time negotiating with her."

"You think you know a lot, but you don't know nearly as much as you think," the President said cuttingly, but he was pleased with the interruption when his Chief Science Advisor came in the door, shaking himself, dripping mud as he got out of his oilskin slicker. "Well, Harry?" the President demanded. "What did they say?"

The Vice President moved the good pillows to one side so Harry could sit down on the couch. "It's terrible out there," he complained. "Anybody got a dry cigarette?" The President threw him a sack of makings, and Harry dried his fingers on his shirt front before he started to roll one. "Well," he said, licking the paper, "I went to every boat captain I could find. They all said the same. Ships they talked to, places they'd been. All the same. Tides are higher than they've ever been, all up and down the coast. They don't think they're rising much anymore, but they're way high already."

He looked around for a match. The President's wife handed him a gold cigarette lighter with the Great Seal of the United States on it, which, after some effort, he managed to ignite. "It don't look really good to me, Jim. Right now it's low tide, and that's all right, but it's coming in. Even if the tides don't come up higher, there's going to be storms. Not just rains like this, I mean, but you got to figure on a tropical depression coming up from the Bahamas now and then, these next few months."

"We're not in the tropics," the Secretary of State said suspiciously.

"It doesn't mean that," said the Science Advisor, who had once given the weather reports over the local Top Forty FM radio station, back when there were FM stations and charts to be in the Top Forty of. "It means storms. Maybe hurricanes, coming up the coast from the Bahamas. Maybe the ice has stopped melting, who knows about that? But even if the water doesn't come up any higher, it sure isn't going to go down any *lower*, and any little piss-ant storm could have us swimming."

The President drummed his fingers on the coffee table, which was glass-topped, covering photographs of F.D.R., Ronnie Reagan, Harry Truman, and about six other ex-Presidents surrounding his own image. It often soothed him, but not this time. Suddenly he shouted: "I don't *want* to move my capital!"

No one answered. His temper outbursts were famous. The Vice President became absorbed in counting stitches, the Secretary of State picked up his cards and began to shuffle, the Science Advisor got up to retrieve his slicker and hang it carefully on the back of a door.

The President said, "You got to figure it this way. If we move out, then all those local yokels that claimed to be a President are going to look just that much better on their own turf, and the eventual reunification of our nation is going to be just that much more delayed." He moved his lips for a moment, and then burst out, "I don't ask *nothing* for myself! I never have. I only want to play the part I have to play in what's good for all of us, and that means keeping up my position as the *real* President, according to the U.S. Constitution as amended. And that means I got to stay right here in the real White House, no matter what."

His wife said hesitantly, "Honey, how about this? The other Presidents had like a Summer White House, and Camp David, and like that. Nobody fussed about it. Why couldn't you do the same as they did? We could pick out one of those old farm houses by Fairfax and fix it up real pretty."

The President looked at her with surprise. "Now, that's good thinking," he declared. "Only we can't move permanently, and we have to keep this place garrisoned so nobody will take it away from us, and we have to make sure of title."

"Oh, there's good titles to those places I have," the Secretary of State assured him hastily.

"I wasn't talking to you, I was talking to Harry. We have to come back here once in a while to show we own it, so is there going to be any problem there?"

The Science Advisor said thoughtfully, "We could rent some boats, I guess, if we couldn't get the horses in."

"No 'guess'! No 'if'!" the President yelled, looking at his Chief Science Advisor with irritation. "That's a national priority. We have to do it that way to keep those bastards in the rest of the country paying attention to the real President."

"Well, Jimbo, honey," said the Vice President after a moment, emboldened by recent praise, "you have to admit they don't pay a lot of attention to us right now. When was the last time they paid their taxes?"

The President looked foxily at her over his glasses. "Talking about that," he said, "I might have a little surprise for them anyway. What you might call a secret weapon."

"I hope it does better than we did in the last war," said his wife, "because if you remember, when we started to put down that uprising in Frederick, Maryland, we got the pee kicked out of us."

The President stood up, indicating the Cabinet meeting was over.

"Never mind," he said sunnily. "You go on out again, Harry, and see if you can find any good maps in the Library of Congress where they got the fires put out. Find us a nice high place within, um, twenty miles if you can—if it happens to belong to somebody we know, we'll get an appropriation for it. Otherwise we'll get the Army to condemn us a Summer White House, like Mae says, and maybe I can sleep in a bed that isn't moldy for a change."

Alerted by his tone, his wife looked suddenly worried. "Jimbo, what are you going to do?"

He chuckled. "I'm just going to check out my secret weapon."

He shooed them out of his study and, when they were gone, went to the little kitchen and got himself a bottle of Fresca from the six-pack in the open refrigerator. It was warm, of course. The Marine guard company was still trying to get the gas generators in operation, but they were having very little success. The President didn't mind. They were his personal Praetorians. If they lacked a little as appliance repairmen, they had proved their worth when the chips were down. The President was always aware that during the Troubles after the bolt from Alpha Centauri he had been no more than any other Congressman—appointed to fill a vacancy, at that—and his rapid rise to whip, majority leader, Speaker of the House and heir apparent, finally to the presidency itself, was due not only to his political skills and merits, but also to the fact that he was the only remotely legitimate heir to the presidency who also happened to be the brother-in-law of the commander of Washington's Marine garrison.

The President was, in fact, quite satisfied with the way the world was going. If he envied Presidents of the past (missiles, fleets of nuclear bombers, billions of dollars to play with), he certainly saw nothing in the present, when he looked at the world around him, that surpassed his own stature in the world he lived in. Oh, there were places where improvements could be made—the Science Advisor was a loser, and his brother-in-law had been better as a Marine major than he was as a Secretary of Defense. But he had plans for making improvements.

He finished his soda, opened his study door a crack, and peered out.

No one was nearby. He slipped out and down the back stairs.

In what had once been the public parts of the White House, you could see the extent of the damage more clearly. After the riots and the trashings and the burnings and the coups, the will to repair and replace had gradually dwindled away. The President didn't mind. He didn't even notice the charred walls and the fallen plaster. He was listening to the sound of a distant gasoline pump chugging away, and smiling to himself as he approached the underground level where his secret weapon was locked up.

The secret weapon, sniffling and sneezing although the weather was hot, was trying to complete that total defense of every act of life that he called his memoirs. His name was Dieter von Knefhausen.

Knefhausen was less satisfied with the world than the President of the United States (Washington, D.C.). When the power nets collapsed with the loss of all the nuclear plants, and transportation broke down for lack of power, and communications stopped mattering in any way because there was no effective means for anyone's will to be enforced past the visible horizon—then the world as Knefhausen knew it had come to an end.

This new one was far less pleasing. Knefhausen could have wished for many changes. Better health, for one thing. He was well aware that his essential hypertension, his bronchitis, his arthritis, and his gout were fighting the last stages of a total war to decide which one would have the honor of destroying their mutual battleground, which was himself. That was not unexpected. He was eighty years old, after all. But there were ills against which one had a right to complain. He did not much mind his lack of freedom, but he did mind the senseless destruction of so many of his papers.

The original typescript of his autobiography was long lost. But he had wheedled his superiors at Johns Hopkins, who had granted him a precarious haven for nearly two years, into making a search for what could be found of them. A few tattered and fragmentary Xerox copies had turned up, some sent from institutions far away. He had begun to restore the gaps as best he could when the raiders of this present President—the pretender, that is, who called himself by the name "President of the United States"—had found him and carried him here. And left half the papers behind, of course, and no amount of pleading seemed to make them willing to bring them to him.

Still—the essential story was there, of how he had planned Project Alpha-Aleph, with all the details meticulously itemized as to how he had lied, forged, and falsified to bring it about. Earliest training lasted longest, and Knefhausen was a thorough record-keeper.

He spared himself nothing. He admitted his complicity in the "accidental death" of Dot Letski's first husband in a car smash, thus leaving her free to marry the man he had chosen to go with the crew to Alpha Centauri. He explained de Bono's experiments, and related how he had decided to carry them out in the large. He confessed he had known the secret would not last out the duration of the trip, thus betraying the trust of the President who had made it happen. He put it all in, all he could remember, and boasted of his success.

For it was clear to him that success was already a fact. What could be surer evidence of it than what had happened ten years ago? The "incident of next week" was as dramatic and complete a proof as anyone could wish. If its details were still undecipherable, largely because of the demolition of most of the world's technology it had brought about, its main features were obvious. The shower of heavy particles, whatever particles they were, had drenched the Earth, and every radionuclide had leaked its energy out as heat.

Also there were the messages received and understood; also there were the still more significant messages for which there had unfortunately been no translation; and, take them all together, there was no doubt. The astronauts had done precisely as predicted. Well, almost precisely. They had developed knowledge so far in advance of anything on Earth that, from four light-years out, they could impose their will on the human race. They had done so. In one cloudburst of particles, the entire military-industrial complex of the planet perished.

How? How? Ah, thought Knefhausen, with envy and pride, there one posed the question! One could not know. All that was known was that every nuclear device and concentration—bomb or ore dump, hospital radiation source or power-plant core—had ceased to exist as a source of nuclear energy. The event was not rapid and catastrophic, like a bomb. It was slow and long-lasting. The uranium and the plutonium had simply melted in the long, continuous reaction that was still bubbling away in the seething lava lakes where the silos had stood and the nuclear plants had generated electricity. Little radiation was released, but a good deal of heat.

Knefhausen had long since stopped regretting what could not be helped. Still he wished, wistfully, that he had had the opportunity to make proper measurements of the total heat flux. Not less than 10^{16} watt-years, he was sure, just to estimate from the known effects on the Earth's atmosphere: the storms, the gradual raising of temperature all over, above all the rumors about the upward trend of sea level that bespoke the melting of the polar ice caps. There was no longer even a good weather network, but the fragmentary information he was able to piece together suggested a world increase of four, maybe as many as five or six degrees Celsius already, and the reactions still seething away in Czechoslovakia, the Congo, Colorado, and a hundred lesser infernos.

Rumors about the sea level?

Not rumors, he corrected himself. No. Facts. He lifted his head and stared at the snake of hard rubber hose that began under the duckboards at the far end of the room and ended outside the barred window, where the gasoline pump outside did its best to keep the water level inside his cell low enough to keep the water below the boards. Judging by the inflow, the grounds of the White House must be nearly awash.

A great triumph!

In the long run, it was only an annoyance that the triumph had been not quite complete. It was planned that the astronauts should develop such knowledge. It was not planned that they should use it against their benefactors, or fail to share it with them.

It was ungrateful to God to complain that the triumph was not perfect—but in his heart Knefhausen could not stop complaining. *Wir siegen uns zum Tode*. We have won so many victories!—and they have destroyed us.

The door opened. The President of the United States patted the shoulder of the thin, scared, hungry-looking kid in green Marine fatigues who guarded it, and walked in, closing it behind him.

"How's it going, Knefhausen?" the President began sunnily. "You ready to listen to a little reason yet?"

Knefhausen stood as straight as he could. "I will do whatever you wish, Mr. President, but as I have told you there are certain limits. Also I am not a young man and my health—"

"Screw your health and your limits, Knefhausen!" the President shouted. "Don't start up with me!"

"I am sorry if I have given offense, Mr. President," Knefhausen whispered.

"Don't be sorry! Sorry doesn't cut the mustard. What I got to judge by is results. See that pump, Knefhausen? You know what it takes to keep it going? It takes gasoline. Gas is rationed, Knefhausen! Takes a high national priority to get it! I don't know how long I'm going to be able to justify this continuous drain on our resources if you don't cooperate!"

Sadly but stubbornly, Knefhausen said, "Up to the limits imposed by the realities of the situation, Mr. President, I cooperate."

"Yeah. Sure." But the President did not push the matter. He was in an unusually good mood, Knefhausen observed with the prisoner's paranoid attention to detail. The President changed the subject. "Knefhausen, I'm going to make you an offer. Just say the word, and I'll fire that dumb son of a bitch Harry Stokes and make you my Chief Science Advisor. Now, how do you like that? Right up at the top of the heap again! An apartment of your own. Electric lights. Servants—you can pick 'em out yourself, and there's some nice-looking little girls in the pool. The best food money can buy. A chance to perform a real service for the U. S. of A., helping to reunify this great country to become once again the great power it should and must be."

"Mr. President, naturally, I wish to help in any way I can. But we have been over this subject before. I will do anything you like, but I don't know how to make the bombs work again. You saw what happened, Mr. President. They no longer exist."

"I didn't say anything about bombs, did I? Look, Kneffie, I'm a reasonable man. You say you can't make bombs; all right, but there are other things. How about this. You promise to use your best efforts *in any way you can.*"

Knefhausen hesitated. "What other things, Mr. President?"

"Don't press, Knefhausen. Services to your country." The President locked his hands over his belly and smiled benignly. "You give me that promise and you're out of here today. Or would you rather I just turned off the pump?"

Knefhausen's head-shake was not so much negation as despair. "You do not understand the difficulties! What can a scientist do for you today? If there were anything, do you think I would have spent these last years writing memoirs?"

"That's why I took you out of that, Knefhausen."

"Yes, you took me from Johns Hopkins University, where I was fulfilling some function until your band of looters came along."

"Watch your mouth," the President said in righteous indignation. "That was an IRS field team."

"*Natürlich,* Mr. President, tax collectors, not looters—a distinction not always easily made. Nevertheless! The preconditions for what you want no longer exist. Ten years ago, five maybe, yes, something perhaps could have been done. Now, no. When all the nuclear plants went out— When the factories that depended on them ran out of power— When the fertilizer plants couldn't fix nitrogen and the insecticide plants couldn't deliver— When the people began to die of hunger and the pestilences started—"

"Yes or no, Knefhausen," the President cut in.

The scientist paused, looking thoughtfully at his adversary. A gleam of the old shrewdness appeared in his eyes.

"Mr. President, you know something. Something has happened."

"Right! You're smart. Now tell me, what is it I know?"

Knefhausen shook his head. After seven decades of life, and another decade of slowly dying, it was hard to allow himself to hope again. This terrible upstart, this lump— he was not without animal cunning, and he seemed very sure. "Please, Mr. President, tell me."

The President put a finger to his lips, and then an ear to the door. When he was convinced no one could be listening, he came closer to Knefhausen and said softly:

"We're not such hicks here as you think. I have contacts all over the continent. Would you like to know what one of them just brought me?"

Knefhausen did not answer, but his watery old eyes were imploring.

"A message," the President whispered.

"From the *Constitution*?" cried Knefhausen. "But, no, it is not possible! Farside is gone, Goldstone is destroyed, the communications satellites are running down—"

"It wasn't a radio message," said the President. "And it didn't come from Goldstone. It came from some people from the West Coast, and they got it from some other place. From some observatory in Hawaii, they said, although maybe they just said that to get the price up. They say there's some telescope out there that didn't get smashed, and I guess there's some old fogies that still look through it sometimes, and they got a message. In laser light. Plain Morse code. From what they said was Alpha Centauri. From your little friends, Knefhausen."

He took a folded slip of paper from his pocket and held it up.

Knefhausen was racked by a fit of coughing, but he managed to reach for it. "Give it to me!"

The President lifted it out of his reach. "Do we have a deal?"

"Yes, of course. Yes! Anything you say, but give me the message!"

"Why, certainly," smiled the President, and passed over the much-creased sheet of paper.

It said:

PLEASE BE ADVISED. WE HAVE CREATED THE WORLD ALPHA-ALEPH. IT IS BEAUTIFUL AND GRAND. WE WILL SEND A FERRY TO BRING SUITABLE STOCK AND TO COMPLETE CERTAIN OTHER BUSINESS. OUR SPECIAL REGARDS TO DR. DIETER VON KNEFHAUSEN, WHOM WE WANT TO TALK TO VERY MUCH. EXPECT US IN 250 DAYS FROM THIS MESSAGE.

Knefhausen read it over twice, lifted his head to stare at the President, and read it again. Then he stared into space, the paper dangling from his fingers.

The President snatched it back, folded it, and put it in his pocket, as though the message itself was the key to power. "Do we have a deal?"

"*Zwei hundert funfzig*— Mr. President, when was this message received?"

"About seven months ago, near as I can tell. That's right. They'll be here very soon, and you can imagine what they'll have! Guns, tools, everything—and all you have to do is persuade them to join us in restoring the U. S. of— Knefhausen!"

The President jumped forward, but he was too late. The scientist had fallen limply to the duckboards. The guard, when ordered, ran for the White House doctor, who limped as rapidly to the scene as his bad legs would let him, but he was too late too. Everything was too late for Knefhausen, whose old heart had failed him . . . just in time.

23

EIGHT WENT OUT TO ALPHA CENTAURI AND EIGHT CAME back, but they were by no means the same eight. The pilot's name was Quittyyx, which signified, among other odd things, that he was of the tenth cohort, and therefore only six years old when they left Alpha-Aleph. That wasn't so bad. His deputy, Jeromolo Bill, was not quite two.

Of course, tiny Bill would not be trusted with the guidance of the interstellar vessel Shef had designed for them until he was at least four, but there was not really a whole hell of a lot to do in the first half of the trip. Turnover was the time that counted. All the universe concentrated into a single terrifying starburst of light, watching the very act of Creation, and no other signposts were in the skies. By then Jeromolo Bill was able to take his turn with his elder. They both had what none of the others had, what none of the Original Eight had had, a genetic, built-in capacity to handle relativistic computations in their heads. They were not smarter than anyone else, simply hard-wired to match and measure the asymptotic slopes of mass and velocity and time and convert them into direction.

The long voyage home took all of four years, but at that less than half as long as it had taken *Constitution* on the way out. The reason was that they were in a better vessel than *Constitution*. They were in Sheffield Jackman's masterpiece, built like a basketball and filled with Flo's genetics, Jim's optics, Ski's communications, and, in lieu of any contribution from their researches, Aunt Eve and Uncle Ghost themselves in the flesh—or, in Will Becklund's case, whatever it was he was in rather than flesh. It was a darling souped-up speedster of a ship, all right, and apart from the fact that they had power to burn there was a valuable purpose in burning it. Acceleration was good for them. It was even necessary. Every one of the voyagers needed to accommodate his body to the crushing weight they had to look forward to on Earth.

So the ship started off slowly—relatively slowly, no more than a quarter G. Even so, most of them crept around in walkers. When they fell, not infrequently, there was a rich harvest of fractures and sprains. But the bodies toughened. The muscles swelled. The porous bones grew denser and stronger. Every one of them (Uncle Ghost always excepted) drank from Flo's nauseating sap of harvested calcium-salts solution every morning and every night; and they were at half a G, three-quarters, as much as a gravity and a half of acceleration toward the end, and the ship fairly flew, and Jeron was its captain. He said so himself.

Even so, it was a long, long trip.

For the six young ones in the crew, the voyage was a sort of class trip to an exciting freak show. They bled Aunt Mommy dry of every scrap of geography she could remember, and pestered Uncle Ghost, when they could find him, for stories and sidelights and gossip. When those ran out, they quarreled with each other for amusement; and the long trip grew longer.

Although they never said so, Aunt Eve and Uncle Ghost shared a certain purpose. The first part was clear. The climax less so. It was to find Dirty Dieter, if he still lived, and—and—and do something, though what that something was was the unclear part. Even Jeron carried that unwritten purpose in a corner of his heart—even the younger ones, sometimes—for their childhood lessons had taken. Diabolical Dieter! Kneffie the ineluctably bad! Thinking of him as they drifted off to sleep, the little ones sometimes growled in their throats, and when they realized how terminally *tedious* the long voyage was, it was Dieter von Knefhausen they blamed. When Jeromolo Bill was three years old—old enough to be worth persecuting—the other children invented the game of "Do It to Dieter" and made Bill their quarry in long whooping chases all around the ship. Even Jeron sometimes joined in, out of boredom, while Uncle Ghost retreated to invisibility and Aunt Eve to her latest crop of malt-nuts. They consoled themselves by thinking that the exercise, at least, was good for the young muscles.

Hopes of revenge could carry one just so far. Dreams of curiosity satisfied, not much farther; the concept of delayed gratification takes long to learn, and longer to be felt as real. The voyage was far too long for tiny tots. The good part of that was that, out of boredom, they were willing to learn anything that anyone was willing to teach, and so on good days Aunt Eve sobered up and demonstrated knitting and plant husbandry, and lectured on the subject of The Good Old Days on Earth. Uncle Will Becklund could not demonstrate much of anything, but he explained the casting of the bones for the *I Ching* and taught the true meaning of The Moon in Water. It was not enough. Shef had designed the ship for speed and efficiency, not for pleasure. It was a golden globe a hundred yards through, with two smaller globes bulging from its poles like snowball ears on a snowman's face for landing craft; inside half of it was for living, and storage of the dormant seeds they were bringing to Earth as gifts, and for machinery; and the other half bare floors as big as skating rinks.

When they were only local commuting distance from Earth—the Sun no longer a star but a Sun; the biggest planets now visible with disks—there was work to do at last. So they fed Aunt Eve coffee and kept her sober for a few weeks, while Molomy lashed the littler kids into pulling out the first lots of seeds and cuttings and planting them in the tanks on what had been bare floors. But then it was back to the malt nuts for Eve, not so much from boredom anymore as from fear. The closer Earth got, the scarier the idea of returning there became.

By the end of the trip even the youngest, Jeromolo Bill, was six years old. It was notable that no children had been born on all the long voyage. Partly it was prudence. No one wanted a squalling brat to tie him down when they embarked on the heart-stopping adventure of exploring old Earth. It was also for earthier reasons. In the close quarters of Shef's speedster for four long years they couldn't even stand themselves, much less each other. Their sexual contacts were short, infrequent, and without issue. For Aunt Eve there was no sex at all in the four-year trip, because with the children she wouldn't and with Uncle Ghost she really couldn't, and therefore the malt-nuts. She spent most of her time in her flowered sleeping sack. It took a great deal to get her out of it.

What did it, just as they were about to round the Sun for final deceleration, was a ninety-decibel shout.

It didn't just wake Eve. It woke everyone who was asleep, and pierced the ears of everyone who was awake. Jeron came running into Eve's cubicle, and it was several seconds before either of them realized that the yell was a message from Uncle Ski. "What's he saying?" Eve cried in terror.

"Attenuate it, Eve! Hold your hands over your ears like this!" And when she followed her son's orders, she could make out the words. It was a kind of shopping list!

"—fly agaric, henbane, bladderwort, belladonna, parsley, parsnips—"

"Can't you turn it down?" she yelled over the noise, and Jeron yelled back grimly:

"He installed it himself—I don't know how. That message has been chasing us for four years."

It went on for minutes: "—Venus fly-trap, madder, yucca, Jack-in-the-pulpit, skunk cabbage—"

Eve moaned, shrugged a shoulder up to an ear to release one hand, and reached for another malt-nut. She popped it open with the dagger that lay beside her bed and took a long drink of the milky fluid. Jeron scowled impartially at the malt-nut and the yelling, and then he had an idea. Wincing, he took his hands away from his ears long enough to pull blossoms from Eve's bower bed. He rolled them into fingertip-sized balls, did something with two of them, then reached for Eve's head while holding two more. She ducked away; he snarled at her, and she perceived what he intended, and allowed him to insert the cool, moist plugs in her ears. Thus diluted, the roar from the communicator was merely loud, and she was able to identify the voice. It wasn't Ski, or Shef or Jim; of course it wasn't, for that much plain English prose would have tied any one of them up in knots for hours. The voice cataloguing plants, flowers, and even lichens and ocean plankton belonged to a fifth-cohort son of Ann and Shef named Araduk.

At last it ended: "Under no circumstances," it howled, "are you to fail to return viable samples of all the foregoing!" There was no good-bye; it just stopped.

Cautiously Eve pulled the plug out of her ear, and Jeron stood up, flexing his knees in the pull of the 1.5 gravity. "I suppose you're going to drink yourself back to sleep now," he said.

"Is there any reason not?"

He shrugged. "Sightseeing," he said disdainfully. "We're about to scoot around the Sun."

"For me," she said, reaching for the malt-nut, "that's just a rerun. I caught it first time around."

But she did not mean it, did not mean most of the things she said to Jeron when he took that contemptuous, cold tone to her, any more than, she hoped, he meant it to her.

Shef had built their ship with many eyes and, though most of them were hooded for the perihelion approach, through the multiply filtered smallest of them the entire chip's crew gazed wonderingly at the immense sea of flame below.

The ship whipped around the Sun, shedding velocity, and eased back to Earth's orbit from the inside. Quittyyx and Jeromolo Bill were relieved of their responsibilities for a time—the ship was no longer relativistic, and had not yet begun orbiting maneuvers. Jeron took command. Since they had done their job well, he had little to do. The ship crept toward the point in Earth's orbit where Earth would be when they got there; and there it was, old green Terra, the mottled blue and white marble with its honey-colored child spinning beside it.

By the time they were half a million miles away—only twice as far as the Moon—their speed had dropped to two hundred miles a second. They were well within the safety margins for the ballistic program. They entered a low-Earth orbit, killed the rest of their surplus velocity, and shut down the drive.

All Shef's built-in eyes were open now. The most powerful of them, visible from outside only as a slotted patch on the gleaming gold sphere, gave them magnification enough to make out surface objects only a few hundred yards across. The difficulty was that most of the objects were usually covered by clouds. All of them had heard of "clouds." None but Eve and the late Will Becklund had ever seen them; in the habitat, moisture was leached out of the air by condensation and rain rarely fell.

They clustered around the narrow magnifying port. "All right," piped Jeromolo Bill, standing on tiptoes to see what the taller, older ones could see without effort, "so where do we go, dad?"

Jeron quelled him with a look. Jeron was fully a man now, especially in his own opinion. He had attained his six thousandth day just a week or so before, and besides he was captain of this vessel. Having put by such childish things as the nasty sniping ridicule in Jeromolo Bill's voice, he snapped, "Shut up, kid," squared his shoulders, and prepared to issue commands.

For this he was well qualified, since he had been secretly studying stories about ship's captains out of the tapes transmitted by open-time communicators from Earth long ago. "Um, *hum*," he said thoughtfully, out of Horatio Hornblower, and, "Is the crew assembled?" out of Nicholas Monsarrat. But the crew was long since assembled, even fumbly, blowsy Aunt Eve, and he really hadn't a clue. Damn clouds! How could you make a plan when you couldn't see what you were looking at?

Of course, there were the maps.

They were good maps. They had been assembled out of the recollections of the Original Eight, but their memories were good and some days of shrill bickering had mediated their differences. Unfortunately the maps lied. They pretended that there were differences in color between sea and land, and even between one nation's land and another, and Jeron could see none.

Gradually, however, he began to realize that those sections of the globe with visible shadows and folds could not be sea, and therefore must be land. Then he began to perceive shores and peninsulas—that one, no doubt, was Yucatan, protruding into the Gulf of Mexico. But where was Florida? Where, in fact, was the Atlantic Ocean?

At that point he realized he was looking at it the wrong way up. The maps always presented themselves with north at the top. The planet itself was not so obliging. That peninsula just disappearing over the horizon was half a world away from the Yucatan. "Ah, yes," he said, nodding sagely, "you see, that is Italy just going out of sight; of course, you must have recognized the Mediterranean Sea?"

"I think I see the Pyramids," Aunt Eve said, hiccoughing slightly. And it was true. Although there were clouds over the eastern Mediterranean, farther south the skies were transparent. Those sharp-angled blocks were unmistakable.

It was time for action. "Molomy," he ordered, "see that our first batch of gifts is in the landing craft. Bill! You will navigate us to a landing. I advise that you get some sleep first, so go take a little nap."

Jeromolo Bill whistled scornfully but, after waiting enough of a second to indicate that he was doing it because he thought it was worth doing, not because he was told to, he turned and headed for his cubicle, leaving Jeron to study the slowly turning globe. Molomy reappeared and drafted the rest of the children to help her stow the landing craft. Aunt Eve, with a malt-nut in her hand but no longer drinking, stared apprehensively over his shoulder; and Uncle Ghost, thrilled and uneasy as any of them, allowed himself to be seen beside them.

"The Horn of Africa," he whispered, and Eve shuddered. The field of view shifted ever westward as the ship orbited, the Indian subcontinent with the pearl of Ceylon hanging from its tip; a muddle of islands; then the broad Pacific. Australia was clear enough, and the smudge just at the southern rim of the Earth might easily be New Zealand . . . but what, Jeron wondered, was this astonishing sprinkling of white? Could they be ships? Ocean liners? Immense ones?

He said nonchalantly to Aunt Eve, "I did not believe so much technology had survived until I saw the cruise ships."

She gazed blearily at the sea, and shook her head. "Don't see them. Hard to pick them out among all those icebergs, I guess."

Jeron kept his face masklike as he nodded, but he was thrilled. Icebergs! It was as though she had said, ah, yes, dragons. "But icebergs are not the question, Aunt Eve. We must decide on where to land."

Aunt Eve sighed. The prospect of meeting von Knefhausen and all those others down there was pressing heavily on her. "Well," she said doubtfully, "pretty soon you'll see a sort of twisty thing up *there*, I think, and that'll be the Isthmus of Panama. Pretty much straight up north from there is where we ought to go."

"Oh, yes," he said, nodding wisely, "Florida."

"No! Who wants to go to Florida? But once we find Florida then we just go up the coast to Chesapeake Bay, I think I'll know that when I see it, and then it's just up the Potomac River to Washington. Where dirty old Dieter lives. Lived. Whatever. But," she added, "I think I will make myself presentable before we land."

"Next orbit!" Jeron called after her back. "Ninety minutes! See you're ready! And then"—he swallowed—"we're going to be there."

When an early spacecraft came back to Earth, an Apollo or a Salyut or a Shuttle, the timing had to be precise and the entry window was tiny. Great banks of computers in

Houston or some Russian town took the readouts from a thousand sensors and converted them into simple yes-no instructions: "Burn." "Stop burning." "Burn for 1.3 seconds." "Burn yaw thruster." "Pray."

The returnees from Alpha-Aleph had no such ground support going for them. They had only two things, though either was enough. First they had the landing craft itself, with Jim's power plant and Ski's plasma, and so they could have come down like an elevator if they chose. And they also had Jeromolo Bill.

The six-year-old was in his full power now. His genes had been edited for mathematics, and not merely the relativistic phase-shifting of the high-speed voyage itself. As a matter of pride he plotted a course. It required him to take into consideration the shuttle's geocentric position vector, the gravitational parameter of the Earth, the gravitational force due to the Earth's nonsymmetric mass distribution and the time-varying contributions from tides, the perturbing force due to the effects of the Sun and Moon, the force due to the effects of atmospheric resistance, and the force due to solar radiation pressure. Since he had no data on many of these, he had to deduce them as he went along, from the perturbations observed in the very ship he was flying. He did it in his head. He was able to feel the responses of the sensors and convert them into attitude and thrust instructions as well as any IBM or Cray-1 monster in old Texas, and it did not even raise a sweat.

The difficulties were quite other than that. The difficulties included the fact that the world did not look the way it was supposed to.

There wasn't any Florida, for instance. Where there should have been a peninsula, there was only a string of tiny islets. All up and down the coast, and all to the west, there were broad, ragged bays where there should have been river mouths and deltas. Clearly the world's water level had risen. The question was, was there still a Washington, D.C.?

As they felt the first gentle shaking that told them their shuttle, for the first time in its life, had an atmosphere around it, Eve appeared and buckled herself in. She was sober, clean, and dressed in her best clothes.

Jeron was captain, Bill was pilot, but Eve was Aunt Mommy. She leaned forward to gaze at the approaching globe, and the others waited on her word.

There was a thunderstorm over the Virginia shore and a line of squalls all the way up into Pennsylvania. It was no real problem for the landing craft that Shef had designed, but the fact that the integrity of the ship was assured did nothing for the integrity of the stomachs of the crew. None of them had been exposed to that sort of lurching, staggering motion for a quarter of a century; most never had. Eve did not seem to notice the turbulence. Through a break in the clouds she saw the river, grossly swollen, an island with a marble monument, a hillside covered with grave stones, a bridge nearly awash, and from them recognized the marsh that had been Washington National Airport. She placed a finger on the port. "There, Bill," she said.

By the time they landed the inside of the shuttle was thick with the smell of airsickness, and six-year-old Jeromolo Bill was sickest of all. But he got them there.

Aunt Eve pulled herself together and stood up.

"We're going out now," Jeron guessed, watching her face.

Eve looked around at her corps of hardened adventurers —average age, nine; average height, not much over four feet. She smiled and shook her head.

"Not just yet," she said. "We're going to be good guests. We're going to stay right here in the lander until something happens outside, to give our hosts time to get ready for us."

24

IT WAS THE MIDDLE OF THE NIGHT AND IT HAD STOPPED raining. The President's Press Secretary was grateful for the latter, if not the former. She had been up all night printing the President's announcements, and now had the job of hand-delivering them before daybreak. There were only about eight that really had to be delivered, because their recipients were the important ones. But you never knew which eight were important in the President's eyes. So she had to deliver them all, forty identical little white envelopes, each containing a card that said:

THE PЯESIDENT
of The United States
Takes pleasure in inviting

To attend the Reseption
Of our Visitors from Alpha Cent.
R.S.V.P.

As she bicycled along the broad, empty avenues she could see lights in some of the windows. A whickering from the stables of the Pennsylvania delegation, where the lordly Amish had deigned to interrupt their sleep. Everyone knew. Everyone could see. Any minute now— Yes! There it was! The storm past, the skies had cleared, and the news was there in the sky for all to see, a great new golden star that swung through the constellations at the rate of four degrees a minute, the width of the full Moon every eight seconds. She slipped an envelope under the door of Blair House (yes, lights there, too, as the people from Puget talked among themselves about the great event), and headed out toward the less important stops by the mosquito-ridden margins of the river—the homes of the Supreme Court justices, the lesser Cabinet members, the so-called "delegations" with suspect credentials who had turned up for the advertised Tenth Anniversary gala, and found themselves present for something far greater.

The satellite was almost out of sight again at the far horizon by the time she had finished the last of them and walked her bicycle to the top of the levee for the easy ride home, and there was the lander. A great gold marble. Sitting there across the river and waiting for morning.

It was not cold, but she shivered.

By dawn the city was wide awake. "They're getting ready to come out!" everyone was shouting to everyone else, but each time the rumor was false. There was a spotter leaning out the windows at the top of the Washington Monument with Army field glasses and a battery-powered walkie-talkie, and he kept everyone posted on what was happening. Which, so far, was nothing—fortunately, in the opinion of the Vice President, trying to get things ready for company. Half the Marine guard had been impressed into peeling potatoes for the great welcoming banquet planned for the evening, and the other half was sewing buttons on its uniforms for the grand dress parade on the White House lawn; and, in the middle of it all, the President sat like a stone.

"Oh, Jimbo," his wife cried as she came breathless into the Oval Office and found him unmoving there. "Can't you get yourself going?" She felt his coffee pot and found it was cold, nodded to the orderly for a refill. "What a day, honey! I been down to the levee to see them. Jimbo, that thing is *big*. And it's got no *wings*. All it looks like to me is the darlingest big flying pumpkin you ever saw—but please get yourself dressed, will you?"

She sat down happily, pulling off her galoshes. Even with the sandbags all around and the dikes along the banks of the river, the White House grounds stayed soggy. "You know, honey, this is going to be the nicest time we ever had! Better than your Second Inaugural. Better than when the wine ship got stuck down by the Kennedy Center. Better than anything!"

Her husband shook his head. He said, "We weren't bothering them. What they got to bother us for?"

The Vice President scratched the soles of her feet, studying her husband. "It's going to be all right, honey. You'll see. Whatever it is you got on your mind. Now, you got to get out of that thing and get yourself dressed up." He was still sitting in his robe. It was made of pure silk and it had the Presidential seal on its breast, but it did not close across his belly; it had been made for a much smaller man. "Come on, Jimbo! What's the matter?" she demanded.

He said bitterly, "What should be the matter? I hear you got troops around the spaceship."

"Well, sure, Jimbo. Just Cousin Buzz's company. They look real nice, and you could look at it like they're a kind of guard of honor for them."

"I hope you don't get them sore at us."

His wife sighed. "If they're not sore now," she said reasonably, "I don't really see what we could do to make them that way. Now change your clothes. The gray suit's clean, and you've got some nice white shirts in the closet that I brought down from Virginia." She picked up his desk clock and shook it, then decided it was running. "You have time to take a shower, honey. Company won't be here for a couple hours, easy."

The President nodded thoughtfully, moving over to the window. His face was somber. He stared toward where the spaceship was, though of course it was not in sight—too many buildings, too many overgrown trees. "Everybody been told they got to dress up for this?" he demanded.

"Course they have, honey." His wife came up behind him and put her hand on his shoulder. "Listen, put your happy face on, Jimbo. This is a *party*. We're going to give these folks the nicest damn formal reception this town's seen in twenty years. The fire department's got three big pumpers ready, and they're going to squirt hoses in the air, and that skinny little chick from Puget said she got some fireworks for us."

"Fireworks?" said the President, smiling for the first time.

"You bet. And we're going to have a real fine state banquet. Smell the cooking?" He nodded, but did not turn around, and the Vice President said softly, "What is it, Jimbo? Something to do with that fellow you buried a couple-three weeks ago? Is that it?" He shrugged morosely. "You been real edgy ever since then," she persisted. "You want to tell me who he was?"

The President turned and looked at her, then shook his head. The President was not a bad man. He wasn't a particularly good one, either—you couldn't be altogether good and still do what you had to do to rise to the top in the yeasty bubble of the world as it was—but he tried to deal fairly with everyone. Usually. And a little more than fairly with his Vice President-and-wife.

He threw off the brocaded robe and scratched his chest for a moment before heading for the shower. "Let it lay, honey," he said. "You're better off if you don't know."

The skinny little chick from Puget, whose name was Darien McCullough, was busy deploying her forces. She had come to Washington with a party of five—you hardly traveled across a continent with fewer than that these days

—and every one of them had a job. The present job of the two strongest of them was to carry the load of skyrockets and Roman candles she had picked up in York State on the way down to the White House. Another was being wired for instant communication, as Darien was herself, and the fifth was given the job of staying home and keeping an eye on things while Darien gave in to her curiosity.

It was a good long walk to the banks of the Potomac, but if you stayed to the main streets you could manage it without getting your good shoes wet. Of course, you had to climb the side of the dike of sandbags to see across the Potomac, because the tides were now running six feet above what used to be the riverbank. But it was worth it.

The golden globe lay there, faintly luminous, in the shadow of what had once been the Eastern Airlines shuttle terminal. Darien was not alone as she stared. The levee was filled with sightseers, members of the delegations who had come for the President's Tenth Anniversary gala as well as Washington natives. She joined them in studying the great globe. It was, after all, precisely what she had crossed the continent to see.

"Good morning to you, Miss McCullough," said someone beside her, and she turned to greet the head of the Amish delegation, a tall old man with a beard and broad-brimmed hat. There was a whole wagonload of the stately Amish there, and heaven knew how many back in the Amish embassy on K Street. After the disaster the Amish, along with the Mennonites, the Doukhobors, and a few other sects, came into their own. They hadn't needed much from modern technology even before the power plants slagged down; they needed even less later on. While Iowa corn farmers stared in dreary despair at the fields they could neither plant nor sow without power for the tractors and a whole spectrum of chemicals to feed the plants and kill the pests, the Amish brought out their teams and prospered. Darien spoke politely to the Amishman. She was on good terms with their government, as she was with nearly every government in North America and a few which were not; that was one of the reasons why Puget stayed as healthy as it did.

Darien McCullough had been a teenager when the world as she knew it came to an end. She was in high school in

Ottawa, firmly intending to become either a nuclear physicist or perhaps a world-champion tennis player . . . unless she went into the family business. Which was politics. Like all good Canadians, she both despised and loved the wretched giant to the south. She had seen a lot of the United States from her father's embassy residence in Washington, D.C., as a small child. She was not anxious to see more. Quebec was more interesting. So was tennis. So were boys. When the kaons sluiced into every fissionable atom on the surface of the Earth, Darien's first thought was that it was a pretty good joke on the U.S.A. The mighty American muscle had simply melted away. All over the hemisphere U.S. bomber crews were parachuting to the ground, dozens of them over Canada, as their nuclear warheads dissolved their casings and the aircraft became uninhabitable. School closed early that day. At home, the telly showed CBC reporters following stunned generals around the Pentagon, asking questions that had no answers at all.

Then even CBC went off the air.

Forty percent of North American, not just Canadian, electric power came from nuclear reactors. As the cores softened and slumped, the turbines stopped turning. CANDUs were no luckier than the Westinghouses or the breeders. The power net failed. The grid died.

There was a bad week then, even in Ottawa. Nothing at all, compared to Detroit or L.A. But bad. When it became clear to her parents that it would be easier to stay alive in their home province than in Ottawa, they simply bought a train ticket and got on board. (A few weeks later it got harder.) The rail trip was normal enough—wheat fields do not riot—although there were delays and the restaurant car offered little choice. But Vancouver, when they got there, was wholly blacked out.

Saunders McCullough, Darien's father, was well equipped for the problem. He had been given the ambassadorship as a reward for political service, and the best of his service was with the national power authority, with an engineering degree from McGill before that. He was the one who put together the hydroelectric network that gave most of British Columbia and parts of the former states of Oregon and Washington a head start on returning to industrial civilization—or something fairly like it—after the disaster. Darien's mother was also an exceptional individual. Burned-out women's-rights revolutionary turned housewife, she sparked to life again and led the secessionist movement that put Puget together as an independent nation. The McCulloughs were certainly the first family of Puget, and the daughter was the logical choice to pick up the torch when the old folks died. Puget didn't have a President. It had a Council, but if there was a first among equals among them it was Darien McCullough. And when they unscrambled the Hawaiian Kingdom's message from space, she was the logical one to bring it to Washington.

A remote *beepbeepbeep* interrupted her thoughts.

The Amishman glanced disapprovingly at her purse, where the sound came from, but approvingly enough at Darien herself as he removed himself a few paces for politeness' sake. She held the purse up to her mouth to respond, then to her ear. It whispered to her, in the voice of Jake Harris, the anchorman back at Blair House, "Darien? You better get back here, ay? Looks like they're going to have a parade and we're supposed to be in it."

She frowned at the thought of walking down Pennsylvania Avenue behind the President's prized cavalry. "They don't need me, Jake."

"Course not. But you know how His Nibs gets."

"He's got plenty on his mind today. He won't even notice I'm not there." She peered past the Amish family to judge distances and then nodded to herself. "Look, I'll pick up the procession at the Arlington Bridge if I have to. So make my excuses till then, right? I have to sign off now."

There was a faint squawk of protest from the walkie-talkie in her bag, but she paid no attention. Like a proper sightseer, she concentrated on the great golden globe across the river.

The soggy ground beneath the sphere was cracked and dry. Tremendous heat had boiled the water out of the mud, between and over the old runways, for a distance of fifty yards around the spacecraft. Darien studied the caked mud thoughtfully. That meant waste heat, surely, but from what? Some immense energy had cushioned the fall of that globe, but there was no external sign of how it was applied. It had no wings, no visible rocket nozzles. Jake, who had watched the orbiting parent sphere the night before, thought that there had seemed to be some huge, wavy sort of aurora behind it—plasma? Darien could not guess, and shook her head regretfully. It was more important than ever, she thought, that she get to the people in the globe before anyone else did.

There were mottled irregularities on the globe that might have been windows, but if they gave a view at all it was only from the inside looking out. What did they look like, the people who undoubtedly were peering at her even now? Great golden gods and goddesses, as bronzed as their spaceship? Two-headed mutants? She felt a shudder run up her back, in spite of the muggy heat.

What the spacefarers were seeing was far less impressive. The pathetic rabble that was the President's picked corps of commandos was knotted around the ship, their oddly assorted weapons pointed at the ship, at the sky, at each other in random directions as they whispered to each other and strained to look inside the ship; and it was beginning to rain.

Darien sighed, rummaged in her purse, and took out a camera. It did not look any different than any other of those Japanese minis that still existed in quantity; cameras were not rare. But she attracted glances when she peered through its viewfinder at the ship because it was rare enough to see one used; film had not been in the stores for twenty years. For Darien's camera that didn't matter. It didn't use film. She clicked away, as a dozen generations of tourists had before her in that spot, and then she noticed what images she was storing on the magnetic tape.

A door in the golden globe was opening.

There was a gasp, then a shout, from the watchers on the levee. Even the Amish. Darien saw one of the levee policemen turn and wave frantically toward the top of the Washington Monument, but even he turned right back to see the most exciting group of tourists to enter Washington D.C.'s National Airport in at least two decades . . . or ever!

"What a funny bunch!" cried one of the Amish women, earning a reproving look from her husband.

But she was right. They came strutting out of the entrance and each one—at precisely the same point—stopped, and stared slack-jawed at the immense sky overhead, and was bumped out of the way by the person behind him. It was not just the infinite overhead sky. Most of the interstellar wayfarers were experiencing rain falling on their heads for the first time ever.

They were all very young. Not just young. The operative word, Darien thought, was "weird." Some of them were darker than the President himself, some almost albino white. They had features that ranged from emaciated aquiline to puffy blobs of noses surrounded by bulging cheeks—and yet, Darien thought, how could that be? There should not be such differences! They were all children of the same eight astronauts. All of them had been white, looking about as interchangeable as any NASA crew. How did the kids come to be all so different?

And, above all, how come they were so *young?* Barring one middle-aged woman, they were children—some of them surely no more than three or four years old. She had expected perhaps the original eight, now surely in their fifties or beyond, with perhaps a leavening of the more mature teenagers . . . but not this kindergarten!

All around the ship was now a scene of confusion. Half a dozen state coaches were being galloped across the taxi strip by agitated drivers, the unmatched teams surging and tangling with each other under the whip. The guards were trying to come to attention. All the old rifles were at port arms now, not actually pointed at the visitors but ready, and the soldiers were looking to their lieutenant for orders—who, in turn, was peering through opera glasses at the top of the Washington Monument. Darien caught a flicker of light from one of the little windows under the shaft's aluminum cap. If it was a signal, the lieutenant did not seem to find it helpful. He was arguing with a teenager from the ship, trying to keep his eyes on the Monument at the same time, and the discussion collapsed entirely when the horses and carriages pulled up. The children from the ship wailed and fled. Only the physical obstruction of the older woman at the door, trying to calm them, kept them from retreating into the ship. The teenager had joined the panicky retreat, but he recovered quickly and began shouting commands. Slowly the others came back toward the carriages. Those huge snorting animals in the traces were less terrifying than the teenager, it seemed.

Darien picked up her purse and held it to her lips. "I'm going to the bridge now," she murmured.

"Good idea, Derry. They're starting to move here—" The voice was lost in a blare of band music.

"Say again, Jake," she ordered, wincing at the noise.

"You can hear for yourself," his voice shouted. "Jesus God, what a racket! But you'd better get on over there, because they're on their way!"

The head of the President's parade was approaching the bridge by the time Darien got there, and the traffic congestion was considerable. Darien pushed her way through a knot of government employees in dungarees and cotton flannel shirts, no doubt given the day off to swell the crowd, and found herself behind a line of twenty or thirty soldiers doing traffic duty. They were keeping farm wagons off the bridge but allowing pedestrians to pass. Darien glanced at the approaching parade, studied the reviewing stand just across the road which was obviously where it was going to wind up, and decided the pedestrians had the right idea. For one thing, they were farther from the parade's two bands.

She walked out onto the span just as the first mounted soldiers in the escort appeared at the other end.

From the District end of the Arlington Bridge you could see right up the weedy hill that had once been America's best-kept cemetery. A later administration had built a small cinder-block fort commanding the bridge itself, and the outriders turned aside to gather under the fort, leaving the carriages with the visitors to enter the bridge alone.

And there they stopped.

There was some argument going on. It appeared the people from the spacecraft were arguing with their drivers, and, although Darien was too far to know which side won, the debate was resolved by the spacefarers' getting out of the carriages and lining up to cross the bridge on foot.

Even from that distance, Darien could see that they were not enjoying themselves. The rain had more or less stopped, but what was left in its place was a muggy, buggy heat. Some of them were sneezing violently, and had to be helped along by soldiers from the guard detachment. All of them were swatting at the insects.

Even so, they started off across the bridge bravely enough. Before they were halfway the bold marching step had slowed down, and even the arrogant teenager from the scene at the airport was beginning to limp. They reached the point where Darien stood, and that was the end of it. Two small children sat down in the middle of the road, weeping. The teenager snapped angrily at them without effect, then shrugged. His gaze wandered over the crowd on the curb, with incurious loathing, pausing briefly to meet Darien's eyes.

Darien McCullough could count on her fingers as well as any neighbor gossiping about a pregnant bride. She knew that it was unlikely that any of the children could be as much as twenty years old, yet there was a grownup ferocity in the man's stare. It shook her. She looked away quickly, but when she glanced back his eyes were still on her.

The carriages were beginning to approach from the far end of the bridge, and the noise distracted him, freeing her to look more attentively at the rest of the group. There seemed to be seven of them in all, two quite small boys, three young girls surrounding the age of puberty, the angry-eyed young man—and, good heavens!, Eve Barstow!

For Darien McCullough, the sight of Eve Barstow was a personal shock, saddening and complete. How different she looked! The slim, smiling bride who had taken off so bravely for Alpha Centauri was now transmuted into a plump, faded woman who limped as though her feet hurt. No doubt they did. Even her Earth-born muscles had lacked practice for twenty years. And there, behind her, there was—

There was what, exactly? Darien could not be sure. The day was still warm, but surely not hot enough to be producing mirages over the pavement. And yet there was something behind Eve Barstow, between her and the approaching carriages, that was making the hillside across the bridge creep and waver, like a view seen through flawed glass. It was too small to be heat refraction, too well defined to be a blurring of her own vision—why, she thought in amazement, it almost looked like the outline of a human form!

That was the first time anyone on Earth saw Uncle Ghost.

25

You knew that your nearest and dearest had fired a wad of devastation at the Earth. You knew that the consequences had to be awful. But you didn't know, until you saw with your own eyes, that what resulted was not so much tragic as tacky. The majesty of the Presidency had boiled away with the nukes.

There was this matter of the parade, for instance. You want to talk about parades? Eve Barstow had seen real *parades*! Dozens of them! Parades that took four hours to pass a given point, with regimental bands blaring in perfect sync and drum majorettes doing baton whirls and cartwheels down the avenue, and the people lined up twenty deep for miles on end. Fourth of July parades and Pasadena Rose Bowl parades and Armed Forces Day parades, and the least of them could have swallowed this pipsqueak affair up in between a Boy Scout troop and a Lithuanian-American Ladies' Marching Society delegation and never noticed it. And yet, truly, this was parade enough for her to participate in. She got to the White House simply worn out, even though they had been in carriages most of the way, and the kids were worse off than she. Strength is not endurance. The man who can clip seconds off a four-minute mile may fall over in total exhaustion before he gets halfway through the Boston marathon. And although they had carefully strengthened themselves for the unforgiving pull of 32 ft/sec^2, they had not practiced long marches, because in the spacecraft where was there to walk to?

So some of the kids were carried into the White House, and even Jeron and Molomy limped, and none of them were really happy. "Aunt Eve! Why does anybody need a house as big as this?" "Aunt Eve! Can't they get rid of these 'bugs'?" "Aunt Eve, you won't believe the *toilets!*" She did, of course, because she had seen flush toilets before, but none of the children had ever experienced a waste-disposal system that did not recycle. Or spicy, humid breezes, or, above all, so many hundreds, even thousands, of *people*.

As soon as they were in the White House, the Vice President whisked them away to a private room, firmly barring the door on the guests and visitors outside. No doubt she had her reasons, Eve thought, but it was a kindness all the same. And when the President appeared, proudly holding a tray with two bottles on it, a J & B and a Jim Beam, Eve felt her heart flutter. Real drinking whiskey again! She let him pour her half a tumbler full of bourbon, accepted a splash of water, and had it halfway to her lips before her conscience stopped her. "President Tupelo," she said—

"No, no! Call me Jim," the President urged.

"Jim, then—the first thing we want is to have a word with Dieter von Knefhausen."

The President's face fell. Standing next to him, his wife reached out and took his hand. "Well, there's a problem there, honey," the Vice President said. "See, Dr. Von Knefhausen passed away a while back. He's got a real nice plot there, out in the old Rose Garden. I can take you to see it if you want to."

Eve looked over the glass, into the face of the woman, frozen in that position. Behind the Vice President Eve could see an agitated shimmering against the drapes; Uncle Ghost had heard it too. At length she sighed and took a sip of her drink.

"What a pity," she said. "Tell me, did he die peacefully?"

What a pity. . . . An hour later, back out among the crowds of invited guests, Eve still had not got over what a pity it was. What she would have said to Dieter von Knefhausen had never been clear, but now she would not have the chance to say anything at all. It was strange that she should feel that as strongly as she did, considering that she seemed to be having a chance to talk to everybody else in the world at once. Or at least to listen, or to shake their hands. So many people! And every one of them, it seemed, with but one goal in life, and that to touch the visitors and talk to them.

It was a pity it was so warm, Eve thought; it made it hard for the children, some of whom seemed obviously unwell.

It was not just sweat. In the close confines of the ship all of them had been exposed to all varieties of natural odors, from the botanicals in the food chambers to the stinks of their siblings, friends, and selves. But there were smells here that were entirely new: Cigars. Charcoal fires on the patio. Above all, the many smells of cooking.

On the habitat, cooking was not very important, because most of what Eve grew could be eaten raw. Natural Earth foods were less kind. They had to be stewed or boiled or roasted or fried, and all processes seemed to be going at once. The immense meal was full of animal protein and saturated fats—right there, matters almost out of the experience of the children. The flavors were odd, the textures unfamiliar. The "meat," as the children learned to call it, was rich with blubber and laced with little cartileginous nuggets of gristle and, good heavens, they discovered, often fastened to a sort of gray-white stone called "bone" that nearly broke the teeth and was not meant to be swallowed at all. In theory the children knew what bone was, but it certainly was not the kind of thing you expected to find in your food!

The visitors were given a sort of corral to eat in, surrounded by Marine guards with flitguns, trying to keep the mosquito population down and visitors out at the same time. When the meal was over their protection vanished, and, one by one, the visiting dignitaries were brought up to the undignified visitors for introductions. Eve Barstow, who had washed down her spareribs with bourbon, found herself giggling out loud as she contrasted this reception with that long-ago one before the launch of the *Constitution.* Instead of the President of France, they had the Chairing Freeholder of the Carolina Confederacy; instead of the Russian ambassador, a slip of a girl from Puget Sound. Most of them brought gifts, the Amish a fletch of home-smoked bacon, the Puget girl a carved miniature totem pole, which she ceremoniously draped over Jeron's neck. By the time the sordid meal was over, the last bug picked out of the greasy food, the last plate picked up from the shrubbery and carried away, the last VIP greeted and dismissed, it was full dark, and Eve was feeling the bourbon. Her malt-nuts ran no more than six or seven percent alcohol; what she had been drinking was four or five times as powerful, even diluted, and she had been swallowing them pretty fast.

The realization came almost too late; Eve barely made it to the bathroom under the great carpeted stair.

Eve stayed in there for a long time, and when she came out the party was visibly dwindling. Not enough so. It was more than she wanted to handle. She turned away from the party sounds and wandered through the damp, shabby rooms, now deserted. None of this was the way she had planned it! Never mind that Kneffie was dead; that was probably better that way, since they really hadn't known what to say, or do, to him anyway. But the whole thing was a disappointment. She thought about the gifts she had planned so carefully, all of them still carefully wrapped in their moist seed pods and ready for germination or planting. Did she really want to give them to these people? There were fifty different kinds of wonders. The vegetable womb, to relieve women forever of the pains of parturition. The supercannabis, euphoria and analgesia without penalty. The bunny-fur plants, fibers with the porous structure of wool and the washability of cotton; the seeds were the size of peanuts and, as the gossypols had been bred out, they could be roasted to make a tasty snack. The malt-nuts, the squash-citrus-protein baby food, the meat substitutes—not to mention the ones that just looked pretty, or smelled sweet.

Not to mention the secrets of how to do all this, which she had once intended to share, the gifts that could change the genes themselves, and thus change the human race forever. But did she want to give all this to the likes of President James Tupelo?

A crash of china distracted her. A skinny young girl in Marine fatigues had entered the room, caught sight of Eve, and dropped the dirty dishes she was carrying to the kitchen. "You scared me," she said reproachfully. "How come you wandering here all by yourself?"

"I'm sorry," Eve offered.

"Sorry don't cut the mustard, miss. Listen. If you don't want to go back to the beer bust, why don't you let me show you upstairs? You got a real nice room. All ready for you. You only have to share it with one other person. Used to have the Carolinas in it, but they rousted them out this morning so's you could have it, and we changed the sheets and everything."

Suddenly a bed sounded like a good idea, and Eve followed willingly enough.

The other person turned out to be Molomy, sound asleep in one corner of a huge bed. It was the only bed in the room. Eve sighed and climbed into it, trying not to disturb Molomy, who grumbled and thrashed over to a new position. Eve closed her eyes. The bed was impressive without being comfortable, far lumpier and damper than the flower sacks Eve had bred for herself, but the fact that she was exhausted made up for a lot—

It did not, however, make up for the noises on the other side of the plywood partition that divided the room. Eve listened, then became aware of motion beside her and opened her eyes.

Molomy was sitting up, grinning. "It's Jeron," she whispered. "And he's got somebody with him."

When Jeron noticed that Aunt Eve was missing he thought briefly of looking for her, then decided against it. He didn't need her. What he needed was to get away from all these people, not least the people he had flown four light-years with, and think things out. He found Molomy, glassy-eyed with fatigue, and set her to shepherding the smaller children, who were more exhausted still, off to bed. Then he returned to what was left of the party and stared out over the lawn, wondering if he could get away long enough to take a walk through the strange, oppressive city, and wondering even more if his legs were up to it.

He did not get the chance. The young woman who had looped that unpleasant carved-wood object around his neck came up to him. "I'm Darien McCullough," she said. "Would you like to dance?"

He looked her over carefully before he answered, because Jeron had learned his lessons well. Aunt Eve had explained to him that dancing was a social ritual in which young men and young women experimented with touching each other and arousing each other as a preliminary to sexual intercourse; and for a young man whose entire universe of possible lovers was limited to about thirty possible partners, almost all of them by now so familiar as to be tedious, the prospect was enticing. So was Darien McCullough. She was tall, dark, slim—and new. He did not have any way of guessing her age, but it would not have occurred to him for that to matter. If they were big enough they were old enough. "Of course I can dance," he said. "Where shall we do it?"

Her expression faltered for a second. "Well," she said, her look strained, "the usual place is probably on the dance floor, you know."

Although he could see no reason for it, he was in no doubt. She was laughing at him. He nodded carelessly. "Of course," he agreed, "but at this moment I wish to remain here to study, ah, the incrustations on this pillar." He had in fact been looking at the white rime on the pedestals beside him, wondering if it were intended as art. For some reason that amused the woman even more.

"It's called bird lime," she said. "I wouldn't touch it, if I were you."

"I did not intend to touch it," he said frostily. "You speak of birds. Do you know that in my home there are no birds? I have never seen a bird until today," he went on, proud of his ability to make social conversation and pleased that she no longer looked as though she were laughing at him.

"Why don't we walk around the garden while you tell me about your home?" she suggested, and then, without pause, "Oh, hell." She was looking past him.

From behind him, the voice of the President of the United States (Washington, D.C.) said, "There you are, boy. Having a good time?"

Jeron said politely, "Yes, thank you. Darien McCullough and I were talking about these birds." He picked up an overlooked French-fried potato and tossed it toward a pigeon on the lawn, but, instead of eating it, the bird flew off to the top of the pillars. "They behave very strangely," he commented, craning his neck to stare up. He could hear a cooing sound from the birds overhead, but it was too dark to make out what they were doing.

"Ah, sonny," the President said diffidently, "I wouldn't gawk up at those pigeons so close."

"Would you not, then," Jeron said. To demonstrate his

independence he found a fork in the grass and shied it at the pigeons overhead. The fork came nowhere near, but forty startled birds flew off in all directions, and Jeron felt something hot and damp strike down along his ear.

The President grinned broadly. "Now you know where all that white decoration comes from, Mr. Jeron. Well, I was about to invite you to come in for a little sit-down with the Vice President and me, so why don't we take you into the Oval Office and get you cleaned up a little? Nice to see you, Miz McCullough," he added politely, steering Jeron away. The woman looked angrily after them, to Jeron's great pleasure.

"She wanted to make love with me," he remarked to the President. "After I'm cleaned up, I think I'll come back and permit it."

"No, no," the President said earnestly. "Take my advice, boy, those wild people from the West are all full of the worst kinds of VD and everything. You just leave her be. There's plenty of nice American girls right here in Washington, D.C., that'd be proud to be with a man like you—but not that one, no sir!"

If there were indeed all these nice American girls lusting for his flesh, Jeron could find no sign of them in the Oval Office. Once he had got himself cleaned up he was led to a couch, the Vice President fluffing up pillows for him and offering a tray of sweet little cakes in paper wrappings and bottles of lukewarm, acidy, bubbly brown drinks. The President pulled up a chair to face him and said, "Now, my boy, let's you and me talk turkey. You didn't come here for nothing, right?"

Jeron nodded. "That is correct. What we want—"

"So we can make a deal," the President nodded. "I knew when I saw you that you were a reasonable man. You're the kind of person that puts your cards right on the table, just like me, right? Mae! Put a little sweetener in this good man's Coke while we talk us some business here."

"It is already quite sweet," Jeron objected, but the Vice President was already shaking her head.

"I don't believe he's much used to drinking, Jimbo honey," she said sweetly. "Isn't that right, Jeron?"

The President shrugged amiably. "Then let's get right to it. I imagine you folks came here with trading goods, right? Mind telling us what you've got to offer us?"

"Offer?" Jeron was finding the whole interview confusing, rather like a conversation in a foreign language that he barely understood.

"What you brought for us, son," the President amplified.

"Oh, to be sure," said Jeron, glad to have understood him at last. "Yes. Aunt Eve has a great many things for you. Different kinds of plants and vegetables—some of which I helped her breed," he bragged.

The President's expression seemed to turn in on itself. "Plants and vegetables?" he repeated.

"Yes. Of course, some of them might not grow properly here—the gravity is so strong, you see, and you do not maintain good control of temperature and humidity, I think."

"Uh-huh," the President said. "I see. Actually, I was thinking more of weapons."

"What would we be doing with weapons?" Jeron demanded, scandalized.

"What anyone else would be doing with them! You mean you don't have any? —No, don't say that, 'course you do. Why, that ship of yours all by itself would have pretty good military applications, used right."

"You want the ship?" Jeron thought for a moment, then shrugged. "We would have to send someone back to orbit to get the other one, but, yes, why not? And in return I have a list of what we require. It is in the lander, but as I remember it includes strawberry, coconut, papaya, tobacco, redwood, sugar maple—"

"Son, I don't know if we can exactly get you a whole redwood tree."

"Seeds alone will be adequate; there are about six hundred vegetable species, I think. Also animals, including possum, gorilla, rattlesnake, dolphin—"

"You gonna have a real Noah's Ark, boy," the President said uneasily, revising his estimate of the size of the ship in orbit.

"There too, genetic materials will be enough. We would prefer sperm and ova, though we can make do with other cells. I do not expect you to ask a female gorilla to let you investigate her private parts," said Jeron, laughing to notify them that that was a joke.

The President laughed too, but he looked at his wife and almost shrugged. "That's all you want? Just some livestock?"

"No, no. I also wish recent publications, on microfiche by choice. *Philosophical Transactions, Science*, the *Journal of Astrophysics*, and about one hundred fifty others."

The President's wife said, "We don't have much of that kind of stuff, Jeron. I think we got some copies of *Popular Science Monthly* down to the Marine dayroom, but they've mostly got pretty tatty by now."

"No, no! *Science*. Or any equivalent journal of recent research in the physical sciences."

The President cleared his throat. "I think you better have a drink after all, son. There's no magazines like that coming out anymore."

"There must be! How else would scientists exchange information about available instruments, for instance?"

The Vice President put her hand on his arm in real sympathy for this young boy who was so evidently feeling frustrated and angry. "I'm real sorry, honey. We don't get any magazines like that—or, tell the truth and shame the devil, most any new magazines at all. Don't need that sort of thing anymore, you know. The only instrumentation we need's maybe a stick to measure how high the water's got."

Jeron scowled, rubbing the area around his navel. The thought of returning to Uncle Shef and Uncle Ski without the journals they had ordered was giving him a stomachache. He said stubbornly, "I just can't believe there isn't any scientific research going on."

"Oh, hell, 'course there is," the President said with pride. "I got over twenty-five people over to the Defense Department, making gunpowder and such, and Mae's got a whole bunch in the Department of Home Economics and Cooking, don't you, hon?"

"Well, yeah. But that's not quite what the young man means, Jimbo. There's none of that fancy stuff here. I don't think there's any of that anywhere in the world—" The Vice President hesitated. "Except maybe in Puget," she finished. "They're more into technology there. I mean, if that's really what you want," she added, catching her husband's chilly eye.

"What she means," the President explained, "is you don't want to mess around with the Pugets. They still take scalps, you know."

The Vice President had never had any children, but all that proved was that nature made some silly mistakes. She was as motherly a type as had ever occupied that high office, and she frowned, leaned forward, and pressed the palm of her hand against Jeron's forehead. "Jimbo," she declared, "this boy doesn't need any more talk of taking scalps and making deals. He's wore out. What he needs is to go right off to bed."

The President looked rebellious, but only for a minute; after all, he would have plenty of other chances. "One last thing," he said jovially. "And I'm gonna insist you put just a drop of this mountain dew in your Coke for it. You and me and Mae here are going to drink a toast. To our eternal friendship between planets! And to our common goal, the reunification of the U. S. of A., and then of the whole doggone world!"

Jeron had a flickering electric light in his room, but all the rest of the furnishings looked ancient. He pulled back the covers, regarded the narrow canvas cot he was supposed to sleep in with distaste, and climbed in. What a place! And what people!

There was hardly a word they said that did not seem to reflect so basic a difference in orientation and desires that communication was almost hopeless. That "toast" of the President's, for instance—was that what the President thought they were here for? To help him "reunify" something that Jeron really thought was a lot less troublesome left fragmented? There was really only one reason they were here—because he and Aunt Eve had idly dreamed up the trip, and Shef and Flo and Ski had seen enough practical value in it for themselves to help build the ship.

He sighed heavily and flounced over in the cot, trying to get comfortable . . . and then sat up.

Someone had opened his door.

"It's only me, Darien McCullough," whispered a female voice.

"How did you get in here? What do you want?" he demanded.

"You always ask at least two questions at once," the woman complained. He could hear her moving around, and then the light went on—she had known, he perceived, exactly where to find it. "Satisfied?" she asked, spreading her hands. "See, no guns, no knives. Now I better turn the light off again, so nobody will come up to see what's going on." As the light went off, she added, "I just wanted you to know. We aren't, and we don't."

"Aren't what? Don't what?" The only illumination now was misty moonlight coming in through the window, but Jeron could see her well enough as she came to sit on the edge of his bed.

"We aren't riddled with VD, and we don't take scalps. Jimbo's a liar, you see."

Jeron said, "Huh." He pulled his ankles up under his thighs and studied her. It was very hard to tell how old these Earthies were. She could have been anything from his own age to Aunt Eve's. Dressed simply in denim slacks and a patterned blouse, her fair hair short and curly, she looked principally female. She smelled that way, too, in ways that none of the women of his experience had ever smelled. Jeron knew it was called "perfume" from reading, but until now his knowledge of it had been entirely theoretical. "I think," he said, "that you could not know that the President had said such things of you unless you used electronic instruments. Is that correct?"

"It's none of your business, Jeron," she said, pleasantly enough. "We do know a lot of what the President says when he doesn't think we're listening. Some of it worries us, and it ought to worry you, too."

There was something about the way she averted her eyes as she spoke that made Jeron suspect he was violating her nudity tabus; he pulled the stiff sheet up over him, and she relaxed. "Jim takes that 'President' stuff pretty seriously," she went on. "He won't be happy until he's President of fifty states again, all the way to Hawaii, and I think you ought to know that he's counting on you to do it for him."

"That's silly," Jeron said dispassionately. "We would not involve ourselves in these petty disagreements."

"You may not have a choice, buster!" Her tone was suddenly sharp, but softened as she went on. "You ought to get out of here while you have the chance," she said seriously. "That's why I came trekking all across the continent. To warn you. And to invite you to Puget."

"Huh," said Jeron, sniffing a little more deeply. The smells of sex he knew and the scents of flowers he knew, but this combination was something new. He moved, and the sheet fell away, and Darien McCullough glanced down.

"Oh, for God's sake," she said, "shame on you. Why, I'm old enough to be your mother."

"So is my mother old enough to be my mother," said Jeron, "but that does not keep me from wanting—"

"I don't want to hear!" She was laughing, but she was embarrassed, too—one more way in which she resembled his mother, Jeron thought. She clung to her subject. "So will you come? To Puget, I mean?"

"Huh." Jeron pulled the sheet up again. "How far is it?"

"About four thousand kilometers, I guess, more or less." He scowled with the effort of trying to imagine four thousand kilometers in a straight line. "We'd have to go in your ship," she added, "but I guess there's room, and anyway you want to get it away from Jimbo as soon as you can. Unless you want to take the road, train, boat, and portage, the way I came?" She stood up, suddenly, and listened for a sound outside. Then, more softly, "I have to go. Think about it, Jeron. It's important. . . ."

When she was gone, leaving behind only that disturbing scent, a shimmer of moonlight told Jeron that he still had company. "I really thought you were going to get laid that time, boy," Uncle Ghost whispered fróm the draperies over the windows.

"I didn't know you were there!" Jeron said indignantly.

"No, I guess you didn't. Jeron? You know, I get the impression that she's telling the truth about this President person. I don't like this place."

"Fat lot of difference it makes to you," Jeron sneered. "You've been hiding the whole time."

"And I'm going to go right on hiding, and I don't want anybody telling these people I'm here." Jeron sniffed, rolling over and burying his head in the musty pillow. "You hear me, Jeron?"

"Of course I hear you," Jeron said into the pillow.

There was a pause, and then the faintest whisper of a

sigh. "I thought," mused Uncle Ghost, "that it would be more fun than it is. I even thought that after we took care of Knefhausen, we could help these people. Now I don't know."

Jeron lay sullenly in the damp heat, waiting for Uncle Ghost to go on. When he didn't, Jeron said, "Help them how? And why?"

But there was no one there to answer anymore.

26

THE VICE PRESIDENT OF THE UNITED STATES HAD BEGUN her career as a diet technician, Spec. 5, in the 456th Infantry Battalion. The other name for her job was KP pusher, but Mae Prewick was the gentlest overseer the kitchen help ever had. They got the work done all the same, because they liked her. Everybody did, especially the platoon leader as it turned out.

When Mae Prewick married Lt. James Braddock Tupelo it did not really interrupt her career. It simply gave her a new one. Her career became not so much a matter of advancing her own status as of keeping James B. from screwing up his, as he made the transition from Army officer to government flunky, to Congressman—ultimately to where he was now. She was happy in her work. James B. was a good-hearted man, with a few exceptions.

She was hoping very much that these people from Alpha Centauri were not going to turn out to be one of the exceptions.

They were really a freaky lot, in the Vice President's opinion, but not a whole lot freakier than the creatures from all over North America she had been dealing with for a decade now. Farmers and freebooters. Romantic voyageurs from Canada Française and arrogant embassies from the West Coast. Pipsqueak potentates from what used to be Appalachia, kings of three hills and half a valley—she had entertained them all. And all about the same way. She pushed her White House KPs into producing lavish meals, made sure there was plenty of drinking liquor to make the negotiations run smooth, nursed the hangovers on the mornings after.

It didn't really make much of a change from what she would have been doing anyway, if James B. had stayed in the Army and by now she had been setting up Saturday-night poker games for his company officers. The stakes in the games were higher now, and they weren't played with cards, but those all-night sessions were still bluff and call, sweep up the pots or take your licking. It did not matter that now she was sometimes called Mrs. Vice President instead of Hey-Mae! Especially since what she was Vice President of was really bounded only by Norfolk, Baltimore, and the Shenandoah National Park. But it mattered, a little anyway, that this new batch of gamblin' friends didn't seem to know how to play the games. So many of them were kids. Mae Tupelo had never been able to have kids of her own, and she was sentimental about them. All of them. Even weirdos like this batch. And the ones that weren't children, or next thing to it, like that funny Jeron—well, Eve Barstow had been a fine woman at one time, the old pictures proved it, but she had sure let herself go. Five little kids. One half grownup. One fat lady that gasped every time she climbed two steps . . . the Vice President frowned to herself, because she didn't really know, and nobody else seemed to know either, whether or not there was another member of the crew. Sometimes seemed like there was. Sometimes seemed like there wasn't; and you couldn't get a straight answer out of any of them. There were times when you'd swear before God you heard a grownup man talking. And then you'd say something to them, not nosy but friendly, and you'd get one of those laughs.

They really knew how to laugh nasty when they wanted to, and at those times the Vice President told herself she didn't care a bit what her husband was up to. Serve them right! But then she'd see how little they were, really. That one they called Molomy. Fourteen at the most. Never had a dress-up doll until Mae Tupelo gave her one. And then, come to find out, that littlest one, the only one with the sensible name, Bill, was her kid!

And the seesaw of the Vice President's feelings went back to not caring a bit what happened to them.

You had to admit, though, that in some ways they had been raised up pretty well. You invited them, they invited you. You welcomed them to Washington with a big party, and they invited you to a picnic in front of their ship the next day. Not the kind of picnic Jimbo had much use for, all greens and fruits and things, but real pretty the way they were spread out. You took them for a cruise up the river to see Mount Vernon, and they came back with asking you to come see the inside of their ship the next day. That had cheered Jim up some, although he wasn't invited in the ship—ladies only, Eve Barstow said, as though it was some kind of a joke. Funny, but Jimbo took it as a joke, too, or at least laughed that way he had when somebody did something he expected them to, and didn't really like. There was something going on, all right. What proved it was that the President didn't even get mad when he found out that the girl from Puget and one of the Amish ladies were invited too.

And then the next morning, when she started out for the ship, half the guards around the White House were missing and the other half wouldn't meet her eye.

So Mae Tupelo was not entirely at ease as she entered the ship, but as soon as she got inside she forgot to worry. What a funny place!

Although it looked forbiddingly large on the outside, it was quite cramped on the interior. "That doesn't really matter," Eve Barstow told her, "because we only have to be in it for a few hours at a time."

"The big ship is still in orbit," Jeron offered—evidently "ladies only" did not refer to the ship's crew. "That one we stayed in for four years."

"You fixed it up real nice," the Vice President said automatically, but not very sincerely. Much of what she saw was simply confusing. The padded seats, the toilets, the wonderful windows for looking out—that she understood easily enough; and the control board, worse than any washer-dryer in the Officers Quarters in the old days, she could accept without having to understand. But what were those ragged clusters of things that looked like—like what? Seed pods? Rotting tamales? They hung along the walls like garlic buds in a delicatessen. Eve Barstow pulled some of them out with pleasure.

"They're going to be presents, Mae," she said, unwrapping some to show to her, others for the other women. "It won't be much of a surprise now, but here they are. These are lamb. You have to give them plenty of nitrogen and phosphorus when you plant them. These are marshmallows, we use them mostly for sugar. These are different kinds of decorative flowers—I'm not really sure which is which right now. It's hard to tell from the seedlings—"

"Not for me," Jeron corrected. He placed his finger on one shoot. "This one will bloom red, white, and blue," he said. "Eve thought you'd like that. This one blossoms with a picture of me on it. I bred that one myself," he said offhandedly, no longer looking at Mae Tupelo. His eyes were on the woman from Puget as he stripped the damp husk from the seedling. "Would you like it?" he asked. "I don't know if it'll grow in all that snow in Puget, though."

She laughed in surprise. "We get less snow than they do in Washington."

"That's ridiculous," Jeron said with scorn. "I can read a map. You're as far north as Maine, and Uncle Shef told me about Maine winters. You don't have to take it if you don't want it," he added, and carelessly tossed the husk back in its rope basket.

The Vice President sighed softly. Aunt Eve took pity on her. "The red, white, and blue is for you, for sure," she said. "Now, do you want to see how this thing works?"

There was a sudden air of tension in the ship. "You mean go up for a flight?" Darien asked after a moment.

"Sure, why not?"

But the Amish woman looked so startled and worried that the Vice President shook her head. Jimbo would kill her, but she said, "No, really, I mean thanks a lot but no. Do you think you could tell us a little bit about how it runs, though?"

Jeron reached back and pulled young Bill forward. The boy instantly piped, "Well, those are the seats we sit in. It's pretty easy to fly this thing, but sometimes your delta-Vs get pretty hairy if you're operating in an atmosphere, so we tied ourselves in." He frowned as he noticed an expression of incomprehension on the faces peering at him, and Darien McCullough cut in:

"That doesn't exactly explain what makes it go."

"Oh, that." He patted a white enamel cylinder about the size of a domestic hot-water tank. "It's just thermonuke, inside here. There's a plasma cord in there about the size of my finger, and it's real hot. Ski says it's about a million Kelvins—of course, it's turned off now."

"I think they mean how do we contain that much energy," Aunt Eve offered. She sighed and scratched her head. "Let's see. I helped draw up that Gödel message that explained the whole thing, but it's a long time ago. . . . The first thing to do is renormalization. Do you people know what that means?"

Obviously they did not; Darien was looking intent but unsure, the Amish lady skeptical and somewhat unhappy, only the Vice President seemed comfortable. "Good lord, no," she said, "but I do like hearing those words, so go right ahead and explain it."

"All right." Eve thought for a second. "Well, everybody knows that quantum field theory says even empty space has to contain infinite energy, right? That's just Heisenberg. In a practical sense that does not usually make any difference, because you don't get work done from *energy*, you get work from *changes* in energy states or *differences* between energy states. So when the old physicists wanted to do mathematics about energy in space they dropped out the term for the infinite energy; that was called renormalizing it."

Darien raised a hand. "Are you saying that you, what is it, renormalize equations?"

"No, no, no! We renormalize space." Eve looked around to the children for help, but they were as perplexed as she. None of them had ever been exposed to human beings, at least to human beings over the age of two, who did not understand simple physics. She said, unsure of herself but unable to find a better way, "If you read the Gödel message, you probably remember something Ski put in; it was a quotation from John Wheeler. It went like this: 'Geometry bent one way describes gravitation. Rippled another way somewhere else it manifests all the qualities of an electromagnetic wave. Excited at still another place, the magic material that is space shows itself as a particle.' Do you see? It's all geometry. All we have to do is arrange the geometry properly and the rest takes care of itself; space is renormalized, energy flows, and we move."

Jeromolo Bill giggled, "Look at them, Aunt Eve!" he squeaked. "They're not taking in a word of it, are they?"

The Vice President could find it in heart to love even bratty kids; she patted Bill on the head, looked at her Mickey Mouse watch, and sighed, "Oh, my goodness! Look at the time! Thanks for the tour, but if you folks are going to get any lunch I better be getting back to the White House."

Lunch was only Chesapeake Bay oyster chowder and a nice salad from the Vice President's own kitchen garden. Her KPs didn't need to be supervised for that, so what she said was not true; and as she walked back to the White House she was worrying.

Little bitty untruths, of course, never worried the Vice President. Social lies rested lightly on her; she was not a theoretician, and abstract arguments in that area were as meaningless to her as what that John Wheeler, whoever he was, had said about gravitation, whatever he meant by that. She knew what gravitation was—it was what made you puff when you went up a flight of stairs. It wasn't geometry, and neither was matter, and what difference did it all make, for heaven's sake? Mae Tupelo did not deny that in some theoretical sense all that stuff might be true—but who cared?—or even that there might be some abstract rule requiring truth-telling rather than falsehood, say when you were testifying under oath. None of that affected her life. It often turned out that the truth hurt people, and a pleasant lie left them at peace.

The truths she was carrying around right now were very likely to hurt. The truthful thing to have said to the visitors was, "My husband's up to something tricky and I have to find out what it is," but a person couldn't say *that*. And the truthful thing to say to her husband, when she saw him, was, "You're never in this world going to be able to handle that ship, so forget it." And maybe she would say that; but before she tried any truths on James B. she was going to find out what falsehoods he had been laying on her.

Mae Tupelo did not expect her husband to have no secrets at all. He had plenty. She could name three of them right off—their names were Rose and Diane, and that little Marine orderly, Sylvia. That didn't mean anything. That was just the dog in any man. No, the kind of secrets she didn't want Jimbo keeping from her were like that bad thing with Dieter von Knefhausen—Mae Tupelo was sure she could have kept him alive, good thick stews and fresh greens, instead of whatever he got in that silly old dungeon—and, most especially, whatever it was that was going on now.

The question was, what could she do about it?

One way was to ask him. That was the wrong way. The Vice President had better ones, and so by the time the President was up in the Lincoln Room digging out his ears and buttoning his shirt to be ready for lunch, she had already had a few words with her own personal CIA. "Jimbo," she said, "you got to have the White House Guard off practicing commando tactics in Rock Creek Park, and it's not going to work."

He scowled like a thundercloud. "What's not going to work?" he demanded dangerously, but she stood up to him.

"Hijacking that spaceship. That's what's not going to work. Not counting it's a really mean thing to do, you can't get away with it."

He sat down and reached for a Fresca, his gaze calculating as he looked at his wife. "You think not?" he inquired.

"I know it, James B.!"

He shook his head. "How they going to stop me, Mae? They've got no guns. You see any guns there anywhere?"

"There's worse things than guns! Besides, how do you know what they've got up in that big ship up in orbit?"

"Up in orbit's not here. Besides, once we get this one, we could just run up there and take that one too, right? What's to stop us?"

"We-don't-know-how is to stop us, for one thing."

He grinned. "*They* do, honey."

"Jimbo! They're company! How's it going to look if you make slaves out of them?"

He finished the Fresca and tossed the bottle out onto the

overgrown lawn. "You know," he said sweetly, "you might be right at that, Mae. I'm going to have to think this over, but right now it's about time to eat lunch."

The President joined his guests for the drinks on the porch and then wandered off for a private word with the guard commandant, and that was all the Vice President needed. She had not moved more than five yards from Jeron, waiting for her chance. Of course he was talking real close with that Puget woman—same dog in every man—but there might not be another chance. "Mr. Jeron, honey," she said, low and fast, "by this time tomorrow night my husband's going to have armed men in your ship, and you're not going to get in it until you do what he wants you to."

"That's silly," said Jeron scornfully. "He can't do that!" But the Puget girl put her hand on his arm.

"Yes, he can, Jeron. Listen to Mrs. Tupelo—what should Jeron do?"

The Vice President smiled and bobbed her head as though they were talking about the drinks or the other guests or the weather, her eyes never off the door her husband had left through. "Though it gravels me to say it," she said, "I think you ought to take that little flight you were talking about, and don't come back for a while. Do it soon. Do it before he gets up tomorrow morning, because after he's had his coffee it's going to be too late."

27

WITHOUT DARIEN MC CULLOUGH'S HELP THE ALPHA-ALEPHS would never have made it to the spacecraft, much less succeeded in sneaking past the dozing guards, but even so by the time they got there they were pitiably exhausted. Eve Barstow's Earth-born muscles were beginning to come back into shape and she was the least damaged, but even Eve plopped herself into a seat and croaked, "Let's get away from here, Bill."

Darien looked around. "—Five, six, seven," she counted. "Is that all of you?"

"Close enough. Go!" grunted Jeron, and Darien barely had time to seat herself when little Jeromolo Bill expertly whipped the ship off the ground and up.

The kind of thrust involved was entirely out of Darien's experience. She weighed twice, three times what she had ever weighed before, and when she turned her head as it leaned against the back of her seat she thought her eyes would be twisted out of their sockets. She knew in theory that sharp acceleration produced G-thrusts, but theory did not persuade her body that everything was proceeding normally. For a moment she thought she would throw up—but couldn't—and then the pressure eased and she could, but didn't any longer need to.

There was a shrill gabble of children's voices to celebrate the fact that they could now get up again. Darien winced at the noise, and then realized that the reason she could hear it was that there was no noise from the ship itself. No roar of motors, not even a scream of air passing around the ship itself. How very strange! She was near enough to the white cylinder that held the power plant to reach out a hesitant finger to touch it. Cool. Also strange. Everything strange; and strangest of all the people, who did not know how strange they were.

Although they had some very grownup ways, most of them were still children, and you could see that in the strain on their faces, the pouting lips, the way they flew at each other. The youngest of all was the child who seemed to be flying the ship! Not yet three feet tall, with sweet, plump skin and eyebrows almost invisibly blond—how could he be trusted with such a thing?

Perhaps it was good for him. He seemed calm enough, whereas the two youngest of the girls—their names seemed to be Ringo and Tudeasy—were shrieking at each other, and close to tears. The older girl, Molomy, and the boy called Quittyyx were trying to quiet them down, while Jeron cursed them all impartially.

It was Eve Barstow who restored order, with a simple, "Shut up, everybody." They obeyed. "Bill, where are we going?" she asked.

"North Pole, Aunt Eve," said the six-year-old.

"Why?"

"Want to see what it looks like," he offered. He hesitated, baby teeth nibbling at baby lip, then grinned. "Also it's the only place I could think of that I know how to go to."

"That's ridiculous," said Jeron scornfully, and the hubbub broke out again until Darien McCullough called over it:

"I have a suggestion. Come stay with us in Puget for a while."

Silence, with everyone looking at her, then another burst of raucous noise until Jeron quelled it. "I think that sounds interesting," he said, and his eyes said why he thought so.

"Hell with that," cried Molomy strongly. "You can get sex anywhere, Jeron, you don't have to go among the savages to get it. You! Darien-McCullough! You're not supposed to be here in the first place, so be quiet."

There was enough truth in that to slow Darien down. She'd sneaked them through the sleeping city of Washington, but when they got to the ship there was no invitation to come inside. It wasn't until the argument threatened to wake the guards that Jeron pulled her in and shut the door. Eve quieted the new outbreak and said, "I don't want to be offensive, but how do we know we won't get into the same problem in Puget?"

"Well, you don't," Darien conceded. "But you can leave one person in the ship all the time if you like— Or maybe just one or two come out with me at a time until you get a look at us— Or you could just trust me? Listen. I *knew* you were coming, and that's why I made that whole damned long trek to Washington. It's important!"

"Trust you!" sniffed Molomy; but the little pilot piped up:

"*I* trust her." Everybody was talking at once again until Eve's deeper, slower voice cut through.

"The best way to make up our minds," she said, "is to roll the bones."

There was a silence. Then Molomy said, "We don't do that anymore, Aunt Eve. Only the old folks do it."

"The old folks made some pretty good decisions with the *I Ching,* Molomy. I say let's read the hexagram and see what it says."

"We don't have any bones," Jeron objected. "Could use a coin, I guess, if we had a coin. Have you got a coin?" he asked Darien.

Talk about strange—! But she found a coin, or at least a Puget retail token that had both heads and tails, and Molomy was elected to flip it.

First flip: Heads. Jeron drew two short lines with his thumbnail on the skin of his knee.

Second flip: Heads again. Jeron nodded. "Pride stirred up because of somebody else's transgressions," he said, making the same mark just below the first.

Third flip: Heads again.

Fourth flip: Heads. "You walk in the midst of others, but you return alone," Molomy sighed.

Fifth flip: Heads. Darien was watching in fascination. "In Puget," she said, "when they do that, they do it the other way. From bottom to top."

"On our ship," Jeron said, "we do it our way. Shut up."

Sixth flip, tails—and the hexagram was complete as Jeron drew a solid line at the bottom:

— —
— —
— —
— —
— —
———

Eve straightened up. "It's K'un over Chen," she said. "It's 'The Turning Point.' "

Jeron rubbed at his knee and nodded, but Molomy cried indignantly, "Same old garbage! You can read it either way—see why we don't cast the hexagrams anymore?"

Eve sat down in her chair and began to belt herself in. "Dear Molomy, that's the nature of the hexagram. But the nature of important decisions is that you have to decide them. One way or the other. If we don't go to Puget we haven't made a decision, we've just postponed one."

"But—"

"But, but, butt out," Jeron interrupted. "We cast the hexagram and it's over. Bill! Take us to Puget."

* * *

By the time they had made their decision the craft, according to Jeromolo Bill's built-in navigation aids, was somewhere over Lake Erie. He studied a map for a moment —strange map, north was not at the north and it had no political markings at all, only coasts and mountain ranges— and then nodded negligently. "Belt up," he piped, and barely gave them time to settle in before he whipped the ship around in a sharp left-hand turn. Then he unstrapped himself and began to play a game with his chief pilot, Quittyyx, using Darien's coin. He didn't need to guide the ship anymore; it was going in the right direction. It was not a difficult sum—there were no relativistic factors to be considered—but it made Darien nervous. She didn't want to criticize the boy's piloting, so she said instead, "Isn't that an awfully wasteful way to travel?"

He looked up. "Wasteful of what? Oh, I see. Energy." He laughed, and called: "Aunt Eve, is there anything to eat?"

That started another battle, Eve insisting that he really should sleep instead, since they had, by his own calculations, an hour and fifty minutes before they reached the Pacific Ocean and it was well past his bedtime. Darien withdrew from the discussion and tried to reconcile herself to the bumpy ride. Shef's landing craft was not an aerodynamic shape, and so the buffeting was considerable. It did not seem to bother anyone but Darien—was not, in fact, a patch on the turbulent landing they had had a few days earlier. It was simply what you had to expect when you were moving fast in air, and all the spacefarers had learned to accept it.

Darien divided three thousand-odd kilometers by an hour and fifty-five minutes in her head and realized that they were traveling at nearly twice the speed of sound. Then she understood why there was so little noise. The noise was there; they were simply moving too fast for it to catch up. All across the continent no doubt people were waking from sleep and jamming their fists in their ears and running out into the open to see what catastrophe was splitting their skies, but inside the ship the greatest noise came from its occupants, now squabbling over which ones got the ripest fruits Eve Barstow was unwrapping.

Darien McCullough was old enough to remember jet

planes, and all the other resources of the great age of technology, but it had been a very long time since she looked down on a continent. It puzzled her that, as they crossed what must have been Lake Michigan, it seemed to be growing lighter; and then, minutes later, she saw the Sun rising—queerly in the west! They were outracing it! The rest of the crew had no preconceived ideas of where sunrise should occur and did not understand what she was exclaiming at, but all of them clumped around the viewing angles to see the marvelous light. The rising Sun illuminated the sky from the top down. Just below them clumps of altocumulus floated at forty thousand feet like luminous pink and white cotton candy, with tiny white cumulus clouds floating in the shadows far below. Even Jeron thought it was beautiful.

In his own surroundings Jeron did not seem quite as arbitrary and scornful as he had in the sphere of the President of the U.S. (Washington). He was not a handsome boy—man, she corrected himself; regardless of calendar age. Too skinny, too dark, and above all, even on his best behavior, too belligerent. But inside that belligerence was the person who had bred a flower with a portrait etched in its chromosomes, and as he stood silent beside Darien McCullough she discovered that he was holding her hand.

The clouds were thickening up, but she could see mountaintops. She shivered. "I think that's Blackfoot Country," she said.

Jeron studied the ground thoughtfully, then leaned back and regarded the map. "Aunt Eve? What's this part here?" he asked, pointing.

She got up from where she was stroking Jeromolo Bill's sleeping head and came over. "South Dakota?" she said doubtfully.

Darien shook her head. "That was when there used to be states, when there used to be a United States. It's all Blackfoot now. Cornbelt south of us, Prairie Confederation up in what used to be Canada, Rocky Mountain Republic just ahead—but that's Blackfoot. We detoured all clear up through Saskatchewan on the way East, just to miss them."

"There must be roads that go straighter," Eve offered, frowning at the map.

"Probably are. But you'd be crazy to use them. Two

hundred years ago the Blackfoot were the meanest bastards in the West. Never did get along with settlers—not that you can blame them. Now they're coming back."

"Indians? Oh, wow!" Jeron's youth showed in his awed face. "I thought they were all extinct!"

"Not a bit of it—especially since the Blackfoot let other Native Americans immigrate. Not to be citizens, you know. They don't go that far. But the Blackfoot have plenty of food, they've even got the buffalo coming back, and it's not so good in, for instance, the Desert Countries. People can't really survive there. They could for a while, when there was plenty of power and they could import everything they needed, but you folks showed them the error of their ways."

Eve fell silent, and Darien was aware she had been tactless. Jeron gave her no opportunity to think what she could do about it, because he was tracing the map with his thumb. "Huh," he grunted. "You came all that way on horses?"

"Oh, Jeron, what do you think we are? Not on horses. By car—alcohol fueled—as far as the lakes, then down by water to the New York Thruway." She sat for a moment, remembering, and then conceded, "It wasn't always that comfortable, of course, but we had a good reason." He looked a question at her. "To see you people, of course," she explained. "We didn't think Jimbo Tupelo would have got your message—and if he had God knows what he would have done—so I brought it to him in person. There're still a few observatories going, you know, though not of course in the East. So—I decided to take a little trip."

He scowled at her. "It is not a 'little' trip and you didn't do it just to give that man the message."

Darien looked at him for a moment. "I never know how to take you," she observed. It was true. He was startlingly self-confident for someone barely out of his teens; most of the people she knew did not get that self-assured manner until middle age. It was not really an attractive trait. "Well," she said unwillingly, "I never meant to lie to you, I just haven't had a chance to tell you everything. We've been having a few problems in Puget. Volcano problems; we've had two bad ash eruptions in the last five years, and both of them hit when the crops were vulnerable. That's not too serious—I mean, if it doesn't happen every year it won't be—but it leaves us a little exposed. We've had to make deals with our neighbors for food. Even the Blackfoot. And Jimbo's a problem."

"Him? So far away?"

"He doesn't want to stay so far away, Jeron. He wants to be President of everything anybody else has ever been President of, and maybe a little more. He's making deals and alliances, and if he had this ship— If he had whatever else you people can give him— He'd get smashed, of course, because he's just a pipsqueak tyrant, but if he started a real war everybody else would start maneuvering too, and while his neighbors were eating him up the SoCals and the Rocky Mountain boys and a few others might get the fever. It's been pretty chancy ever since the sneak attack."

Eve looked up from her thoughts. "The sneak attack? Is that what you call what Shef did?"

"Oh, God," said Darien penitently, "nobody's *blaming* you."

"I'm blaming me."

"No, really! You folks did us a kind of a favor."

Eve frowned and shook her head.

"No, really," she said again. "I don't think you know what shape the Earth was in. Talk about armed camps! There were missiles under every front porch, and it was only a question of time until they went off. You messed us up, sure. But there were plenty of survivors—and if you people hadn't wiped out the worst of the weapons, I'm not sure there would have been *any*."

Jeron said, almost apologetically, "I do not think we meant to do you any favor."

"We certainly did not," Eve said bitterly, with a look of decision in her eyes. "Maybe we can now, though. I think we owe you something, and. . . . I wish I could talk to Uncle Ghost."

There was something worrying about the way she said it, Darien thought. "Who? Someone you left back on Alpha Centauri?"

"Not exactly," said Eve Barstow, and then, suddenly, "Oh, look! That must be the Pacific Ocean! We'd better wake Bill up to land us!"

28

Sometimes I walk among you in a form of flesh and sometimes hover like an airy cloud. My name is Willis Becklund, and I died twenty years ago. More or less. I don't mean more or less twenty years, I mean more or less "ago." When you stand where I stand it is not easy to see what is "ago."

Since it is important that you understand what I am saying, let me give you an illustration. When I was alive and standing on the face of the Earth, I could see ahead of me and behind, but only as far as nothing got in the way. To see farther I had to rise higher; but the higher I rose the more distant what I saw became, and the harder to make out. Thus in space. So in time. I am on neither side of Chandrasekhar's other limit, but above it as you might say, and you would be astonished at how tiny you all look from here. Multiplying embryos in one direction. Moldering corpses in the other. And I am not always sure which way I am facing since, once you rid yourself of the myth of causality, it makes no difference at all.

—No. That is not true. It makes a difference.

I think the difference it makes will surprise you, for it is no more than public opinion. Let me find an analogy. You can, if you wish, paint your body green, dress in your wife's undergarments, and make indecent gestures before a mirror. Do you do this, ever? I wouldn't be surprised if you did, in the privacy of your own home. But if you were to do it, say, at a baseball game or in the middle of a veterans' convention, *that* would surprise me. You would not. You *could*. But you wouldn't, for you adapt to the conventions of the group. And so do we all. Even I! The event that cost me my physical body gave me in exchange a kind of freedom I had never imagined, but for twenty years I stayed with my fellows and my progeny and was dragged along with them into their myths.

I could, of course, have followed my whilom wife Ann.

There was a good reason why I did not, however. The reason was simply cowardice. None of us dragonflies can ever come back, but once in a great while one of us—I am one—can see just a bit of the other side, and it terrifies me.

So when we came back to Earth I found a chance and I seized it. I escaped. I stole away from the children and the churls who were making them welcome and I roamed, ah, God, how I roamed this dusty planet!

It was not as much of an escape as I had hoped, because in spite of the best we had done the planet was still full of people, and all of them followed the causal myth. Wherever I was. Unseen guest at a lynching in Wheeling, W. Va., or riding a charcoal-burning bus down Fifth Avenue—also unseen—they were there. I found some pleasure in their pleasure, when they had any, and even in their pain; and then I decided to seek some lost familiar pleasures and pains of my own. Why not?

So I recreated some of the lost loves of my youth. There are ten thousand of them or so by now, including the childhood, the almost, and the ones I made up out of my own mind—the last category is far the most numerous. There was Jenny, classmate and briefly bedmate at I.I.T., all love and hunger to please; and just yesterday I stood by the overgrown weeds by the waterworks, for she was my Chicago love, and made her live again. She was in the water of Lake Michigan, under it, swimming toward me. I could see her twilit and distorted face under the ripples, upturned and afraid. I formed a current in the water that swept along the sides of the peninsula and drove her away. I fear for my soul that I let her drown, but of course she was not real. Not even as a standing wave. There was Sharon. When I did her it was only an abstraction, a sense of loss and deprivation, a stain on a pillow and a smear on a sheet; she hurt me, and I will not give her any life at all. Rosemary. She was my least and longest love, in the next seat in high school and for a quick screw two weeks before we boarded the shuttle orbiter, in a motel at Cocoa Beach. We saw each other, oh, a hundred times, over years, but only to go to bed and then claw wittily at each other afterward. I am sure she is deader than I now. I brought her back for a week this morning. When we kissed it was like dry bones clashing. So, all in all, since we came back from that very ingenious place we manufactured near Alpha to this very crude place of our origin, I have recreated fifty sexual partners of my youth, five real and the rest only wished for. It gives me no pleasure, less pleasure than when I amused the children by creating inch-high elephants and candy-colored Tiger tanks for them to play with. Amusing myself was harder. It gave me so little pleasure that I masked what I was doing, even to myself, as a "survey trip," to "scout out the lay of the land" and to "report back" to my kith on what structure survived in the compost heap we had made of a world.

But when I came to report, they were gone.

I knew they would be. There was no question in my mind that they would get in trouble with that oaf Jim Tupelo and have to flee. And I knew that they would not wait for me, for who worried about someone who is already dead? Not even I, who happen to be the corpse.

Ah, you say, trying to sound as though you are following this, but you still move and talk, so how can you be a corpse?

Well, *sigh*, I will explain. After I died, the particles that made up my physical body were so rearranged that they could no longer support each other, but something remained. This "I" is what remained, and "I" am a soliton. A soliton is like a wave. Not a *wave* wave—in the sense of surf on a beach, or the wiggling vibrations of light or sound—but what a matter wave would be if there were a matter wave that resembled a light wave. If you do not follow what I have just said then you need to go back to freshman physics. Solitons are not a theory. They are a fact. You can see soliton waves in water if, for instance, a big boat suddenly stops and you see the lump of water at its prow continue indefinitely. That is a standing wave. A soliton. It is nondissipative, and so am I.

You, on the other hand, are an instanton. An instanton is a soliton that does not survive very long, and that describes you to a T. You are a pattern, like a giant jigsaw puzzle. As long as the particles of your body exist in the proper geometrical relation to each other you also exist. When you sweep the pieces off the card table back into the box, you have reduced the pattern to randomness and it is gone. I am a persisting pattern, like the orographic clouds over a hill. Break me up if you can, but I will return. In order to be nondissipative, a wave's motion must be nonlinear, and I am that, too. Therefore I am here. While Jenny and Sharon and Rosemary—and you, too—are gone. Got it? Fine. Glad to clear that up for you.

But under certain conditions I can bring you back, you see. I had had enough of lost familiar joys. I sought a lost familiar misery instead, and his name was Dieter von Knefhausen.

So I elevated myself over the city of Washington, D.C., studying what you call the lay of the land. There it sprawled in the watery moonlight, here brooding Lincoln, there Washington's phallic shaft, there the cutesy gingerbread that celebrated Thomas Jefferson. The Potomac was a lot broader than it used to be. Foggy Bottom was Soggy Bottom. There were lights burning bright in the White House where Jimbo, no doubt, was screaming at his evaded aides, and a few others, here and there; and it was, in some sense, sad.

Time was when this city held the spark that stirred the world, for good or evil, when all those circles and avenues were solid with cars and each marble building held its thousand industrious tamperers with everything. It was not like that anymore. The world no longer respected the District, or feared it, either. It was just another weedy marsh, stretching from Arlington to the Maryland line, and if ever I have taken pleasure in the loss of the flesh it was when I heard the steady song of mosquitos all around.

Knefhausen was not buried in any Arlington. Not he. Not in view of the low status he enjoyed at the time of his death. It didn't matter. I knew where they had planted him, close enough. It was not strictly necessary for me to find his wretched remains to do what I wished to do, but I like to do things properly. One never knows what is "necessary," and so I sought out the wretched dog's trough where all the physical facts of the body of Dieter von Knefhausen lay, in the tangle of the White House rose garden. It was easy to find his grave. The tangled thorns grew two feet above the jungle around them: so his corpse found its function. I felt for him. I found him; and in a moment I had him there, as large as life, rising spectrally above the sodden turf.

"Why, it's Dr. Becklund," he said, after he had blinked at me for a moment—self-possessed devil! "What a great pleasure, my dear Willis! I had thought you were dead."

"So I am, Kneffie. So we both are, and what else is new?"

He peered at me with that opaque, nearsighted smile I had seen so often, in Huntsville and at the Cape and all the places in between, masking whatever quick reassessments were going on in his mind. He was even uglier than he had been at the launch. He was also quite shabbily dressed. They had not valeted him well in his ultimate prison, and of course the natural chemistry under the swampy ground had not improved his appearance. "So I have died," he said, nodding as he comprehended and accepted the position. "To be sure. It is only what I had expected. And yourself, my dear Willis?"

"Even deader. Or at least, I have been dead longer, though perhaps not as thoroughly."

He gave me the ghost of that tolerant smile, the look of being apologetic that masked his utter confidence that he had never had anything to apologize for. A Peace rose bobbed annoyingly through his mouth as he spoke. "I do not think I quite understand. If we are not alive then, please, what are we?"

"We are nonlinear equations, Kneffie, and it is not important that you understand. I didn't rouse you to answer your questions but for you to answer mine."

"To be sure." He pursed his lips. Decay or none, he still possessed that broad, clear brow, so awfully and proudly the mark of the master race, and he smiled with the expression of a person addressing an inferior whom it is not yet time to chastise. "Please do ask what you will, my dear Willis," he said warmly.

"I shall," I said, but the truth was that I was not sure how to proceed, although I had formed the questions a hundred thousand times: What is it like to be a dragonfly, rather than a worm? What does Chandrasekhar's other limit look like from the far side? But I could not concentrate for, among other reasons, the rose was still annoying me. He had moved slightly and now it was dipping in and out of his ear.

That at least I could deal with. I gave us both substance. He sprang away as his form took flesh and the rose's thorns ripped across his cheek. "That was wickedly done!" he cried, rubbing the wound.

"I have done it to myself too, old man," I said, since the thorns had found me; but the experience was interesting as well as painful and I let it stand. "Be grateful that you can feel at all," I advised.

He glowered at me, then quickly controlled himself. It was the old, known Kneffie who rapped: "Your questions, then, if you please."

"Very well." I glanced about the dim and moonlit jungle, as though there were someone who might hear this Walpurgis conference, before I plunged in. "I want to know if, after you died, you were judged?"

Knefhausen looked at me opaquely, and then at the blood on his fingers. "What a curious question," he murmured, ripping the lining out of a pocket to wipe his hand clean before he replied. "But I understand the curiosity, it is only that it is strange coming from a person in your position. Nevertheless! The answer is that I have no recollection of meeting the Herr God. I have no recollections at all, after coughing very severely and feeling very ill, until I saw you standing here."

"Not even—" I hesitated.

"Not anything at all," he said firmly, "and certainly no sort of what you would call 'judgment.' What would I be judged for, my dear Willis?"

I had thought I was past anger, but even as a revenant he was insufferable! "You have the arrogance to ask *me* that, Knefhausen?"

"Ah, I see," he said, nodding, "you refer to my experiment. To be sure. One can see that, from the point of view of the subject, the exercise was, what shall I say, quite disconcerting—"

"Disconcerting!"

He stood up to my anger. "Disconcerting, yes! As a subject, one could not enjoy it, naturally. But the purposes, dear Willard! The sublime purposes! It was purely an experiment, conducted with great ends in view, and you must admit that it succeeded for you yourself are the proof. Judge me? Of course, if you wish! Anyone may judge me, but the success of the experiment, that is my defense!" It would have been sensible of him to stop there, but the old peacock could not help but preen: "To be sure," he smirked, "one does not expect the schoolboy to welcome the birch."

"Shut up!" I shouted—not only in words.

So, of course, he could not help but shut up as ordered. He stood frozen there, neither wave nor motion, while I calmed myself down.

It was a temptation to send the old bastard back to his grave! Dead or alive, Knefhausen was a slippery and evil person—enough to piss off a preacher, as we used to say; enough, enough, to anger as dead a person as I. The fact that I have lost the flesh does not mean that I do not feel its fury. Throb of blood in the temple, rush of adrenaline, trembling of the building of rage—I feel them all; if I am an illusion I create for myself, at least I create it in all details.

Even feeling rage is better than feeling nothing. Any feeling is welcome, when you have known very few for some time. It was like the physical circumstance of my having given us flesh. I itched. My skin stung where the roses had pricked. The back of my neck was a target for blood-seeking bugs. (And what did they gain from *that*?) An orgasm, after all, is nothing but the explosive easing of an almost unbearable itch. These itches I could end at any moment, by dissolving away the flesh; so I could almost enjoy them.

Not, however, so tranquilly that I did not want to hurt von Knefhausen. I took my revenge. "You are an arrogant son of a bitch," I told him, "so try a little humility." And I caused him to shrink to half his height and twice his breadth. I lengthened his nose to a Roman hook worthy of the worst posters of his childhood.

"Vot? Vot?" he gasped. "Vot are you doink to me?"

"I'm teaching you a lesson, Knefhausen," I told him, pleased with my joke.

He clapped a hand to his forehead. "Oy veh! Lessons I need, a dead person already?"

"It doesn't matter what you need. A lesson is what you're going to get."

He shrugged immensely, and I could see the half-snarl fading into his usual opaque smile. What control! "So ven is comink de lessons, bubbeleh?" he demanded.

"You bastard," I said, but what was the use of anger in this situation?

"Such a mensch," he sneered. "One deader plays tricks on another!"

"All right," I said. "I'll let you off the accent, but I won't change the way you look. I want to discuss something with you."

"Thank you," he said stiffly, squinting to look at his nose. "But you have no grounds for this. It is unjust to charge me with the deeds of others, which took place when I was only a child. Still! You are the person in authority, is that not so? And so I must play this game by your rules. Tell me then what you want of me."

I said unwillingly, "I want to know what to do."

"Do? My dear Willis! Whatever you wish, of course! In what respect?"

"I would like to help these people," I said, "and I don't know how."

He nodded slowly, his fingers feeling the shape of his nose and lips. "I too wanted to help these people," he said. "And with your help I believe I did. Do you follow me? No? Let me explain. It is necessary to cut in order to cure, and I was willing to cut. The world you left—with my assistance—was on the verge of destroying itself. It had almost no hope of surviving. I made the assumption that the knowledge that could be gained—by you!—from my little experiment might in some unpredictable way save it. And so it did! You made the final cataclysm impossible. Now are you going to throw away your success?"

"Our success? What success is that, man?"

"The chance to remold the world!" he cried grandly, the Prussian voice no longer sounding strange out of those thick caricatured lips. "The world is yours now, Willis, to form aright! Peasants and petty tyrants—there is no force on

Earth that can prevent you from bringing a wonderful new order to the human race! Peace and wisdom and the fruits of the mind, in tranquility, for a thousand years!"

And suddenly my little game was turning out poorly. We were on no mountaintop, but that devil was offering me everything!

I resolved to end the game. It was simply done: "Go away, Dieter," I ordered—again, not only in words.

So the tears dried, the triumph on the hideous face turned into an apprehensive, placatory half-smile. The smile turned into fear, and became transparent, and so did all of him.

And then the last of him was gone—I do not think it is profitable to ask the question "where?" Back into my own memory, maybe. Once again a revenant, returning to his dissolving corpse under the roses . . . perhaps.

But he had left a seed in my mind, and I could not help but feel it grow.

The poison in the pill was its truth. I could not deny it. If I wanted the world reborn, I could give it parturition—with Eve and Jeron and the others if I chose, and they did. Or without them, by my sole self.

I rose up into the sky over Washington, D.C., and hung there for a long time, as the Earth turned and at last the eastern sky softened into pearl gray.

I do not like being instructed by myself. Yet I had been taught a lesson by Dieter von Knefhausen, or by the simulacrum I had created out of memory and rage. Should I follow it? Should I grasp the sorry scheme of things entire—I had already shattered it to bits, with Shef's help, and the remolding would be easy. And if I did, would what came then be only another construction of my mind?

And there I was, back to the ultimate question. What is reality?

Maybe all the universe is only the other half of the inside of my mind. For sure Dieter's specter came out of my mind, and would not have existed without it.

So, when I spoke to him, who was I talking to?

Or—generalizing—who am I talking to when I talk to anyone, including you?

29

THE SUN WAS VERY HOT, EVEN THIS FAR NORTH. WHY? (JERON had not quite grasped the concept of "summer.") The stuff beneath his bare feet was hot, too, so hot that he winced and howled until Darien showed him how to scoop down to a cool place—and the stuff it was made of! Crushed rock, sharp shell edges—like a hydroponics bed before you sludged it and wet it. And the things out in the harbor, great-bellied floating houses with tall sticks—sometimes as they moved swelling out with white "sails" on the "masts"; other, leaner floating houses with metal stacks that sometimes emitted "smoke" and "steam"; smaller ones with oars or paddles, apparently just for fun—some of the people in them were children. "The clipper ships," Darien said, stripping down to the bikini bra she wore for comfort and the G-string for modesty, "they belong to the King of Hawaii, but they're ours on lease; we trade him timber, potatoes, and apples for pineapples, sugar, and rum. The ocean-going steamers are Japanese. They had some idea of colonizing here for a while, but we talked them out of it—" She pointed to a rusting hulk across the bay, and Jeron realized with a thrill it had been a warship. "The kayaks are for pleasure, the dories for commuting to islands across the bay. Coming in for a swim?"

He had automatically been removing his own clothes as she took hers off—when in Rome!—but he stopped with his tunic just over his head. "A what?"

"A swim. In the water," she explained. "Come on! I won't let you drown."

Jeron looked after her in amazement as she ran down the pebbly beach. Swim? In the water? But one could not see into it! One could only speculate what other "swimmers" there might be, for he was, oh, so fully aware that under that pleasing sinusoidal blue there were a great variety of sorts and kinds and sizes of living things. Who *ate* each other! Who might well wish to eat *him*! Things with bony shells and crushing claws, things with tentacles that stung, things with great jaws and teeth—and all of them, always, hungry!

But still—

It certainly *looked* like fun, as Darien hurled herself into a wave and other swimmers laughed and splashed nearby. He screwed up his courage, hesitated on the firm wet sand the retreating waves had left, squealed as a new wave splashed him to his thighs. "Come on, dummy!" she shouted, but he still hesitated; in Jeron's imagination every wave concealed a triangular fin and every shard of shell was the claw of a sheep-sized lobster, about to lop off a leg for its dinner.

And yet, the sheer physics of the thing was fascinating. At home, the whirled gravity was so light that any motion at all, in the few bodies of open water they had yet created, kept even a skinny child afloat; the tiny positive buoyancy of the human body was not important. Now hip deep, he felt the queer sensation of lifting and dropping as the waves passed him; and when a bigger one came and lifted him off his feet entirely, he no longer resisted. He coughed and splashed and spluttered, but he stayed afloat; then he forgot about lobsters and sharks and splashed together with Darien, laughing, until at last she was the one to drag him out. They flung themselves on the hot sands, breathing hard.

For a primitive technology, they had some pretty neat stuff, Jeron admitted to himself. The beach, the sky, the Sun, sometimes the rain—a very interesting set of phenomena, when you had never seen them before. More than that, they had kinds of technology the Alpha-Aleph people had forgotten existed. Darien's perky little alcohol-fueled car. Elevators in the buildings. Television! With situation comedies and game shows!

Darien pushed herself up on her elbows and shaded her eyes. "See that big ship just coming through the narrows? It's a tanker. From Japan. Oil."

"Oil! I thought all the oil was used up!"

"Oh, no, not all of it. It's too expensive to burn, but we use it for feedstock—fertilizer, industrial chemicals, some plastics."

Jeron marveled at the sheer size of the ugly thing, and

listened to all she had to say. The oil was from China's offshore fields originally, but it was Japan's canny businessmen who had financed the drilling and marketed the product. They had survived the kaon stream very well. It was only the end of their world as they knew it—but Japan's World As It Knew It seemed to end about once every other generation, regular as the flick of a digital clock. The nation that had coped with Commodore Perry and Hiroshima, with the God-Emperor and the Meiji rebirth, with the samurai and the Economic Miracle—with incalculable change, always when least expected—simply picked itself up and rewrote its habits. Their electric power net was wholly wiped out and, as the seas rose, much of the low-lying shore area became swamps and uninhabitable tidelands. But just inside the beaches the archipelago's islands rose steeply to mountains. Most of the country remained dry. The Toyota plants became food warehouses. The night-soil carriers once again replaced the agricultural chemists. Surprisingly few starved. In China, even fewer—industrialization had not gone far enough for its loss to shock—but farther west the losses of life and property had been appalling. But then, they always had been, in good times and bad. Nothing worse than Calcutta's slums and the Bangladesh floods had happened, because nothing could.

"So," said Jeron, nodding, "you have brought back International Trade. Uncle Ski taught us about this. Imperialism. Colonization. Trusts and cartels and dumping."

Darien laughed, but only out of friendship and good humor, not in the wounding way that would make the boy bottle up inside his sneering face. "It hasn't gone quite that far. I don't think anybody wants it to; I expect we're making plenty of mistakes, but I hope not the same ones all over again. No. What we trade is mostly food, some raw materials—and now and then information. Did you ever wonder how we knew you were coming?"

"We sent a message," Jeron said.

"You sent it by laser light. From Alpha Centauri. Did it ever occur to you superbrains that Alpha Centauri is never visible from the continental United States? It's too far south. But there are still telescopes on the mountains of Hawaii, and the King of Hawaii graciously allows the astronomers to use them—and graciously traded us the message. Cost two hundred pounds of liquid nitrogen, though by the time he got it I suppose half of it had boiled away. Suppose you were worth it?"

The scowl flickered briefly back on his face—was she making fun of him? He did not want her to do that. What he wanted was for her to like him, very much, so that he would be able to like her as much as he wanted to—as much as he was coming to like all this complicated, strange, huge planet—

He was relieved to see that her smile was still friendly. Then it changed to concern. "Oh, hell, you're burning up, Jeron! You're just not used to this sun. Hold on a sec while I grease you up."

As she spread the sunscreen oil over his body he stretched slowly, pleased with the softness of her touch. No one had stroked him so gently since, at least, Aunt Mommy cared for the very young child he had been—

"Why, Jeron," she said softly, glancing at his face and then lower. "You seem to be falling in love again. Tell you what. It's about time I showed you where I live, eh? It's only up the hill. . . ."

Up the hill was what had once been a huge, rambling motor hotel, saunas and swimming pool, banquet rooms and lecture facilities. There weren't enough transients or sales meetings to keep it busy anymore, and so it had become housing for nearly fifteen hundred Pugets. Mostly the occupants were singles, though there were some childless couples and, in the larger suites on the upper floors, a few families.

In energy terms it was a good bargain. Half of each picture window had been silvered over to keep out summer sun and keep in winter warmth, and the building was sturdy. It was true that the upper floors were unattractive without elevator service; the winches that pulled the cars imposed a considerable drain. But most of the inhabitants used the stairs by choice, except for moving furniture or carrying heavy loads of groceries, and lifting was energy-cheaper than heating. Things that go round use less energy than things that heat up; and "smart" cybernetics traded from the chip people down south in Santa Clara economized on trips. Each room had huge beds, a small refrigerator, a little stove, its own bath—it was not a bad life for a single. You didn't have much space for keeping knickknacks and family heirlooms, but who wanted all that stuff anyway?

Above all, the beds! How different from President Tupelo's soggy mattresses, or even the flower sacks back home! And what wonderful things one could do on them!

Although Darien was twice Jeron's age, it was at least an open question which brought more craftsmanship to their lovemaking. Or more puzzlement. Jeron's peculiar twitches and pokings in the middle of everything—they were off-putting, but how was Darien to know that they were what Jeron had picked up of the sex-as-communications modality the *Constitution*'s grownups had evolved? The attempts were wasted on her, but not much else was; it was good. Explosively good, and then when at last they rolled apart and their breathing slowed it was Jeron's turn to be puzzled. His voice almost tender, he said, "Perhaps we should save this one."

Darien, who had been playing with the long, straight hair that lay across his shoulder, propped herself up to look at him. "Save what, Jeron?"

"The baby," he explained. "Aunt Eve's probably going to want to plant some of the cabbages pretty soon. Of course, you'd have to carry it for a few weeks until the vegetable womb grows out—"

Darien had not yet switched her reasoning mind back on. She was slow to respond; but then the meaning of the words penetrated and she sat up. "*What* baby?"

"What do you mean, what baby? *Our* baby. I've been thinking it might make a nice cross." He sat up too, nodding as he thought it out. "See, I'm Eve and Jim Barstow—you can tell that by the name—"

"Tell *what* by the name?"

"Breeding. All the first ten cohorts or so show their bloodlines in the name—then they began fooling around, but my name, for instance, shows E for Aunt Eve and O for Uncle Jim. The J means I'm from the third cohort, R just means I'm unedited. The N has no significance, that's just for pretty. 'Jeron,' you see? Well! A lot of the younger kids, like Jeromolo Bill, have been edited some—there are plenty that have been edited more than him—but basically, there's just been the same four male and four female lines to play with. So what I'm saying is, I think it's a good idea to breed out a little."

The last time Darien remembered blushing she was six years old, tripping on her skirt as she curtseyed to the most famous people she had ever met; but she could feel her shoulders and throat reddening. Sexuality never made her blush. But such light talk of childbearing! "I'm thirsty," she said, getting up to fetch two bottles of beer out of the tiny fridge. She showed Jeron how to pry off the cap without damaging it, so that it could be used again, and took a long swallow.

She seemed doomed to go on repeating *What strange people!* to herself for the rest of her life. She had been doing it now, she counted, for a week and a day, the brief meetings in Washington, the quick flight across the continent, showing the visitors around Puget—and still they had the capacity to astonish! Or this one did, anyway. "Jeron," she said, "around here we don't get pregnant that easy, in fact a lot of us don't ever expect to get pregnant at all. But when we do, we take it pretty seriously. Sounds like you folks do it a little different, eh?"

His astonishment was equal to her own, and for ten minutes they exchanged data on childbirth and rearing. They let the actual foetal development take place in a surrogate vegetable womb, he explained. Obstetrician? Was that some kind of doctor? No, of course not. What would they need a doctor for? Most everybody knew how to do it, just as in the old world most everybody knew, for instance, how to give mouth-to-mouth resuscitation or perform the Heimlich maneuver. Finding the ovum was a little tricky, he admitted, but there was a douche with a selective stain that made it easier once you got the speculum and cannula deployed. Then you had to check if it was fertilized. If not you could always do it all in vitro—if you wanted to do any editing or cross-linking you pretty near had to—but mostly it seemed more fun to knock each other up in the old-fashioned way. Then you transferred the embryo to the vegetable womb. Any time in the first thirteen weeks was plenty of time, he assured her—you could let it go later if you wanted to, but who would want to? Then, for the next six or eight months, you could watch it swell with your child.

"Yes, but— Yes, but—" she kept saying. "Yes, but what about overpopulation?" (Not a problem when you were filling up a solar system!) "Yes, but suppose you don't want a child?" (Why wouldn't you?) "Yes, but suppose you don't even like the other person?"

He stared at her in increasing astonishment. ("What strange people!") "Now, what difference would that make?" he asked. "There's always somebody who likes to take care of babies. Don't you have any Aunt Mommies around here? Although," he added, with what Darien construed as a touch of embarrassment, "I did sort of teach my first two for a while. Not Bill, though. There was a second-cohort woman named Odirun who kind of liked to do that— Of course, I wouldn't interfere if you wanted to take that on . . ."

She shook her head. "It isn't going to happen, Jeron," she said, and explained why. Years before she had had a kid-not implant in her Fallopian tubes, as had nearly every nubile teenaged woman in Puget. Childbearing in Puget was almost always intentional, requiring an act of decision on at least the woman's part. He looked skeptical, then tolerant.

"We could always do it in vitro," he pointed out. "Or Aunt Eve will know how to reverse it. Or we could do tissue clones, like with Uncle Ghost's old blood specimens when we wanted to breed him after he died."

"Who's Uncle Ghost?"

"The one who died," he explained, and then, his face brightening, "Oh, Darien! We can do so much for you people!" He took another quick swig from the bottle, while Darien reflected that the last person who had said anything like that in her hearing was the commander of the Japanese warship across the bay. He swallowed hurriedly and went on. "Like Uncle Ski taught," he said, "Zen! You go through a couple of years of that and you're really able to handle things! Anything! And we can teach you— And all that waste space we flew over, why, with the vegetable wombs, we can fill that up in no time. And—"

"Can we come in?" piped a voice from the door, interrupting him. The voice didn't wait for an answer but opened the door and entered, the oldest of the girls, Molomy, and one of the younger ones, perhaps the one called Ringo. "Been fucking?" Molomy asked politely. "They said you were up here, Jeron. Listen. You better come down to the ship. Uncle Ghost's there, and you won't believe what he's got with him!"

30

ON THE MORNING OF DAY 9563 I WOKE UP NEXT TO A perfect stranger. Well, I think it was Day 9563—somewhere around there, anyway—maybe as much as ten days after we had finally set down on Earth—how can you tell for sure, with all the relativistic corrections and complicated counting? Close enough. And Toby wasn't wholly a stranger, and not *absolutely* perfect.

But close enough.

He had sprawled one big thigh over my (big enough) thigh, which was friendly but inclined to cut off the circulation. My whole leg was asleep but, as I slid myself out from under and sat briefly on the edge of the bed, the part of me I sat on was happily awake and reminiscing of good fun gone by. Not perfect? Compared to what I'd been waking up next to for the past twenty years or more, Tobias Pettyvass was perfect enough.

So I woke up feeling like rather a different woman—no, not like a different woman. Like the woman I used to be when I was saucy young Eve Barstow, Queen of the Space Rangers, back around Day 250 or so when we were all young and medium innocent and very very scared of what we were into. Those were about the best days of my whole life, with Jim and me taking our turns in the Honeymoon Hotel and Eve and Ski tossing the ruble and Flo just beginning to play games with the hydroponics plants. Up to then, growing up. After then—God! But in that little time while we still thought we were doing something fine and never suspected anyone was manipulating us, yes, those were days to be glad to be alive in. . . .

And the funny thing was, when I caught a glimpse of myself in Toby's bathroom mirror, I *looked* like that little fresh Mrs. Eve Barstow! I had lost at least five kilos. I looked like somebody who was getting laid nicely. I wasn't any spring chicken—you might guess I was past the big Five Oh and you might even suspect the ten thousand liters of alcoholic bevs that had poured past those cupid's-bow lips. No Miss America! Not with the sagging stuff behind the cheekbones and under the chin, not to mention the eyes— And yet, you know, not bad! I wasn't a puddle of Silly Putty that walked like a woman any more. The drag of one-G exercise had sucked some of it off me, and there was a sparkle in the old blue eyes.

The sun was well up over the gorgeous blue Pacific, which meant it was late morning, pushing noon; I thought about waking Toby, but that peaceful bearded Toby mug lay so happily on the pillow that I didn't bother. And in the shower I found I was singing to myself. Softly. I didn't want to wake the man who had been guiding me so nicely around the wonders of Puget by day and the wonders of his bedroom by night. It was really astonishing what a few days had done for me, not just physically, not just mentally, not just emotionally— I don't know in what way. For instance. I'd been clinging to the illusion that I was the one person around Alpha Centauri who was essentially the same as the common run of humanity on Earth. Not flying off into the peculiar, like the rest of the grownups. Not raised to be bent, like the kids. Just *normal*. . . . But I wasn't! The experience had changed me too. Although I was the dummy of the group, I had learned the knack of learning and there was much to be learned: Toby was impressed, I could tell, by how much I knew and how much I could do as he showed me around the sleepy police station and the self-tending sewage plant and the parks and the bars of Puget. I wasn't Aunt Mommy—the kids were off on their own. I wasn't the wife of the famous astronaut, or even the local drunk and easy lay; I was just me, Eve Barstow, and me, Eve Barstow, seemed by then to be a very good thing to be. Good enough, it struck me, to have goodness to share.

Why not share it?

Why not spend the rest of my life right here in Puget, helping these people get their world together?

The more I thought of it the better I liked it; and so I stepped out of the shower, wrapped a towel around me, and shook Toby's shoulder. "Wake up, it's morning," I caroled, "and I'm going to stay here in Puget!"

There was another nice thing about Toby Pettyvass. He woke up nicely. He didn't snort and struggle, like my whilom husband, or jerk like a galvanized frog leg, like Ski, or sulk, or glower, or do any of the other things my few recent bedmates had taught me to expect. He just opened his eyes and woke up. "That's nice," he said.

"But you'd better get up!" I leaned forward to let my hair hang down, then wrapped it in the towel. Toby was just lying there, admiring me. Fair exchange. I was admiring him, too: big man, former football player, now Darien's Chief of Special Services, which meant, mostly, that he was in charge of Puget's police and firefighters. And squiring around visiting ladies. "Look at the sun," I scolded.

Then I looked at it myself. The confounded thing was distinctly *lower* than it had been. "Oh, God," I said, "wrong ocean! It's the middle of the afternoon! We've been in bed all day!" So much for the swift and impressive Eve Barstow. . . .

But it was not for my brain alone that Toby admired me. "I like your outfit," he said, and grabbed. Since my outfit consisted of a soggy towel wrapped around my hair, I understood at once what he had in mind. Quel homme! Older than I was, waking up out of a sound sleep after an unusually active night, and he grabbed! Well. I knew what to do about that. I grabbed back, and the sun was lower still by the time we were conversational again. He at least had known well that it was afternoon, because he had been up for a couple of hours in the forenoon while sated Eve replenished her powers in sleep, had checked with the department to see if he was needed, wasn't, came back to bed without waking me.

"But don't they need you now and then?"

He shrugged. "They'll call me on the beeper if it's

important. There was a little brushfire in the hills—we don't get them often, and they kind of appreciated the chance to handle it by themselves. How else are they going to learn?"

Now, do you see how quick and intelligent Eve Barstow is, after all?

I wasn't listening to him, I was listening to the urgings inside my own head. "I guess you didn't hear what I said," I told him, taking his hand off my breast and kissing him to show that he wasn't to take it personally. "I'm going to stay here, Toby."

He grinned and gave a good answer. "I'm glad."

"And I'm going to help you people!" I threw my arms around him—nice hard warm male skin over nice hard strong male bones—but he didn't exactly respond. He looked as though he thought, but wasn't sure, that his message beeper had gone off.

When I am naked and put my arms around a naked man I expect more of his attention than that, no matter how many times we have been making it. I was feeling really good, and it was a downer to suspect that Toby didn't seem to be. "What is it, love? What they say, Omnes triste post coito or something like that?"

He looked at me as though I had suddenly begun speaking Greek, but of course it wasn't. "That's Latin," I explained, "meaning all men seem to get gloomy after making love, only if that's what it is how come you never showed any signs of it before?"

"Oh, no," he said, stirring himself. "I was just thinking about—something. Say! Aren't you getting hungry?"

Well, of course I was, once he mentioned it, but it didn't answer my question. It did change the subject, because we certainly couldn't go out to eat the way we were.

You hear a lot about how long men have to wait for their lady friends to get dressed. It wasn't like that with us. I was out of the shower and into a dress and sandals and perched on Toby's nice, solid window ledge, watching nice, solid Toby lace his boots, in about seven minutes. He was slower. He had to buckle his belt with the big Puget medallion, and load it up with his beeper and his handcuffs and his flashlight, and then he had to call in on the beeper to say he was back on duty. I just sat there admiring him, and working up an appetite. "Don't you have to blow-dry your hair or something?" he asked, while he was checking the cartridges in his gun.

"Not with hair like mine. Do you ever shoot that thing?" I asked, because guns make me feel as though I'd eaten tuna salad that had been in the fridge a day too long.

He grinned. "Not usually, not counting snakes and now and then a wolf, up in the hills. What do you want to eat?"

"Seafood!"

"What else?" he sighed, and took my arm as we went out the door. Of course, the fruits of the sea were old stuff to Toby because he'd been eating them all his life. Not me. We had had five meals together, and had them in five different fish restaurants. I had scored sand dabs, crabmeat cakes, abalone, poached salmon, and that thing they call dolphin, although it isn't, and I was ready to run right down the menu, one by one, to make up for twenty-some years of eating nothing that didn't come out of the garden patch. Even the kids had taken to Earth food, especially seafood; when we took Jeron along the night before he'd ventured oyster stew, and loved it until he found a whole oyster in his mouth. I didn't blame him for that. I'd finished his plate for him, and all that that did for me was make me want some oysters of my own. So when we got to the new place Toby had picked out, nice ramshackle frame building looking right out over the bay, I ordered them fried, and a shrimp cocktail to start with, and when Toby ordered a beer I virtuously declined. I hadn't even cracked a maltnut in forty-eight hours. Didn't need it. I was intoxicated enough just with being where I was and thinking about all the great things we were going to do for these poor people in Puget—and with Toby. I explained all this while he worked on his beer. That took us through the shrimp and well into the fried oysters and home-fries. And there it was again. He wasn't lighting up with joy. He was just nodding, and staring out over the bay at the sailboats and the big lumber vessel and the wreck of the Japanese cruiser across the water, and it was enough to make a girl wonder if her deodorant had failed to work.

So the first oyster was a delight, crisp outside and gummy and sinewy inside, with that marvelous iodine Pacific taste;

and the second very good, and the third nice enough, but by the time I got to the fifth the salt had lost its savor. I put down my fork. "Toby?" I said.

He turned to look at me. "Yeah?"

I said, feeling my way, "Listen, love, I'm not talking about getting *married*, or anything like that. I mean, I'm not claiming any kind of *rights*."

He had a forkful of crab Louis halfway to his mouth, and he stopped there. "Ah, no, Eve," he said. "It's not that."

"Then it is something, right? What?"

He put the crabmeat in his mouth and chewed thoughtfully. An ox could have finished a mouthful of hay before he got that mouthful pulpy enough to suit him. "I was thinking about all you people staying here to, what you said, help us."

"Right!" I cried. "You've had a tough time, and we want to make up for it! We're going to show you ways to live you never even dreamed of—not just the vegetable womb and the other presents we brought—although you wouldn't be drinking that stuff out of a bottle if you'd ever tasted a malt-nut! No. A whole new life-style, Toby dear. We've had twenty-five years to work it out, and we've got a lot to teach you—"

I stopped, because his beeper had beeped. He spoke into it, put the plug in his ear, listened a moment, and then frowned. He put it away and glanced at me. "You finished with that?" he asked.

"What's the matter?"

He rubbed two fingers across his lips. "Your friendly ghost is the matter," he said. "He's at the ship, and so is everybody else. And they're not alone. There's something pretty funny going on."

Now, the term "pretty funny" could easily be applied to almost anything involving us. I admit that. It's all a matter of perspective. If you grow up with a cross-eyed kid sister you get used to her, but you know that strangers are going to look at her in a different way. So it was with our little family. Sassy Jeron, flabby me, weird littler kids—but the prize for funniness had to belong to Will Becklund.

However, there was something funny in a different way,

and that was that Toby had known that Uncle Ghost existed. We'd been having fun about that, all of us, dodging questions in Washington and letting the President and Darien and all the others wonder if their eyes had played tricks on them; but Toby had not been fooled. And I didn't know why not. In his bright red little gas-burner, cruising along the bay front to the beach where the golden ship nestled on the shore, I tried to figure out how that was. I didn't succeed, and then we were there.

There was a crowd of Pugets surrounding a smaller crowd that was all the rest of us from Alpha-Aleph, just in front of the ship. People who have never seen Willis Becklund have many varying reactions. The Pugets had them all, but mostly what they had was narrowed eyes and closed-in expressions. Not me. My jaw dropped. Because there really was someone else. Someone no more than four feet tall, with a great hooked nose and blubbery lips. When it moved its nearly transparent head around to stare at the staring crowd I could not fail to recognize it. Although it looked like a baggy-pants burlesque version of a Jewish comic, I knew who it was. Had been. Was again. Whatever! It was none other than Dieter, or anyway the ghost of Dieter, the dreadful von Knefhausen.

"My God," I said, hopping out of Toby's three-wheeler and almost falling because I wasn't looking at what I was doing. When Toby came around the car I grabbed his hand to steady myself and tugged him through the crowd of silent Pugets.

Dieter and Will and the kids turned to me at once, all excited and kind of glowing, and, oh, what a clatter of words and clash of tongues! We were talking so fast that it was almost quick-speech, and, of course, everybody was talking at once.

Twenty-plus years with our little extrusion of the human race had trained me to certain expectations. One of them was that whatever I wanted to do, the next person I talked to would want to do something else; whatever I thought or felt, most of the rest of our bunch would disagree. With me; with each other. But not this time! The least-mean-square measure of difference was almost undetectable, because all our great minds had run in the same channels. Jeron had been brainwashing the younger kids, who were wild to try altruism and beneficence now that they'd heard of it; Will had roamed the Earth all by himself until he came out of the wilderness with the same idea. And with this curiously malformed version of Dieter von Knefhausen. I couldn't help it; I had to ask. "Why'd you bring this funny-looking ghost, and why—"

"Soliton!" Will corrected angrily; he never did like those race names.

"This funny-looking soliton, then, and why does he look that way?"

"I almost didn't," he whispered, while Dieter's ripply face expressed polite interest, "but then I figured he ought to have a chance to mend his karma with the rest of us."

"And for this," Dieter von Knefhausen said politely, "I am quite grateful, although the alterations you have made in my appearance are, you could say, most disagreeable."

"Shut up, Kneffie," Will whispered. "Just count yourself lucky you're here at all. Anyway! Listen. Here's what we've decided! Jeron, Bill, and the two girls are going to stay here, and so am I, for a while. Molomy and the others will take ten Earthies back to Alpha-Aleph for training. We'll radio for some more ships to be built. Lots of them—what?"

Knefhausen coughed and indicated the Pugets. The indrawn look was tighter than ever. Will sighed with a sound like a distant air-brake—an irritated one. The happy villagers were supposed to be dancing and throwing flowers by that point, but the script wasn't playing.

Will sighed. "How annoying it is," he remarked, "when you strike a spark and the audience does not catch fire. Well. If I can't tell you, then I will show you," he whispered, and flung a glassy arm toward the sea.

I will say for Uncle Ghost that he can put on a great show when he wants to. The distant shore began to wrinkle and fade; the setting sun turned glassy, paling from apple to peach to soft shimmering pineapple Jell-O, and then it all melted away. We were looking at a huge fluted shell of color, like what I think Radio City Music Hall used to look like, and within it Will was staging a show that beat the Rockettes.

Oh, none of it was real. The Pugets knew that as well as we did. It didn't even look real, because it was all that wrinkled-cellophane look that was the best Will could manage. Through the paler parts of the display you could see the sun and even the beached wreck of the Japanese warship—but, oh, what a show all the same! He threw a starry sky across the shell. Against it a dozen golden globes slid through space, then a hundred—many hundreds—then one spun directly toward us, growing huge, changing shape. It opened at the side and stretched and flowed and turned into an immense golden cornucopia, with all the treasures of the world—our world—spilling out. Trees that grew into barkless two-by-fours, then cabins, then handsome homes. Luscious fruits in a hundred shapes and colors—you could nearly smell them and touch them, though not quite. Vegetable wombs with cunning cherubs popping out, blinking adorable eyes and clapping fat little hands with glee—oh, Will was stretching it some. No doubt about that. *We* never grew a house like that, although I suppose we could have if we'd wanted to, and babies from the cabbage patch get just as wet and cranky as any from Nature's Gate.

But it was a real five-bell smash performance, and what astonished me was that it was falling flat. The Pugets weren't buying it. Will knew it, too; the vision collapsed and the sun popped out again.

I felt Toby let go of my hand, and realized how terribly confusing this must be for the poor darling. "It's all right," I said reassuringly. "It's good, really—no, wonderful! We've all come to the same conclusion, and we're going to turn your life right around!"

"Turn us around?"

His tone worried me. All the other Pugets were straining to hear, but not crowding around—they stayed back, almost out of earshot. It was all pretty peculiar. I said impatiently, "We're going to give you the help you need. Teach you how to use the *I Ching*, show you how we edit our offspring for any characteristics we like—why, Will might even teach you how to turn your terminally ill people into solitons, so that you don't even need to die!"

Toby sighed deeply and nodded. "I thought it was something like that," he remarked, and his hand went to the butt of his gun. And his was not the only one. All those Pugets lounging around were suddenly a guard perimeter, and half a dozen of them had guns.

"That's it," cried Darien McCullough. "You're all under arrest. Nobody moves, nobody goes near your ship until we get things straightened out."

It was one of the worst moments of my life. I mean, *guns*! Rational adult human beings don't use *guns* to settle differences! And they were all in it together, that hypocritical Darien, my own all but perfect Toby, every one of them; they'd planned it all along and rehearsed it.

Much good it did them.

What they did not know, of course, was that five of the six children had grown up under Zen Master Ski's personal tutelage, and all those years of challenging each other with flower stems paid off at once. *"Hai!"* shouted Molomy, launching herself at Toby's knees, and *"Hai!"* yelled Jeron, spinning like a top with his two fists locked together; the battering ram of his fists bloodied the nose of one of Toby's gunmen while Jeron's foot in the abdomen of another took him out of action. *"Hai!"* and *"Hai!"* and *"Hai!"* and Araduk and Ringo and Modany each marked a target and clobbered them, and even little Jeromolo Bill, who had done most of his growing-up light-years away from Ski, threw himself at the two young women who were heading for the ship. Even I managed to get the old bones moving long enough to lay out the girl behind me, and Will Becklund, who had no body to charge with, blew himself up huge as a Macy's Thanksgiving monster. No Santa Claus or Mickey Mouse, he; he towered like a demon in a Chinese opera, hands the size of mattresses, tipped with talons as long as spears, and out of them he hurled grenades and firebombs, Napalm and fiery coals at the Pugets. None of them were real, of course. As with all Will's shapings, you could see clear through them when the light was right. But they sure were disconcerting. And he yelled—if you can imagine a cobra yelling instead of hissing, immense volume but no voice to give it body—*"Stop it, all of you! This minute!"*

And when we sorted ourselves out, the biggest of the Pugets were rolling on the ground, mostly clutching their testicles, and all the rest of them were staring at a gun apiece in the hands of Araduk and Bill and Molomy, and one in each hand for Jeron.

"Let me up," said Toby from the ground, wriggling slightly under the not very considerable weight of Molomy sitting on his chest.

"For what?" Jeron demanded, trying to point both guns at him simultaneously.

Toby sighed. "Don't wave those things around, will you? We weren't going to shoot you."

"No!" sneered Jeron. "Of course not! You were just going to try to steal our ship and our technology!"

Toby lifted Molomy clear and sat up. "Wrong," he said. "One hundred percent dead wrong. We weren't trying to take any of that stuff from you. We were trying to get you to keep it."

Way, way back, ever so long ago, when I was a happy head in the beautiful California Southland, I made an anniversary present for my dad and mom. The present was me. For two solid weeks before their anniversary I didn't drink a drop or smoke a joint. I washed my hair every morning, and brushed it a hundred strokes every night; I took the money I made from hustling junk jewelry to the tourists and bought a white blouse and a dark skirt, and on the plane ride home I not only didn't take a drink from the airline stewardesses, I didn't even eat their peanuts. And you know what my mom said when I came in the door? She said, "Evelyn, why do you let yourself get so fat?"

I always thought that was the most unexpected stab in the back I'd ever had in my life, but that was before Puget. I just didn't know what to do, say, or think. Neither did anyone else. Jeron was scowling furiously, fiddling with the guns. Molomy was pouting, and the other kids were staring back and forth, trying to figure out what was going on; tableau. Then Darien broke it. "Put the guns away, please," she said. Jeron glowered at her furiously, then disdainfully hurled the guns to the ground. "Thank you," she said. "After all, we can't blame you."

"*Blame* us!" I squeaked. I couldn't help it.

She looked at me, sadly and sympathetically. "Excuse me if I'm hurting your feelings, Eve. I know you mean well—according to your lights. We've been bugging you since the day you landed, you know; we know everything you've said to each other. You think you can run our lives better than we can, and I guess that's natural enough. That's the kind of world you come from. Old von Knefhausen there, he learned how to trick and force and cajole from some of the best teachers in the world, and he manipulated the eight of you, and you manipulated your kids, and I guess you just can't imagine any other way of dealing with people. Any of you. *But we don't want it.* We know you think you'd be doing it for our own good. So were our Japanese friends, when they came around to include us in their Greater Pacific Co-Recovery Sphere, and we had a lot of trouble talking them out of it." She nodded across the bay, to the rusting warship on the beach. "The thing is, we want to make up our own minds what's for our good. And so what we'd like best of all from you folks, please, is if you'd leave. Go back to Alpha. We won't bother you, we promise. And we won't let you bother us, either—because," she finished, "I should tell you, it doesn't make much difference whether you got the guns away from us or not. Up on the rooftops there are twenty more of us with machine guns. If they start shooting they'll likely hit some people they're not aiming at, and some of us will get killed—as well as all of you. Or all of you that still *can* get killed. And you know what? It will be worth it."

We all looked up at the rooftops. Darien had told the truth, all right. I could see a black barrel pointing out over the red Howard Johnson's cupola, and two more over the K-Mart, and others all up and down the beach avenue.

Jeron looked at me. I looked at Jeron. None of us said a word, until I did. I sighed. "Kids," I said to Araduk and Molomy and Jeromolo Bill, "put the guns away. Darien? Toby? Leave us alone for a minute. We've got some talking to do."

31

IN THE EVENING OF DAY 22,305, HOUR 17, MINUTE 22—I CAN give you seconds to the millisecond, if you like, even to that least of all Dirac units, the length of time that it takes light to cross the radius of an electron. At that moment, I say, I watched Nephew Jeron set foot on his own planet. Watched? Watch. Will watch; you know the trouble us ghosts have with mortal temporal fancies. It is all one time, not causal, and it goes on forever. If I pick one moment to consider a "now," it is my own caprice to do so—as you might, strolling, stand on a particular flagstone next to your wading pool to survey your property, rather than the graveled driveway near the mint patch. One place is as much "your place" as any other. One moment is as much "my moment" as any of the myriad alternatives from the instant events began to their remote terminal full stop. Oh, yes! I have been there! But the farther I go from my physical "now" the harder it is, and so I have gone only once to The End, and will not again. Enough of that. I don't want to speak of things that terrify even a ghost. For even the end of events is not the end of time.

So what I seek is friendly, familiar events, the doings of my colleagues and our get. It was just the same when I was in college. I faced the cruel beauty of mathematics and was glad to turn from it to the letter from home, Joan's new baby, Arnie's transfer to California, the leak in the porch roof, and how well the little vegetable garden was doing this year. And so it gives me pleasure that Jeron has found himself a world, and that the Jeron-Molomy cross is doing so well, and that Eve Barstow has her heart's desire.

Jeron surprised us all in Puget, would not stay, would not go home; he had a better idea, he said, and he was right. He went back to Aleph only long enough to build new ships and recruit a new community, and now he has a world of his own. If I had had eyes I would have wept with pleasure when he brought the fleet of golden globes to the third planet of Epsilon Eridani. Rich genes to cross! He had a dozen former Pugets with him, and a couple of the President's old White House guards, to add to the stock from Aleph—including fifteen of his children in body and about a hundred more in stored buds from the cabbage patch. They will make some handsome strains. Molomy was not there; she stayed on Earth with Eve. And that's going well enough, for Eve is fat and frail and happy with her Toby and their lives. She persuaded Puget to make treaties with New York and London and all the other great glamor places of the Grand Tour, and now she drinks tea at the Ritz and eats onion soup on the Champs Elysées whenever she wishes to, and the old mother planet is gradually limping toward ease. Ann? Ann is encrusted inside her own planet. She makes it rumble now and then, throwing up a mountain range or opening a sea. I visited her once, in her crystal catacomb at the core, but she responded to me not at all, and anyway magma is not to my taste. Shef and Flo have built forty navigable habitats and sent some of them flying off to Arcturus and Procyon, with Jeromolo Bill and some of his children and grandchildren to fly them, solving tensor equations in their heads. And I . . .

Oh, I'm all right. More or less.

I'm alone, of course. Now and then I would call up a Knefhausen or a former love to imitate a companion, but it was like making faces in a mirror. I wait and hope. Hope for someone as cowardly as myself, who dares not break through the surface tension to see what is on the other side; but all the other larvae seem willing to turn to dragonflies.

So I roam. Looking for the starburst. Slipping through gas clouds and watching the organic molecules form. Plumbing the hearts of suns. Waiting. As long as events occur I will have something to do, but after events stop . . . oh, after events stop! When the last stars of spongy iron dissolve as their protons melt away and there is only a universal soup of decaying photons—

Oh, then I will have no choice but to spread my wings and enter the place I fear; and then, perhaps, I will rediscover purpose. And the coming of the knowledge of that purpose, yes, that is it: that is what I fear.

About the Author

Frederik Pohl has been about everything one man can be in the world of science fiction: fan (a founder of the fabled Futurians), book and magazine editor, agent, and, above all, writer. As editor of *Galaxy* in the 1950s, he helped set the tone for a decade of SF—including his own memorable stories such as *The Space Merchants* (in collaboration with Cyril Kornbluth). His latest novel is *The Cool War*. He has also written *The Way the Future Was*, a memoir of his forty-five years in science fiction. Frederik Pohl was born in Brooklyn, New York, in 1919, and now lives in New York City.